& OTHER STORIES

Also by Norman Lock

Fiction

A History of the Imagination

Joseph Cornell's Operas / Émigrés

Trio

Notes to 'The Book of Supplemental Diagrams' for Marco Knauff's Universe

Land of the Snow Men

The Long Rowing Unto Morning

The King of Sweden

Shadowplay

Grim Tales

Pieces for Small Orchestra & Other Fictions

Escher's Journal

Stage Plays

Water Music

Favorite Sports of the Martyrs

*The House of Correction**

The Contract

*The Sinking Houses**

*The Book of Stains**

Radio Plays

Women in Hiding

*The Shining Man***

The Primate House

Let's Make Money

Mounting Panic

Poetry

Cirque du Calder

In the Time of Rat

Film

The Body Shop

---

* Published in *Three Plays*

** Published in *Two Plays for Radio*

Love Among the Particles

& OTHER STORIES

Norman Lock

Bellevue Literary Press
New York

First Published in the United States in 2013 by
Bellevue Literary Press, New York

FOR INFORMATION CONTACT:
Bellevue Literary Press
NYU School of Medicine
550 First Avenue
OBV A612
New York, NY 10016

Library of Congress Cataloging-in-Publication Data
Lock, Norman, 1950-
[Short stories. Selections]
Love among the particles & other stories / Norman Lock. -- First edition.
pages cm
Includes bibliographical references and index.
ISBN 978-1-934137-64-2 (alk. paper)
I. Title.
PS3562.O218L68 2013
813'.54--dc23
                                        2012046160

Bellevue Literary Press would like to thank all its generous
donors—individuals and foundations—for their support.

Book design and composition by Mulberry Tree Press, Inc.
Cover design by Alban Fischer
Bowler hat art on front cover courtesy of Bombaert/iStockphoto
Manufactured in the United States of America.
FIRST EDITION

1 3 5 7 9 8 6 4 2

ISBN 978-1-934137-64-2

Contents

For Helen, Meredith, and Nicholas

Love Among the Particles

& OTHER STORIES

The Monster in Winter

He, I say—I cannot say, I.
                    — R. L. Stevenson

1.

Frederick Drayton impressed the superintendent of Broadmoor by an affability at variance with the impertinence he had come to expect of young Americans, especially those whose experience of travel was limited to their own rough shores and the Continent. (The superintendent despised the Continent, by which he meant France; it was, for him, *Les Fleurs du mal*, although he had never read Baudelaire, nor would he ever.) That Drayton might be otherwise than he seemed did not occur to him. The young man carried, besides, a letter of recommendation from someone of importance in the Home Office, endorsing the bearer as worthy of favor. Lord M— had added a postscript in his own hand: "Do what you can for him, John."

The superintendent might have wondered at the interest shown in Drayton by so illustrious a person, but curiosity was not among his "gifts"—a convenient absence in a man charged with the disposition of many whose qualifications for admittance to an asylum for the criminally insane were dubious. Nor was the superintendent offended by the twenty-pound note that Drayton had caused to appear, like a conjuror's trick, on the teak desk this official had purchased while on Indian

service in the Punjab, whose allusive carvings some found
unsettling. The banknote seemed to have arrived there of its
own volition, so suave were the gestures of this good-natured
San Franciscan. The superintendent left it undisturbed, while
he searched the other's face for signs of servility or mischief.
Finding no sign of either, he put the note out of mind and beyond the reach of any mention, inside a leather-bound inmate
census lying on the desk.

"It can be arranged," he told Drayton with the air of one
used to arranging things of greater import than this, a private
interview with one of the inmates. "At one time, he was considered the most dangerous man in England," he added, his
gaze shifting involuntarily to Britannia's portrait. "He was exceptionally vicious." Again his eyes slid off Drayton's, onto his
own hands, which played with the thin-bladed knife he had
employed in opening Lord M—'s crested envelope.

The American nodded his understanding.

"Of course, the atrocities were committed more than twenty-
five years ago!" the superintendent declared with an emphasis
the young man could not interpret. He put down the knife. It
caught the gaslight along its edge in a way that made him stare
involuntarily. "He has—I assure you—repented of his past. He
has applied himself to his rehabilitation."

"His behavior—"

"Exemplary." The superintendent swept the knife away into
the top drawer of the desk. "You will be quite safe with him,
Mr. Drayton."

The American nodded a second time.

"If there is nothing else . . ." The superintendent rose from
his chair.

"No. Thank you."

"I must examine the census."

Drayton stood at the other side of the desk and extended his
hand across it. The impulse to draw his finger down the length

of a darkly oiled swelling in the wood was almost irresistible. The superintendent seemed unsure whether or not to take his hand—aware of the novelty, perhaps, of such a gesture in a place reserved for the instruction of the asylum's staff and the admonition of its patients.

He took it, finally, and looked as one released from an intolerable strain.

"I hope everything will be satisfactory, Mr. Drayton." He let go of the young man's hand only to take his elbow and lead him to the door. "Please convey my regards to Lord M—, when you see him."

"I will," said Drayton in a tone of voice that insinuated an intimacy with the eminent man.

"Tell him that I have been helpful."

2.

Frederick Drayton feared obscurity and the meagerness of a life spent in the shadows. It was not money he wanted; money, like a prepossessing nature, was only an instrument in the attainment of his ambition. He wished for fame and would not have regretted if a portion of it were infamous, so long as that infamy were not predominant in his reputation. He would not be a murderer or even a thief (except in a small way); but he would not mind that people considered him a roué or a rogue so long as admiration as well as censure were mixed in their regard. Drayton did not care if he ended up excluded from respectable company so long as that company came to see him on the stage; it was as an actor that he first had hoped to step out of the shadows he detested—into the green and garish footlights. But he lacked talent in that direction. He had also attempted a play, which failed and took with it the savings of a spinster aunt, whose distress he ignored. He was not discouraged. Drayton had that quality by virtue of which ambitious men sometimes succeed: a high opinion of himself.

After he had been repulsed twice by the more or less legitimate stage, he conceived an idea of such originality that few would doubt its genius, had they only known the dimensions of his brainstorm. But Drayton was shrewd as well as ambitious, and he concealed his thinking from his friends. He determined to make his name in vaudeville, whose stage, he knew, would be open to the kind of grotesque entertainment he planned: a confession so harrowing as to make Dickens's public reading of the murder of Nancy by Bill Sikes a pale piece of fiction, which it was. The confession Drayton had in mind would be the real McCoy—the testimony of a degenerate man—a genuine beast, if beasts may be said to be wicked and perverse.

An idea must have a provenance, and Drayton's originated in a newspaper article published on the twenty-fifth anniversary of the terror that reigned in London (so memorably described by Robert Louis Stevenson), whose culmination was the beating to death of Sir Danvers Carew. Drayton had skimmed the account, his mind occupied by the devising of a lampoon that might, with luck, bring him the fame that he demanded. So apparently slight an impression had the item made on him that he left the newspaper on the seat of a San Francisco Traction Company car, which deposited him at his rooming house near the Presidio. It was not until the following evening that the story of Edward Hyde was recalled to him by a conversation overheard in a saloon.

"They say he ate the living hearts of the women he killed."

"He was a devil."

"Not even children were safe from his rages."

"They ought to have hanged him."

"He's locked up for life in a lunatic asylum."

"I still say they ought to have hanged him. Cut off his arms and legs and hung what was left."

"He is a freak of nature."

"People would pay plenty to see him."

People would pay plenty to see him. This observation regarding the public's inexhaustible voyeurism set Drayton's train of thought on a new track as he sat over his whiskey and water. He remembered the story of Dr. Jekyll and Mr. Hyde from his school days and knew with an impresario's certainty that it represented a far greater coup de théâtre than the worn music-hall sketch he had been trying to reupholster, in his imagination, with naughty innuendo.

AN EVENING WITH EDWARD HYDE

NOTORIOUS MURDERER

ONSTAGE FOR A LIMITED ENGAGEMENT

PRESENTED BY FREDERICK DRAYTON

A homicidal maniac reciting his unspeakable crimes, alone onstage in the sickly light of the gas brackets. What a sensation that would be! Nothing could match it for terror and novelty. Drayton would rocket to the empyrean of celebrity, riding such an indecency. For that was what it was—a gross indecency—and Drayton knew it. *That*—he also knew—was the rancid bait to bring out the public in droves. I will arouse its indignation to fury, will make it howl for Hyde's blood. The public will be in a frenzy to apply rough justice to his neck, in the alleyway behind every theater at which we stop. My God! he thought. Not even Barnum had offered so complete a provocation to an audience! Everyone who sees the author of such crimes will want to leave his own sins sticking to him like a plaster. They will come—each of them—determined to revile Hyde, to vilify Hyde, to daub Hyde over with their own filth so that they may leave the theater with their souls cleansed.

Drayton possessed Barnum's dramatic instinct: He knew how to put on a show. He also knew that a spectacle, no matter how original (that is to say, how deviant), is not in itself enough to produce a powerful sensation; there must also be scandal and a counterbalancing redemption—whether for the spectators or for the object of their antipathy is irrelevant.

Yes, that's the formula! I'll put the monster on the boards and let them bathe themselves in a virtuous hatred. Unless the monster itself be repentant. Drayton speculated on what effect a contrite Hyde might have on his audience. Would it be more profitable, he wondered, to divert the hot blood of the mob into a channel of maudlin rejoicing for a lost soul? To turn a Roman circus into a revivalist's tent meeting?

THE ATONEMENT OF EDWARD HYDE

INFAMOUS MURDERER & RAPIST

PRESENTED BY FREDERICK DRAYTON

FOR THE EDIFICATION OF THE GREAT AMERICAN PUBLIC

Ire or awe, which would be more likely to win an ever-increasing audience—not one, but as many as there are cities in America? And why not abroad? After all, by his public readings the length and breadth of England and America more than by his books themselves was Dickens made famous. By his literary murders—fictions! How much more thrilling the real thing! What if Hyde were actually to strangle someone onstage in front of the astonished crowd? Even if it were only a simulation, such an act would undoubtedly add an unparalleled frisson to the evening for the gentlemen. The brothels will benefit! Drayton was aware that he had felt it himself many times—a prurience aroused by the details of a gruesome murder, especially when the victim was a young woman. He knew himself not to be unique: Why else the nearly universal interest in the Ripper and his Whitechapel Murders?

WITNESS EDWARD HYDE AS HE STRANGLES
A WOMAN ONSTAGE
PRESENTED BY FREDERICK DRAYTON
FOR AUDIENCES IN AMERICA & GREAT BRITAIN

Drayton was on his fifth whiskey and water when the train derailed. With an involuntary movement of his hand, he knocked his glass to the floor, where it shattered—an apt mirroring of the sudden destruction of his ungovernable thought.

What an ass I am!

What smashed his daydream was the realization of the impossibility of releasing Hyde from his incarceration for a purpose no loftier than Drayton's own extravagant aggrandizement.

How could he be released for any purpose? The man was dangerous—may be so still. He is confined for life and condemned forever. His remains can never be given Christian burial—Drayton remembered having read that in the newspaper story—nor any other form of interment that might keep open the prospect of resurrection. And I wanted to take him on tour!

And then—he could not help himself, so mercenary a heart was his—Drayton wondered if, when the time came, Hyde's remains might not be obtained, and at what price.

3.

Hyde did not die upon the scaffold, nor did he find the courage to release himself at the last moment, as Henry Jekyll had hoped during his final hours of consciousness while he waited for his monstrous twin to usurp him. He understood that Hyde was stronger and more cunning in the simplicity of his need, and that he would—when next he arrived within Jekyll's locked laboratory—remain there. Jekyll expected to predecease his rival by months or years. But the coming of Hyde proved too violent; Jekyll perished in convulsions upon the rack of Hyde, and immediately Hyde followed him. Thus were they both dead within a narrow space of each other—expiring, as it were, "in one another's arms"—and (this later proved crucial!) officially declared to be so.

The constables shoveled the body of both, rudely, into the back of a van. But before the corpse could enter the dismal precincts of the mortuary to wait upon the inquest into that "strange case," Hyde woke. Woke from a dream of death or some other counterfeit induced by the doctor's powerful drug. Unless having died on the instant with Jekyll, he had come back to life, having gone only a little way into the dark and not yet been possessed by its chill rigor. In any event, Hyde returned; and Jekyll, because of a ruined health perhaps, did not. As the doctor had feared, he was supplanted by the other, who has survived him now a quarter century. Had the mortuary van been unlocked (why should a corpse need locking in?), Hyde might have gotten away and continued to prosecute his private war against humanity. But the door was locked, and he did not escape.

When the city understood what Hyde had done—what atrocities and enormities—it screamed for vengeance. It demanded (to speak of the city as the nearly homogeneous thing it is in times of hysteria) the most severe punishments, exacted by means that were extraordinary for their invention and cruelty. Hyde the beast and monster elicited the bestial and the monstrous in everyone who contemplated him. Almost everyone. Some few there were who called for mercy, believing Hyde to have been the unwitting dupe and victim of his creator, Jekyll. Enlightened and forbearing, they spoke of "accidents of birth" and "Dr. Frankenstein's Monster." Ironically, it was the law that saved Hyde from hanging. That he had died (ostensibly or in reality) before witnesses and been pronounced dead established a degree of doubt, and doubt gave rise to a faction that declared that a dead man could not be tried. The opposition argued that the fact of Hyde's death was moot; all that mattered was his present status as a living man. Ultimately, the court decided that a legal pronouncement of death could not be reversed without committing a supreme blasphemy. Thus did Edward Hyde enter the limbo in which he was, legally, neither living nor dead, but in a condition partaking of both. Advocates of either side of the legal opinion were in any case agreed that Hyde must be committed, and for life. (The public could not follow the subtle arguments of the case and, in the end, forgot it.) So Hyde was taken to Broadmoor and left to rot.

During the first years of imprisonment, Hyde raved—raved and rioted in his basement cell, making the hearts of his jailers quake. He was the very coin of evil, with the face and bearing of a beast—malignancy made flesh, affecting them like a cold hand upon the heart. To hear him execrate God turned their bowels to ice. To see him was to look on leprosy. And so Hyde lived, unregenerate, cursing God and Henry Jekyll—God for having given Jekyll life, Jekyll for giving life to Hyde.

Early in his second decade of confinement, Hyde changed. He grew quiet, calm, composed, mild. He became pleasing in his demeanor, so that his outward form seemed, almost, to copy an altered nature. *Almost,* for the deformity—the most notable aspect of his appearance (a misshapenness that had been thought the visible evidence of an inward corruption)—persisted. It could not be otherwise, for Jekyll's chemistry had produced the outlines of Hyde's very form. The skull was too large, as if the fontanelles, which had closed in infancy, had been reopened by a gigantic subterranean strain. The hands, too, were overlarge, pelted and sinewed like an animal's. The backbone had been violently recast into the likeness of a heavy swag of iron chain, such as decorates a courthouse entrance. And yet, it was possible now for his jailers to look at Hyde without shuddering, because his soul no longer seemed to them repugnant. Even the asylum's fastidious chaplain, who had fled from Hyde's insistent blasphemies, would stop to give him the comforts of his Savior, for which Hyde would bless him. Hyde's reclamation soon came to the attention of the superintendent and then to that of the Home Office, which recommended clemency toward the prisoner. No longer considered dangerous or insane, Hyde was given a larger, more pleasant cell on one of the asylum's upper floors, with a view of sky and English countryside. He was allowed to take daily exercise on the asylum grounds and given other privileges reserved for the reformed. He would die at Broadmoor: No provision existed for his release. But he might live out his life there in relative ease. The public had forgotten him entirely, in favor of the hated Boer, whose iniquities belittled Hyde's in the popular press and imagination.

This was the Hyde to whom Frederick Drayton was introduced in the winter of 1900, in Hyde's bright, if spare, cell, with an aspidistra struggling on the brick sill and a curtain at the window to keep out the morning light. He was not "the child of Hell" Stevenson had promised and that he, Drayton, had been expecting. The man who rose politely to acknowledge his visitor was reserved, remarkably kempt, and almost gentle in his manner. Hyde might have been a caretaker or a gardener attached to some estate.

He looked his age—seventy-five—but no more than that, or less. Drayton had read, in Stevenson's account, that Hyde's appearance and vigorousness had belonged to a man much younger than Jekyll, who also would have been seventy-five, had he survived. Apparently, Hyde had caught up with his age during a quarter century of enforced retreat from the world, whose stimulations had earlier excited in him youth and an unnatural robustness. During Drayton's visit, he kept his hands hidden.

Hyde must have guessed that curiosity (and fear perhaps) had brought the American to visit him. His instincts remained quick. He might have seen in Drayton's face disappointment, which the young man made an effort to dissemble—not in sympathy for the old man, but because of the duplicity with which he habitually engaged the world. He did not want to put Hyde off! In his mind, Drayton saw the placard he had daydreamed in a San Francisco barroom that announced, in handsome Baskerville: THE ATONEMENT OF EDWARD HYDE. He was versatile and quick-witted and knew that although what was handed him—by fate or accident—might be likely to surprise him, it would not—he swore—defeat him.

"Mr. Drayton, you expected something else?"

"Not at all!"

"The world remembers Hyde the monster, if it remembers him at all."

"I am glad to see you're looking—"

"So unlike an animal?"

"*Well,* Mr. Hyde. Looking so well after your years of hardship here."

"Please call me Edward."

"And you, sir, may call me Frederick."

(Hyde snuffled.)

"I smell winter on you, Frederick."

"It is cold."

(A silence ensued, during which Hyde sat down at the oak table.)

"What is it, Frederick, that you want of me?"

"To give you your say."

(Hyde, perplexed.)

"Your side of it. I hope—with your permission and assistance—to present your point of view upon the stage."

(Hyde nodded—might even have smiled momentarily.)

"But the stage—I'm afraid—is unavailable to me."

"I will record you, Edward—your voice. It will be just as if you were there in front of them. The audience. It will be a *sen*—a most moving testimony to—it will be extraordinary, Edward!"

(Hyde did smile then; but pleased by his own cleverness in so quickly having gained his object's confidence, Drayton did not see him smile.)

"You intend to take down what I say, then have it read out by an actor?"

"I will record it with an apparatus. It will capture your voice as a photograph does a face."

(Hyde turned his face and looked outside—at a vast shadow that a sudden wind had caused to slip over the snow beyond the outer walls, blackening it.)

"Science! Of what is it not capable?"

"I have brought it with me—it is in the anteroom! Shall I go and get it?"

"It will be my pleasure."

(Hyde turned his head toward the window.)

"What's that you are humming, Edward?"

"A favorite air from *Alexander's Feast.* Do you know it? It's by Handel."

"No. I'll get the machine. The spectacle of the Elephant Man will be nothing next to this!"

4.

Frederick Drayton was lucky. Within the very month that he had conceived his plan for Hyde and then realized its impracticability, he had attended a public demonstration of Edison's newest recording device. The lecturer produced waxed cylinders on which sounds had been previously captured. Drayton listened to a cornet solo by Sergeant Smith of the Coldstream Guards, a bassoon solo entitled "Lucy Long," and a solo by the English whistler Charles Capper.

Had the Raising of Lazarus been presented upon that little stage with its sad proscenium and tatty drapes, it would not have created a sensation to equal this. Each who bore witness to the miraculous occasion was amazed.

The lecturer predicted that, in a very little while, people would be relieved of the drudgery of writing letters. Instead, he asserted, they would sit before the phonograph and speak their letters into the machine, which would capture not only their words but also subtleties of tone and emphasis. If the subject were droll, one might laugh; and the laugh would go down on wax. And should a sigh or kiss escape while one spoke tenderly of love—these, too, would be inscribed onto the cylinder.

"Thus will you be able to send a laugh or a sigh or a kiss by post!" the lecturer exclaimed, so great was his enthusiasm for Mr. Edison's device.

The demonstration ended with a recording made three months earlier of "Two Lovely Black Eyes," "Auld Lang Syne," and "Rule, Britannia." It was this last song that brought to Drayton's mind Hyde and how he might be presented on the stage. Not Hyde himself, to be sure—but his recorded voice amplified by a tundish, just as the music and songs were heard in the crowded hall of the San Francisco Philosophical Society.

If so many thronged to listen spellbound to Charles Capper whistle, what would the voice of Hyde evoke in them? What would they not pay to hear him speak or rage or weep?

Drayton approached the lecturer immediately after the demonstration to discover how he might order a machine of his own. The cost was high, but he soon found a man willing to invest in the enterprise. Two months later, Drayton was in New York City, where, in an afternoon, he learned to operate the phonograph and, with the machine and a supply of waxed cylinders bedded in excelsior, he embarked the following day for England.

5.

Cylinder No. 1: 10 December 1900—3 o'clock in the Afternoon

HYDE: . . . was for me at the start of it.

DRAYTON: You must not turn your head away from the machine when you speak. Aim your voice there, at the tube.

HYDE: I don't recall much of how it was for me in the beginning.

DRAYTON: Good.

HYDE: I seem to have been asleep far more than awake. Although it was not sleep. There was no refreshment—no waking afterward to a renewal of my relationship to the things of the world, which had been broken, temporarily, by fatigue. There was no sense of waking up from a dream, no feeling of relationship to anything or anyone. It was—it is difficult to say what it was—as if I were suddenly born. Each time. Born anew, without connection or associations. I had little sense of connection even with my former self—for that is what I felt myself to be: something that had been. Something previous. The merest sketch. Opening my eyes, I was left with the sensation of having been, but without memory of what I was. I did not know that I was bad, for the knowledge of my crimes died with me each time I fell asleep. But I tell you it was not sleep! It was a blackness that overtook me, engulfing and profound. It was death—yes, that is what it was like for me at the start! As if I'd died with all my sins upon me and was born again spotless. I did not know that I was bad! If I had known, I might have chosen otherwise. I mean I might have ended it. But the thing was beyond me—beyond my power to change. I was not myself: I belonged to someone else. To Jekyll! Though I did not know him then. My eyes would open on a shuttered-up room with the stink of chemicals in the close air. Later, I understood the room belonged to Dr. Jekyll—was his laboratory. But it was only a name to me then! The man whose space this was, was never there—never at home, always elsewhere, on his rounds or at his club or at the houses of his friends. I'd wait for him in that stuffy, pent-up, dismal place, growing sick and tired and angry. You cannot imagine what quality and depth of anger. *Anger* is far too weak a word. Rage—I was always in a rage. And he did not come! I would fall asleep—let's call it sleep, for convenience—and Hyde would disappear—who knows where—until he woke again in the empty laboratory. Later still, my eyes would open elsewhere—in a woman's room or an alley—and soon there would be blood upon the coverlet or bricks. I was helpless against the raging, helpless to understand it even, and baffled by the absence of the elusive Dr. Jekyll! May I have a glass of water?

DRAYTON: I will call for one. I must change the cylinder, too.

Cylinder No. 2: 10 December 1900—3:30 in the Afternoon

HYDE: I went in search of Jekyll. I *hunted* him. But in every place he might have been, should have been—he wasn't. Never was he where they said he was. His man, Poole. His friends Lanyon and Utterson. I broke my stick on the head of Sir Danvers because he knew and would not say! If you are looking for a monster—look at him! At Jekyll! He tormented me so! He hid from Hyde, and Hyde—poor Edward—could not understand who or what he was and why he should wake in that laboratory! There was some vital connection between us, which I could not fathom! He drove me to fury and to madness. To murder—murders that I committed and forgot. Except for the blood on my hands and clothes, my broken stick, I would not have known that I had . . . that I had been where blood'd spilled. Later, I did know. Later, I remembered a little of before—I mean before I woke. I did not dream. Poor Edward has never dreamed—not even here. But I seemed to see on the other side of that engulfing darkness a distant coastline, fogged in at first. Little by little, the fog dispelled. And I saw. But that was long after the beginning. The end—it was—when I seemed not to sleep at all but to be Hyde Hyde Hyde for days on end and never sleep at all. Then I knew the meaning of my bloodstained clothes, the ripped collar, and fingernails which looked like claws that had been trying to tear up the alleyway bricks. Christ, what had I done! And why? I knew it was not Christ who knew, but Jekyll, whom I could not find and hunted days and nights in every street and brothel, museum and music hall. I almost caught up with him one afternoon in Kew Gardens. I rushed at him with my sword-stick, ready to run him through, but he turned—the man turned at the noise of my bearing down on him over the dead leaves—and I saw that he was not the man I wished dead. Surely, you can see why!

DRAYTON *(irresistibly)*: Yes!

HYDE: It was Jekyll who drove me!

DRAYTON: They shall find it out! Edward, you will be vindicated!

HYDE: I wish now that he were alive to see it and be hounded and brought down and called a monster and made to endure a quarter century shut up here!

DRAYTON: They will set you free, Edward! When they hear you speak, they will insist you be released. They will demand it. They will storm the walls and break down the door if you are not! They will love you, Edward, for—

Drayton turned off the phonograph and placed the two waxed cylinders carefully into the rosewood case.

"—your martyrdom. We will make them pay. You will be a free man, and rich!"

He was gripped by an excitement that was part indignation for Hyde and part gratitude for his own good fortune in having found in Hyde so amenable a subject, so very eloquent and moving a victim for him to champion. Drayton sensed a triumph far greater than the one he had first imagined for himself. He saw the headline in his mind that would soon be published through the wide world:

FREDERICK DRAYTON EXCULPATES EDWARD HYDE
INNOCENT VICTIM OF THE INFAMOUS DR. JEKYLL!

He imagined himself to be not only a celebrated impresario but also an exalted advocate. He would become the most famous man in England and a hero in America to all those of his countrymen who despised the cruelties and exploitation of the aristocracy.

Already, Hyde sensed the measure of the other man's ambition.

"I know of something else the crowd will love."

Having begun to disassemble the phonograph, Drayton had the tundish in his hands. "What?"

"Jekyll's formula—the one that gave me birth. It will be— what's that word you Americans use to describe a remarkable disclosure?"

"*Sensation.*"

"Yes. It will be a sensation to put Jekyll's notebook on display. It will tantalize the mob. It's yours, if you want it—my gift to you for what you intend to do for me."

"You have it here?"

"Certainly not. It's hidden in the laboratory. I know where. It must be there still."

"How do you know?"

"It's curious, but I know—now—everything that Jekyll

knew. I didn't when I hunted him. But since his death, I have acquired—don't ask me how—his mind. I know, as well, the impurity that had entered the salt. Because of it, he could not duplicate the original mixture. Because of it, he lacked the strength to keep me out, and so he died."

"You and Jekyll are the same."

"Everyone knows that!"

"I had almost forgotten it."

"I didn't understand, at first, that the man I sought to kill was myself. And yet—you know—he was really another man. Whether or not we were locked in the same body, Jekyll was separate from me, and he created me, injured me, and hoped to murder me. We might say—for convenience—that although we were the same, he and I were two different men entirely; and I wish to see him in disgrace."

"Edward, you shall! He will be exposed. Together, we'll restore your good name and blacken his."

"The notebook is in the wall behind the laboratory stove. Eight bricks from the floor, seven from the right wall. Poole will let you inside. Lord M—'s introduction will see to that."

"And the impurity?"

"Cigar ash. A length of ordinary cigar ash that, by accident, had fallen into the salt during its manufacture."

"I thank you, Edward."

(Hyde did not take Drayton's proffered hand.)

Drayton picked up the tundish to place it in the box.

"You might leave it here, Frederick, and one of those waxed cylinders, too. In case I think of something else to say."

6.

Lord M—'s secretary now removes the second cylinder from the phonograph and lays it in its bed of crimson plush with a tenderness ordinarily reserved for a relic of a dead religion, or a vanished love. Throat dry after so lengthy a narration, he pours water from an earthenware jug (incongruous in the luxury crowding Lord M—'s study); and as he tilts back his head to drink, it is not the secretary we see, but Edward Hyde—the bony knuckles of his throat working obediently to slake his thirst. We shudder as if it were blood he were drinking—as if Hyde himself were drinking it—until the secretary coughs once and the spell breaks like a thread of saliva.

"I can't say I really understand Lord M—'s interest in Frederick Drayton," says Roebling, taking from a silver case a Dutch cigar; "why he should have lent Drayton his influence and why he should have bothered to acquire this." He indicates with a hand that holds a flaming match the rosewood box of waxed cylinders and the phonograph.

"His interest was Hyde," the secretary says. Roebling is about to ask for an explanation, but a peremptory gesture admonishes him, and indeed all of us. The secretary closes the rosewood box as if to signal his determination to keep the matter dark. "Drayton produced his sensation; the magnitude of its effect exceeded anything he could have foreseen when he conceived of his exploitation of the Monster Hyde. The dimensions of Drayton's celebrity were enormous. There was not a man or woman in England or America who was not affected by it. I have no doubt they heard the tale in Patagonia, so avid were the journalists to publish details of Drayton's Grand Guignol."

"He butchered the poor girl on her wedding night," Phelps reminds us, who need no reminding.

"He out-Hyded Hyde himself!" says Roebling. "His savagery was worse even than the Ripper's."

"We know everything but why," I say, recalling that the murderer had offered no defense—was, by the time of his apprehension and trial, incapable of reason and coherent utterance, so entirely given over was his nature to the bestial.

"I can hear him howling still inside his cage," muses

Roebling, eyes caught by the barbed light winking on the clock's brass bezel.

Drayton was each day conveyed to and from London's Central Criminal Court in an iron cage, where I am told he raged continuously through the two weeks' proceedings against him.

"His motives are not entirely obscure," the secretary is saying. "After his sentencing, I spent some hours sitting just the other side of his cage. He had been given morphine and was lucid. That is how I came to know his story."

"I can't picture you in the cells," I tell him, "or think what brought you there."

"I went as deputy for Lord M—," the secretary replies, drawing me aside and speaking low. "He could not very well have gone himself, could he?"

"But I do not see why he should have concerned himself at all in the matter!" I nearly shout in my impatience, despising this unnecessary mystery as I would a woman who insists on undressing in the dark.

"We were hoping to discover the whereabouts of the notebook," he says with an insinuation made more emphatic by a hand upon my sleeve. "Jekyll's," he adds in answer to my look of incomprehension. "Do *you* know?"

"How should I?" I bristle.

"I've heard that you've acquired some curiosities in the course of your research into people's Gothic inclinations." Abruptly, his manner relaxes. He turns to Phelps and Roebling. "Like anyone, we are all curious about evil. Are we not, gentlemen?"

He unties a marbled portfolio and draws out a copy of *The Illustrated Police Budget,* whose headline shrieks in seventy-two-point Copperplate:

FIEND SLAUGHTERS JEKYLL HEIR DURING WEDDING NIGHT:
HEART TORN FROM BODY FOUND IN NEARBY MEWS

With more reserve, an edition of *Lloyd's Weekly Newspaper* announces:

FREDERICK DRAYTON TO HANG FOR UNSPEAKABLE ACTS

"He wanted to make a spectacle of himself and profit by it," the secretary concludes drily, like a magistrate at an inquest. "But he could not control his metamorphoses any more than Jekyll could."

"That bit about the cigar ash was a lie, then?" Roebling asks.

Before the secretary can respond, Phelps says, "I heard that, the moment before he was dropped, he cursed Hyde." As he speaks, he is impelled to touch with his finger the word *unspeakable* in the black headline.

"What did poor Hyde have to do with it?" Roebling replies angrily. "He's banged up for life in Broadmoor!"

"He should be let out!" I cry, seized for a reason I cannot put into words by sympathy for Hyde in his winter—I, who am ordinarily indifferent to the miseries and ill use of others.

The secretary's voice is like the crack of ice in a river's sudden thaw. "You must not think to let Hyde loose! You do not know what he is. Not even Lord M— guessed what Hyde . . ." He raises his hands, then lowers them, abjectly, like a naturalist who has been asked to classify something unclassifiable. He opens the rosewood box and lifts a third cylinder from its velvet bed, a cylinder sent to Lord M— "in confidence" by the superintendent of Broadmoor. The cylinder lodged in the machine, Hyde's voice again leaps out into the room. While it apostrophized him, Frederick Drayton never heard this last recording. (What quality is in that voice to make the heart stand still, to fill its chambers with snow?) Now we all listen.

Cylinder No. 3: 10 December 1900—4:30 in the Afternoon

HYDE: You cannot know all that I have lost—what liberty has been mine in being Hyde! What ecstasy and release! To give way without thought or misgiving to the most amazing impulse! To be incapable of the slightest misgiving. To be incapable of any thought that would check the natural propensity to the exercise of power. Having neither ordinary scruples nor a self-censuring faculty, nor any fear of consequences—acknowledging only his insistent need and contemptuous of any moral imperative that might frustrate its immediate satisfaction. This was Hyde—his glory and achievement. You have yet to discover, Frederick, the perfection of such a state, how harmonious a condition, and how much in keeping with a sovereign nature! Hyde was not the beast they made him out to be—no, but a god, or an angel faithful to his own untrammeled self, with nothing to bind him to circumstances or the provisional universe. To have given way to everything that might afford him pleasure, to have yielded nothing of himself, to have been above all laws and sacred prohibitions—this was Hyde! I say you cannot, Frederick, know what it was like to assume his being. But you *will*. I know you, sir, and see how willingly you lean away from the common center toward a larger self. Your hunger for celebrity (which is the wish for power over other men, as it hopes to enthrall their imaginations to one's own)—that is your nature and, as you must know, the instrument of others' inevitable destruction. It is Hyde who sees Drayton removing Jekyll's notebook from its lair and yielding precipitately to the seduction of a formula that will make him singular, extraordinary—which is to say, *monstrous*. Hyde sees Drayton now in Jekyll's house, captivated by Jekyll's niece, whom I did not mention (a lovely young woman by all reports)— now circling around her, now seducing her, and soon—in one form of Hyde—destroying her, as he must, as he must. Hyde sees Drayton becoming Hyde, perpetrating his crimes, perpetuating him—extending the line. And Hyde, now grown invisible, will sing—in his winter—his favorite air from *Alexander's Feast*, on the occasion of Drayton's marriage to Jekyll's niece, followed by her quick obliteration:

Revenge, revenge, Timotheus cries,
See the furies arise,
See the snakes that they rear,
How they hiss in their hair,
And the sparkles that flash from their eyes!

I, Edward Hyde, swear to it!

7.

Late afternoon, the sun fallen already behind the trees. The pale winter light stops at the window of Hyde's cell, unfettering shadows from beneath bed and table. The water in the washbowl, black. Hyde at the window, looking with curious intensity at the field beyond the stone walls, where, here and there, stalks stick up stiffly through the snow. The light going, he leans his forehead against an ice-cold pane and shuts his eyes on the world without.

"Edward Hyde," I say; and in spite of the pains I have taken to rehearse, my voice betrays unease.

He turns; and I seem to hear in that supple movement a commotion that makes me think of the Minotaur, or perhaps of a machine, the single-minded music of its whirring gears.

"Sir, I am at your service," Hyde replies, suavely, as if the distance traveled from the depths of contemplation to the present moment were no further than the six steps that separate us. This distance between us he closes as he walks toward me. I offer him my hand; he does not take it.

"I doubt you know me, Mr. Hyde. I am a writer, of tales. I wish to write of you—your duress: a serial for *The London Magazine* and, later, a novel. I've already begun it." I ignore the silent probing gaze, the glint of teeth, the roaring in my ears issuing from a rapidly accelerating heart. Opening my portmanteau, I show him a manuscript. "It will be—I promise you—a sensation!"

He continues to regard me in silence. Suddenly, although his manner seems benevolent, I am afraid. Do I not see a man, not unlike myself, standing on the gallows' little stage? This is but a momentary impression, which Hyde's smile and the assurance of Lord M—'s patronage conspire to dissipate. "You will want," he says, "Jekyll's formula . . ."

"You know it, then?" Astonished, I nearly shout at him.

Imperturbable, Hyde replies, "I know everything that Jekyll knew."

"And you will tell me all of it?"

"It will be my pleasure," says Hyde.

"And the impurity of the mixture?"

Hyde smiles again, leans close, whispering something into my ear.

The Captain Is Sleeping

1.

The engineers have not been seen for days. I stand outside the engine room, their freshly laundered sheets folded in my arms, and listen to them weep. I wonder at their anguish, at its depths, and shudder at the sound they make on the other side of the iron door.

"What is the matter?" I say through the door. I dare not shout. If I raise my voice so as to be heard, I am sure I will faint. My nerves have been tightly strung, like piano wire, ever since the ship began to act queerly. "What is the matter, men?" I try again, my lips close to the door, whispering into my cupped hands, having made of them a megaphone.

As if in answer, their keening grows more plaintive—the burden of its grief heavier to bear. I turn away.

"Oh, engineers, what is your sorrow?" I cry into the sheets, which smell pleasantly of soap and steam.

Few know of the engineers' sequestration or that of the captain, who shut himself away in his cabin three days ago. I reported both circumstances to the ship's doctor, as I ought. The doctor, whose fastidious whiskers remind me of Dickens's, was denied admission to the captain by the captain's mother, who sits impassively in front of the cabin door "like a veritable Gorgon," and knits.

"The captain is asleep," she says—that, and no more.

The doctor, who studied in Heidelberg under a brilliant, if

controversial, specialist in diseases of the mind, believes that the captain suffers from an acute nervous disorder, characterized by willed sleep and general suspension of animation.

"But what of the engineers?" I asked after he advanced his theory. But he merely shrugged and snipped, with a tiny scissors, a rogue whisker, which was causing his nose to snuffle. "What of their weeping?" I asked.

Snip.

"Unremitting grief may be symptomatic of a disintegrating mind," the doctor declared into the mirror, in which my own face, with its usual look of bewilderment, appeared. "However, I know of no instances in the literature where eight men simultaneously shared in the disintegration."

Snip.

"Especially men in the Corps of Engineers."

Snip.

The engineers are weeping, the captain is sleeping, and the ship seems to fidget in sympathy, or restlessness, or fear, out on the middle of the North Atlantic.

I am the ship's steward. There is little that passes belowdecks that escapes me. Is it any wonder I am afraid?

2.

Last night, after a genial performance by the Light Orchestra Society players, the doctor lowered a young woman into the engine room. Her name is Daphne, she dances in the chorus, and I love her madly. I had objected that the dumbwaiter was never intended as a conveyance, no matter how slight the passenger; that the condition of the rope was unknown; that the pulley creaked alarmingly; and that the good conduct of the engineers could not be relied upon in their present mood. The doctor could think of no other way to assess the situation.

"The situation," he said, "is becoming more dangerous with each passing day. If for no other reason than the safety of all aboard, we must risk it," he said. "And then there is our mission."

Our ship, the *Minos*, was laying a transatlantic cable.

"Our mission is of incalculable importance, Simon. We are embarked upon a great adventure."

I reminded him that, as ship's steward, I had only a negligible role in the adventure: that I saw to the sheets, the pillowcases, tidied the cabins, and brought the members of the syndicate their whiskey and sodas.

"And clean up after those who can't hold their liquor in a beam sea."

The doctor reproached me for my lack of imagination. Infuriated, he would have struck me if McCutcheon, the cartoonist from one of the American papers, had not entered the infirmary.

"I need something for my nerves," said McCutcheon. "I'm feeling on edge. My nerves are . . ." He left his sentence in midair, punctuating it, as it were, with a tear that suddenly coursed down his cheek.

The doctor and I looked at each other. His face registered the barest trace of alarm. From the involuntary displacement of my cheekbones, mine must have, too. The doctor poured some white powder into a paper, twisted it, and handed the "screw" to McCutcheon.

"Thanks, Doc," the cartoonist said with undisguised self-pity.

"I begin to be afraid," the doctor said anxiously as he went to find Daphne and offer her an expanded role in our history.

Daphne agreed. The doctor commended her bravery and commitment to scientific progress, better understanding between nations, et cetera. She folded herself inside the dumbwaiter. I listened to it creak and bang during its slow descent.

"A mere girl—scarcely more than a child!" said the doctor, wanting to shame me.

I hated him and hoped one night he would be carried overboard. In the meantime, I'll short-sheet him when I make up his berth, I promised myself. Tomorrow he will retire into a straitjacket—may he rot there!

Daphne returned from the engine room, trembling.

"What is happening down there?" the doctor cried. "Simon, get the gin."

I poured out a tumbler of the good Bombay, then helped Daphne into a chair. The cleats of the doctor's shoes could be heard tapping on the galley floor, the hanging pots and ladles chiming companionably. We were alone in the galley—Daphne, the doctor, and I—the cook and his gang of kitchen roughs having gone to the casino to squander their week's pay.

The gin proved itself sovereign against hysteria. (In my experience, it is always so.) Having regained her composure, Daphne was now dabbing at her eyes with a napkin.

"Tell us, girl, what it was that you saw!" the doctor demanded pitilessly, so that I hated him for Daphne's sake.

"It was a scene from hell," she said without the least affectation.

The doctor stopped his pacing and looked at her searchingly.

"They are lying in their bunks, their faces in their pillows, crying, while all about them black particles of soot tumble in the hellish light. From time to time, a hiss of steam drowns their lamentations."

The doctor was silent a moment. I gently took the tumbler from Daphne's hand, allowing mine to fall chastely onto her pert breast.

I washed the tumbler in the sink, while the doctor posed a momentous question: "Then who—for Christ's sake—is stoking the boilers?"

"A dwarf, I think," Daphne replied. "Naked, and black with coal dust, and incredibly hairy."

"A dwarf?" the doctor repeated wonderingly.

"Unless it was a monkey," she said.

3.

Later, I walked Dolores to her cabin. For reasons I cannot explain, we came out onto one of the ship's upper decks. We stopped at the rail and yielded to the charm of happenstance. We are young, after all, and susceptible to the prodding of the invisible. We wondered first at the sky—carbon, ermine, black as any sky I have ever seen in my voyages—black as a tropic night is black in spite of its crowding stars. This is not a night one finds in the North Atlantic, I thought to myself, where purity of darkness yields to a sullen, secretive gloom. And the air—so suave and flowery as we leaned over the rail to watch the shining fish.

"*Poisson*," said Dolores, "is French for fish."

I asked her to repeat the word.

"Fish."

"Tell me it in French!" I begged.

"But why?"

"In saying it, your lips look as if they were about to kiss," I said.

She smiled and looked at the moon, which was round and gold as a coin.

"I don't understand what is happening," I said.

She misunderstood my confusion, thinking I meant kisses. "Would you like to kiss me?" she asked. "In this moonlight?"

I forgot about the weather, which was wrong for this latitude, and the fish, which ought to have been swimming elsewhere, and kissed her. I am young, and questions of travel are better left to old men.

The Light Orchestra Society players rhapsodized. I took Dolores in my arms and danced. The gay music, which I had assumed to originate in the ship's ballroom, seemed to be coming from the ocean itself. Straining my eyes, I saw, in the distance, the white hulls of the lifeboats—each occupied by a section of the orchestra. But I was intoxicated by moonlight and the scent of Dolores's hair and could have been mistaken.

4.

Waking this morning, I remember the night—the kissing and the ship's apparent dislocation in space. I swing out of my hammock and land on the ice-cold floor. The room is freezing; the portlight, frosted over. A pale wintry light leaves what looks like frost upon the floor. I dress quickly, putting on a sweater and wool cap, before going to the infirmary.

"Dr. Gordon, last night the ship was not where it was supposed to be," I say. "The night reminded me of the Seychelles, or Zanzibar."

"As to that," he says, "we have no idea where the ship is."

I cock my head as if listening to the shoaling of distant waves.

"The sextant is missing. And the charts."

"What does the navigator say?" I ask.

"He also is missing."

The doctor fastens a tourniquet around his arm and injects himself.

"It is beyond my power to explain, beyond understanding, beyond anything I have yet to encounter in this world."

"I hoped it might be love," I say.

"What does love have to do with it?"

"It could have explained the night."

"And can love explain the unmanning of the engineers, or a captain who never wakes—and now this, our vanished navigator?" The doctor sneers at my ridiculous naïveté.

And I am ridiculous! Love has made me so.

"Last night was incomparable!" the doctor mutters. "I

remember a night under the equator when, like you, I was in love. Last night reminded me of it."

The doctor shakes his head as if to empty it of memory.

"What interests me now is this ship."

We go out on deck to take a rough reckoning of our position. The sky is gray—the sun a small metallic disk that comes and goes according to the wind, which is herding lead-colored clouds across it. Their shadows lumber over water vexed and broken by the wind. We pull our collars up and our caps down over our ears. The bitter wind bites our cheeks and carries rain in its ice-cold pockets.

I look at the deck rimed with frost and frozen spray. Surely, it is not possible that Dolores and I danced, here, while the orchestra played von Suppé!

"Impossible that I kissed Dolores in last night's moonlight—here!"

"I thought her name was Daphne," the doctor shouts into the wind.

"Is it?" I say, my eyes transfixed by the horizon line, which is violently shaking as if with ague.

We go inside and take off our wet clothes, leaving the deck to the men who supervise the unwinding of the cable from the enormous iron spool.

"I am chilled to the bone!" the doctor cries.

Was last night a dream? I ask myself.

"The ship is moving—that's what I do not understand!" the doctor continues. "The cable unwinds. The ship moves—on what course, we cannot say for sure. West. In a westerly direction. But without a captain, a navigator . . . Someone must be stoking the boilers! Daphne said a dwarf, or a monkey. Not a monkey, surely!"

Dolores, Daphne, Dolores, Daphne, Dolores . . .

"Confound it—there is no dwarf aboard this ship! Certainly

not among the crew! I examined them all—every man of them!
I would have noticed a dwarf!"

. . . Daphne, Dolores, Daphne, Dolores, Doris?

"But someone is stoking the boilers," the doctor says. "Then
why does he not unlock the engine room door?"

Last night there were no men on deck, I tell myself, no commotion of the spool. No cable being paid out. Only the insouciant music made by the Light Orchestra Society players.

"How is it possible!" I cry.

"That's what I'd like to know!" the doctor replies.

I turn and hurry along the passageway.

"Where are you going, Simon?"

"I must talk to Doris."

"Your fine romance will have to wait. First, we must talk to
the captain's mother."

5.

The doctor and I make our way into the
interior, where the captain's cabin lies. Each time I move about
the ship, I am surprised by its interior spaciousness. The *Minos*
is listed in the registry as a 160-foot commercial vessel. But inside, it has the capacity of a passenger ship! Its decks and cabins
multiply as I perform my steward's duties, pushing the laundry
cart along apparently endless passages. I am also struck by the
haphazardness of the ship's deck plan; how passages twist and
turn, end abruptly, or open up into two or even three new ways.
I have been amazed to find myself on a deck below, or above,
the one on which I began, without my having taken the stairs.

"Have you noticed how odd the . . ."

But the doctor is nowhere to be seen.

How very strange!

I will leave the captain's mother to the doctor. I know her
obstinacy. Her taciturnity. She will not be persuaded into

standing aside so that the captain's condition may be sounded. I suggested that a party of ordinary seamen be armed and ordered to break down the captain's door, but the doctor feared an incident.

"There is no telling where such a breach of ship's discipline will lead," he said. "What horrors. Besides, the ordinary seamen are all in the infirmary, or else sick in their bunks from alcohol poisoning. We ought to have set a watch on the ship's rum closet."

At the time, I wondered who was performing the duties involved in the ship's operation—the chipping, painting, swabbing, oiling, knotting, coiling, and uncoiling, not to mention the stoking. I thought it best to keep my misgivings to myself.

The doctor can confront the captain's mother alone. Her surliness and enormous skein of black wool—they frighten me. Instead, I will go see Dora.

6.

I spend an hour or more in fruitless search of Dora's cabin. In the end, I succeed only in exhausting myself. On a deck I have never been, far below the waterline, I discover a barbershop. The barber is asleep in one of the two chairs, snoring underneath a striped towel. I decide to rest awhile in the other chair.

I have always been drawn to barbershops: Their relaxed and luxurious atmosphere, the sense of privilege one feels while being expertly shaved, the temporary sanction of self-indulgence, the fragrance of soap and pomade—all combine in a feeling of extraordinary well-being. Barbers are also much admired as conversationalists, well versed in the day's opinions and events.

As I let myself down in the chair, the barber whips off the

towel and levers himself into an upright position. He looks at me in surprise.

"Do you mind if I sit a moment?" I ask. "I've been walking for hours—maybe even days. It feels like days, although by my watch it has only been an hour and a half since I left the doctor up on B deck."

The barber swivels his chair toward me.

"Doctor? What doctor might that be, sir?"

"The ship's doctor—Dr. Gordon! Surely you must know him!"

The barber shakes his head—sadly, I think.

"I don't know any doctor. On B deck, you say?"

"B deck—yes!" I reply impatiently.

"If ever I were on B deck, I have forgotten it."

I look at the shaving mugs arrayed on a shelf beneath the mirror. Each mug bears the name of a crew member. Hunting among them with my eyes, I soon find Dr. Gordon's.

"There," I say, pointing in triumph to a mug snug between the navigator's and the hydrologist's.

The barber gets out of his chair and, picking up the doctor's mug, blows it clean of dust.

"As you can see, it has not been used," he says smugly. "No, sir, I have never shaved a doctor of any sort!" Glancing at the other mugs, he says, "Indeed, I cannot recall ever having shaved any man from the ship. As it happens, sir, you are my first customer."

"I hate to disappoint you," I say with every intention to be cruel, "but I am not a customer. I am looking for someone."

Abashed, he swivels round to his former position and would have levered himself into the horizontal had I not restrained him.

"I am looking for a young woman named Doris," I say roughly, in my increasing annoyance.

"Never heard of her!" the barber replies curtly.

I jump out of the chair and twist his arm. He yelps in pain. Wincing, he says, "People rarely come into this part of the ship . . . cabins all empty for who knows how long . . . without window, calendar, or clock—impossible to grasp the passing of time . . . cannot be certain even of the time of day, or whether day or night . . . sleep when I'm tired . . . nap in the chair . . . read old magazines . . . eat when Peggy beats the dinner gong."

"Peggy?" I ask. "Who is Peggy?"

"Peggy is my wife," he says as a superlatively large woman pushes aside a drapery separating the shop and the barber's accommodations.

"I understood wives are not permitted on board."

"That may be true of those hired under the new regulations," the barber simpers. "But I am exempt because of my long service to the syndicate."

"This is our home!" Peggy says combatively, as if to preclude a challenge to her status I am too indifferent to raise. "I cannot remember having ever lived anyplace else."

Nearly dropping with exhaustion, I climb into the barber's chair and shut my eyes.

"I must rest!"

"By all means!" the barber exclaims, tipping back the chair in which already I have begun to drift, out onto the oceanic expanse of a mind that has slipped its moorings. "The incessant duties aboard a ship, especially one commissioned to undertake a magnificent and dangerous enterprise . . ."

I wake to the noise of pots in the barber's quarters, where, presumably, Peggy is preparing dinner—another extraordinary dispensation, as the rest of the *Minos*'s crew is obliged to eat in the mess. But perhaps a barber and his wife are not crew, per se, but enjoy some other status. But what of the musicians, the entertainers, the hydrologist, the coatroom attendant, the metaphysicians, the magicians, and the newspapermen—they dine with the ordinary seamen and lesser officers in the mess. But are they *obliged* to do so?

"I have never set foot inside the mess," says Peggy, reading my mind. "In fact, since coming here as a bride, I haven't left this deck except once—for a fitting. Otto and I were invited to the captain's ball." A woman as substantial as a flour sack, Peggy shambles round the shop in a tender travesty of a waltz, causing bottles of hair tonic to toll one against the other. "It would have been a lovely gown!" She sighs. "Taffeta, like green sea foam."

"Would have been?"

"I could never find the modiste's again." She sighs a second time, and I am reminded of my own sadness.

"Have you ever seen this girl?" I ask, showing Peggy a photograph of Diana the ship's photographer made of her the night we met. She is wearing an enormous hat. Her face hides in its shadow.

"I can't make out the face. Anyway, I don't think so," she says, handing me back the photograph. "Is she very pretty?"

"Yes, very pretty"; although my heart nearly stops as I realize I have only an imperfect recollection of Diana's face. It is as if a reflection rocking on water were suddenly troubled by a pebble. She must be, I tell myself. Shaking my head to dispel an anxiety that has laid its hand upon my soul, I inquire after the barber, who is nowhere to be seen.

"He went to shave the captain!" Peggy says with the air of someone who has just been given a great happiness. "We can't remember the last time he was called. And the captain was always so fastidious! He disliked beards and side-whiskers, insisting that he be clean-shaven. He was such a handsome man—and still may be, although it's been years since I saw him last."

"Called?"

"Through the speaking tube," she says, nodding toward

an apparatus above the wainscoting, next to a crudely litho-graphed calendar.

I listen through the brass end piece and hear what sounds like ocean and something else, the somber beating of a heart; but this may be only the effect of a molecular disturbance in a bend of the tube, or a sympathetic resonance.

I whistle down the tube, then shout, "Hello! Hello, is anyone there?"

No answer.

I return the end piece to its hook and, glancing at the gaudy calendar, remark, "Your calendar is out of date, you know."

"Is it?" she replies indifferently.

7.

I pass through a tangle of dim passage-ways—desolate, with the exception of a kind of chapel, which I have never before seen, in which three monks play dominoes beneath a mural depicting Christ's bleeding heart. I begin to speak but am silenced at once with a hostile remark delivered in a language that may be Icelandic. I leave them to their domi-noes and walk on, ever deeper, into the bowels of the ship. For I now believe that the answer to all that has made a mystery and an enigma of our voyage lies in the engine room, among the weeping engineers.

May she not have returned there—to them—in the dumb-waiter? I ask myself. Her reason may have been overturned by an irresistible fascination. And then I am led against all rea-son to the dwarf—the thought of whom makes me shudder uncontrollably. For I have remembered the story of Eurydice—how the god ascended and ravished her to his underworld. Might not the dwarf, having first subdued the engineers, have ascended in the dumbwaiter in the middle of the night, stolen to Denise's cabin, then carried her to hell?

I spend what seems hours penetrating to the depths of the ship, aware all the while of an impossible silence. I might be on the surface of the moon! Or, if not the moon, at the center of a dismal, scarcely penetrable forest, enjoined to silence by a sorcerer.

I find the scattered evidence of a rout: a navigation chart, the ship's log, magic lantern slides, a violin, an astrolabe, a ball belonging to one of the jugglers, the magician's handkerchief.

I climb down another of an endless number of companionways, my boots ringing on the iron stairs, turn one more corner, push open a door, and find myself out on deck in the freezing cold of a North Atlantic winter's night!

I no longer hope to find the girl, whose face I can no longer recall, whose name I do not remember.

8.

It is snowing. The ship lies still and helpless within the iron grasp of the frozen sea. The snow whitens the unmoving waves. I look into the black night and see endlessly falling flakes. They are knitting a white shroud for the ship. Its lines and rails are thickly glazed. The shuffleboard court is visible behind a pane of frozen spray. If time any longer can be measured or understood, it was only a week ago the off-duty engineers played the musicians there. The great spool is stopped—its windings iced; the cable cut by the scissoring action of two floes before their drifting ceased. This is a cold to freeze birds in mid-flight and to make the earth stand still!

Looking far out on the solid sea, I seem to see men. One, I think, waves. He is calling to me faintly in a voice of immeasurable sadness. The words, if words they are, are dashed by the gale, which makes the heavy ship lean even in its icebound fastness.

I think it is the doctor who is waving to me.

Or Mary Shelley's monster shambling over pack ice.

But no—how can it be, in a cold approaching absolute zero? In a cold where nothing lives or moves—not even a thing compounded of the dead.

No! I say to myself mockingly. Not even the moon moves on such a night, in such a cold!

I hurry inside, in terror—in terror hurry down the passage leading to the infirmary.

The doctor is gone. The sickbeds are empty.

"Surely not!" I cry aloud.

I must find the captain and wake him; for surely this is a dream, and whose dream is it if not his?

9.

In an instant, I am standing outside the captain's cabin. The captain's mother sits before the door, her stony face inclined toward the wool in her lap.

Click, click, click is all the sound there is: that which her steel needles make as they tease the wool into a lengthening cable. Not tease, *torment*. She has made a black cable with them, which stretches from an inexhaustible skein into the darkness at the end of the passage.

"I've come to wake the captain," I tell her.

"The captain must not be wakened," she replies, without dropping a stitch. "You must know by now that it is in sleep that the ship moves and the cable is laid."

"But the ship does not move!" I cry. "And the cable is severed!"

She smiles into her hands, which ply with remarkable art the needles.

Click, click, click.

"The ship moves nevertheless, and the cable is paid out. The work continues for as long as the captain sleeps."

"But everyone is vanishing!" I shout.

"You remain," she says with a smile more inscrutable than the first.

"Why should a ship's steward remain?"

"Who knows why? Perhaps because the captain is in his bed and feels the sheets against him. Be glad of it!"

"There was a girl . . ."

"Yes?"

"Even the memory of her is disappearing!" I have never known anguish equal to this. "She is slipping away from me!"

The old woman raises her eyes to mine and says, "Perhaps, if you follow the cable? The one I knit."

With difficulty, I turn my eyes away from her, whose gaze is powerful, and trace the black wool to where it loses itself in darkness beyond the far bulkhead.

"Follow it, steward! It leads to all you have lost."

Her voice is sweet—a coaxing, sweet murmur, which is the voice of death. Or, if not death, death's own servant. She sees in my mind the terror with which I beheld on the ice-clad deck the death of the world.

"What you saw outside is simply your own dreaming—the nightmare of a dreamer who is himself a dream."

I feel how sweet it would be to follow the voice, the cable, the lost girl into the dark. I will myself to shake off the enchantment. Desperately, before there is time to surrender to the desire that I be no more, I strangle the captain's mother with the black yarn.

Her head lolls to one side. Her hands open. The needles—the needles continue to knit!

Click, click, click.

10.

There is in the captain's cabin that same cold that would have stopped my blood and sealed the chambers of my heart if I had remained any longer out on deck. The cabin walls are sheathed in frost. The floor is ice. The sheet folds about the captain's body like snow. His body, too, is cold; the limbs are possessed by rigor; the eyes, two stones beneath the lowered lids. His smooth cheeks bear traces of the lather the barber left there before he, too, disappeared. Was it to shave a corpse that the barber was called?

I stare at the sheeted body—my own eyes glazed with weariness and—something else—a fascination for this ghastly sight, for the tracery etched in ice by death's deliberate hand, and for the freezing seawater that is welling up from the bowels of the ship—from the engine room, in which no man any longer weeps. Not even a demonic dwarf can endure this death ship, I think. Not even a lord of the underworld. I strip the body of its sheet and—startled and dismayed—see the marble chest rise and fall. Studying the face, I note about the mouth and nostrils warrants of life.

The captain breathes! He is dead, but nevertheless he breathes!

And should he stop—what then?

He must not; for I know with certainty that my life and his are bound—whether by his sleeping or mine, his dream of me or mine of him—a metempsychosis of our two selves within the space of this grim ship.

I leave the captain lying where he is, afraid to remove the body from the cabin's arctic chill—afraid its life—however minimal—will end, and the body rot, and with it—me. I fetch clean sheets from the linen closet and—pitying him—a blanket. Surely, I think, a blanket cannot sabotage the machinery by which he breathes! I mean only to comfort him—this man, who loves me. He *must* love me to keep me with him, when everyone else has gone! Unless it is for this only that he does: to change his sheets, as is the duty of a steward. Assured of his stability, I go out into the passage and shut the cabin door behind me, because of the cold—the cold is past enduring!

The captain's mother lies crumpled in the chair, dead. The needles knit.

I know the art sufficiently to continue their work. I learned to ply the needles, like others aboard ship, during the empty hours between watches, to make a sweater or a pair of socks. Why should I not take up the needles and the lengthening of the cable of black wool? The truth is, I hate the captain's mother—the hideous sight of her—and wish her away from here. So I drag her off, shut her in the infirmary, and—sitting in her chair—take up the needles.

The Mummy's Bitter and Melancholy Exile

Osiris, God of the Dead

The Mummy is invited to speak on the radio. He is driven from his apartment house through the autumn streets, toward the broadcasting studio. He looks through the limousine window at the street cleaners sweeping the fallen leaves. The leaves are the color of old gold and rust. Of bronze and copper amulets. The limousine driver is drawn irresistibly to the face of the Mummy, which he studies in the rearview mirror with a mixture of curiosity and fear. He would like to ask the Mummy about the women of ancient Egypt. He would like very much to satisfy his curiosity concerning sexual practices in the New Kingdom. He has become something of an amateur Egyptologist since the Mummy's discovery. He and the night porter at the Commodore discuss life in the Eighteenth Dynasty during breakfast, which they take together on Forty-second Street before going home to their rooms to sleep. Intellectually, the driver is prepared to assume a tolerant attitude toward his 3,500-year-old passenger, weeping now in the backseat for a reason he cannot guess. (The driver does not know how the leaves have moved him!) But because he saw *The Mummy*, with Boris Karloff, he is afraid. So he keeps a wary eye on the rearview mirror as the limousine threads its way through the dusky streets toward the studio. And when the Mummy leans forward to speak, the driver feels the hairs rise on his neck and shivers as if with cold.

"Tell me, please—what is Chase and Sanborn?" the Mummy asks.

"Coffee," the driver replies; and the ordinariness of the word comforts him. He no longer looks at the Mummy in the rearview mirror. Instead, he savors the moment when, in the morning, during breakfast, he will tell the porter how he ferried the Mummy down the black Nile of the darkening streets.

"Like Osiris," he will tell him. "God of the Dead."

Clash of the Automatons

"Welcome to *The Chase and Sanborn Hour*!" announces Major Bowes, moistening the microphone with a little cloud of gin and aromatic bitters. While the studio orchestra lurches into the theme of the hour, the major exhumes a handkerchief from a pocket and daubs at his lower lip, where a seed pearl of spit has formed. "Edgar Bergen and Charlie McCarthy are with us tonight," he continues, "and a very special guest who is exciting curiosity from the Bowery to the Bronx. I refer to none other than the Mummy!"

"The dummy!"

"Let's not confuse our radio audience!" Edgar Bergen chastens the little man sitting on his knee. "There's only one dummy on the program tonight, and that, my friend, is you!"

"I'd rather be a dummy than a mummy," Charlie McCarthy sneers. "Here's six bits, Mummy; get yourself a tube of wrinkle cream on the way home."

The Mummy despises the hateful little man, who is squinting down his nose at him through a monocle glinting maliciously in the shadow of his high silk hat. Despises the insolence and cowardice of arrows dipped in acrimony and shot from the safety of his protector's lap.

"A chambermaid at the Chelsea—a dish!—told me that the

Mummy cut the sheets on his bed to ribbons. Jockey shorts aren't smart enough for his nibs."

The musicians guffaw.

"Now, now, Charlie!" Bergen scolds. "Remember, he is from a different time."

"He is our guest, Charlie," says the major, hiding his mirth with his hand. "A guest of Chase and Sanborn coffee." (This last is intoned reverentially.)

If he were once more a man of Pharaoh's, the Mummy would dash the brains out of Charlie McCarthy's head. But, of course, the dummy hasn't any brains, or heart, or any other organ. He, too, is an empty granary, a desert, a vacancy, an empty tomb. Even so, he would have the head off his shoulders with a sword for his insults. But the Mummy is sitting in a room overlooking a firmament of streetlights trembling in the blackness below. It is 1934. Pharaoh is quiet as dust; he and all his princes are embalmed and swathed in bandages—those, that is, who have not been shaken roughly out of their windings by vandals and thieves.

The Mummy thinks, I would pity him, this puppet whose will is not his own any more than mine is, if only he were not so certain of himself. His flippancy enrages me! How he pretends that he is self-sufficient and a man! Unless he believes himself to be. Perhaps he does not know that he is an emptiness, does not feel the god's hand at his back. The dummy is no more a sovereign man than I, who spoke the wishes of Pharaoh, whose hands were extensions of Pharaoh's hands, whose dreams were his—even those! I wish I were in my apartment, sitting in the familiar dark. I wish I were in my funerary chamber, with the companionable cricket and the scuffling mice, with no more light than a shaft of sun or moon might make.

And for the second time that night, he weeps.

Gong!

Falseness of a Chambermaid

"That Charlie McCarthy is so mean!" the chambermaid says. "I never said any such thing about the sheets!"

The chambermaid has brought the Mummy a sleeping powder. He cannot fall to sleep because of the coffee he was given during *The Chase and Sanborn Hour.* He had never tasted coffee before and did not like it. It tasted like wormwood, he thought, like bitter aloe.

"Your face isn't so bad," she says, looking at him with an expression he recalls having seen, thousands of years before, in the eyes of a serving girl in the house of Pharaoh. Her name he cannot remember, but her face was lovely—of this he is sure.

"Live steam hit my brother in the face once when he was working on a boiler; it left him with marks like those," she says, touching his cheek with her fingertips.

The touch—light as it is—awakens in him something unfelt since the elephant hunt in the swamps of Nei. A stirring in his loins. Surprised and pleased, he smiles at the girl in gratitude.

"I would like to tell you what I would have said on the radio, if they had not rung the gong."

"Oh, that major and his gong! It's awful how he makes fun of people!"

The Mummy opens his mouth to speak, but already the sleeping draft is coursing through his veins with the speed of an asp's venomous kiss. His eyes close, the congestion in his loins dissolves, and once more he sleeps the sleep of the dead.

The chambermaid takes a little scissors and pares the Mummy's nails and snips several locks of his hair. A man has promised her one hundred dollars for them, and with it she will buy an evening gown for the New Year's Eve party at the "21" Club.

Snip, snip, snip.

Where's the harm? she says to herself.

The Mummy's Dream

The Mummy Plays the Piano

The Mummy goes to a party on Fifth Avenue. He admires the bare shoulders of the women, who are moving searchingly—dreamily—from room to room. How bright their eyes, how musical their laughter! Their dusky shoulders are powdered with light. He admires also these men, who inhabit their evening clothes as if they wore no other. He feels graceless and unprepossessing in his, and leans on his stick as one would a prop to keep from falling—so heavy the weight of judgment in their eyes. But in this, he is mistaken; their frank gazes are not critical, but curious. They are fascinated by anyone who is a sensation. The Mummy is that, as surely as if he had crossed the Atlantic in an airplane. But he has made a journey even more amazing: He has crossed an immeasurable gulf of time—has, in fact, arrived from the farthest shore, where life's freshwater is tainted by the brackishness of death.

The Mummy is drawn to the piano, where Noël Coward sits playing. Coward is also a sensation; but his fame is not so ethereal as the Mummy's, and the glass wall between him and his admirers is made of sugar, like the saloon windows through which cowboy actors crash. The Mummy's window is of an imperial hardness. Tempered by the occult, it admits light, looks, even handshakes (seldom, however, offered because of the unpleasant dryness of his hands)—but little to affirm, for him, life. Since his arrival in New York, he has come to understand the degree of his separation: it is for this, perhaps, that he weeps.

Coward, whose intuitions are quick, sees in the Mummy's face a yearning, which he interprets as the wish to play; and he makes room for the Mummy on the bench. The Mummy sits and, without a word, begins to play Beethoven's *Moonlight* Sonata because of—who knows?—the women and the particles of light sown in their hair by the prisms of the chandelier.

The Mummy plays beautifully but with a burden of mournfulness Beethoven did not intend.

Now it is Coward's turn to weep because of the depth of the Mummy's accomplishment and for the anguish of a man whose cup is charged with sorrow. He takes the Mummy by the arm. (Both, after all, are estranged from the ordinary and can commingle, if only momentarily.) He leads him as he would an injured man or a blind one onto the terrace.

"Cigarette?" Coward asks, offering him a Gauloise from a silver case.

The Mummy smokes and finds the toasted taste and smell delicious.

"Now tell me how it is you can play Beethoven, on an instrument that did not exist in your time; and why, though your playing is excellent, the music is sterile and so very sad."

The Mummy is grateful because it is this that he wished to say on the radio and, later, to the chambermaid. But gong and sleep prevented him.

"The dead are omniscient," the Mummy tells him as they lean against the terrace wall and watch the automobiles sweep like fiery comets down the streets of light. "All is known to them in the place in which they live. One must not say 'live,' but it is a kind of living in which they dwell—not dwell—*are*. And in being, all knowledge is transmitted somehow through

them as if they were each a radio receiving from the air everything that is able to pass from one man to another. So it was
that I learned to speak the languages of men, understand their
arts and subtleties—understand them without, however, feeling them; for I was, like all the dead, without emotion—that
being an aspect of the human that does not survive into death.
Why this should be so, I do not know, unless—feeling it—
death would prove unendurable."

"And do you now," Coward asks, "feel anything at all?"

"Sadness mostly. Little else. Loneliness, which is for me
the same as sorrow—is the reason for my sorrow. You cannot,
being alive, know the loneliness I feel among the living."

"I have often been alone," Coward says softly, his gaze sliding from the Mummy's eyes to hide from him the remnants of
a desolation felt too often.

"Not like mine!" the Mummy says bitterly.

Coward tosses his cigarette into space. They watch its
ardent ember fall into the street below, which seems now to
the Mummy like the long, wavering line of torches that lit his
way to the doorway of his tomb.

Wrath and His Terrible Yearning for Egypt

Of all the pleasures available to him in the twentieth century,
the Mummy finds cigarettes the most desirable. Its women are
also desirable, but they are not for him. Women do not want
a Mummy, he tells himself; and this realization—however bitter—is the truth. Women shrink from him. The chambermaid,
who resurrected his desire, never again was kind. He watches
her in the arms of a handsome man. The Mummy does not
dance—would not dance the Lindy Hop! He considers the
Lindy immodest, although he claps like the others when the
band concludes. He wants to be like the others—more pre-
cisely, he wants to be thought by others as if he were like them.
Which he is not—he knows this!—nor can he ever be. He is

alone on earth. In each and every corner of it, were he to go there, he would be alone with himself. He has tried more than once to kill himself—with drain cleaner, rat poison, a bullet through the place where his heart used to beat. Once he threw himself out a window. But he cannot die or even seriously injure himself—this being, this *thing* that is already dead and well past injury.

The band makes some other noise. Couples shamble in circles. A drunk wearing a conical hat slumps in his chair. One hour of the old year remains. The Mummy has been too steeped in time to be moved by its passing. Finishing his last Gauloise, he motions with the empty package to the cigarette girl. As she leans over her tray so that he can select another, he steals a glance at the tops of her breasts and sighs.

"Mister, we got only American cigarettes here," she says, mistaking the meaning of his sigh.

He looks from the girl's face (whose cruel and beleaguered beauty reminds him of a priestess he adored in the temple of Isis) to her tray, and his eyes fall on a package illustrated with a pyramid.

"What's this?" he asks.

"Camels!" she snarls. "What's it look like?"

He studies the package as she walks away on the daggers of her heels. He cannot understand why the iconography of his desert country should appear in a city of skyscrapers, taxis, and potted palms. And suddenly, he feels rise up in him a powerful nostalgia—a terrible yearning—for Egypt.

He puts money on the table, as he has seen other men do, and goes, wishing he were like Karloff's mummy, possessed of an irresistible will, an unappeasable wrath, so that he might slay them all—all who have humiliated him since he was awakened, roughly, from his dream.

He leaves the club as the bells begin to toll the New Year— each quickly silenced peal falling to earth like a dying bird.

Nineteen thirty-five.

He steps into a white night of snow.

Transmissions from the World of the Dead

The snow, a labyrinth—its walls, winds that buffet him.

Steel needles tattoo his skin blue for the snow to bandage.

The sky is white as day, white the air. It might be day and not the middle of the night; he could be walking upside down—his feet in air, although his moving, when he moves, is something other than walking, is shuffling, shambling, lurching—is what a mummy does when, by invocation or profanation, it escapes the tomb. Whitely clad, the Mummy might be that mummy now. An unraveling monster for a Saturday matinee.

Once before, the Mummy lost himself within a seeming emptiness, inside a space without dimensions, bequeathed by a malevolent god as a curse to men. Crossing the deserts of Amora, the sand blew up suddenly in the face of the setting sun. Darkness settled over everything, but through its frayed pocket leaked a gleaming copper light. Enthralled, he looked at the swirling amber mist until he had to shut his eyes against the stinging sand and grope (the camel having lain down at last in the lee of a dune). The Mummy—a man then—went with arms in front of him until he stepped into a river—hard and sharp against his shins, like an iron blade. There, after the storm had vanished in a seam of air, he met Tey, who kept her father's house. She was comely and modest, and her slender hand in his solaced him. He stayed to woo and marry her, according to the customs of that place.

He oversaw the workers in her father's field. She moved within his house, calm and elegantly wrought, like the ibis. In the evening, while the wind nuzzled the river, they would walk beneath the palms and listen to the boatmen's songs. Their happiness was brief: She was brought to the house of the dead nearly three decades before he followed her there. The sparrow, which was her soul, never came to him, though he waited for it.

The snow slows. The wind is dropping, and he hears—not singing, but that humming heard in the silence between voices as the radio dial turns. Transmissions from the World of the Dead. He finds a door that opens and goes inside.

The Mummy is alone inside the Empire State Building—or nearly so, for the clinking of pails and the brief cataracts and freshets of gray water on marble or porphyry are proof of an otherwise-invisible occupation. He has heard how this building towers above antiquity's pyramids and obelisks, and he thinks that, perhaps, from the top of it he can see across the world—to Egypt!

He rides the elevator car up—a mechanical ascent toward Horus, son of Osiris and ruler of the heavens. Perhaps now, the Mummy thinks, I will find the sparrow and will know it to be Tey, her transmigrated soul. But the sparrows are asleep elsewhere; and the observation deck is, in its Tibetan isolation and cold, possessed of the enchantments of death. The Mummy stands as if in a bowl of milk and sees neither Egypt nor the ocean, nor even the river where, two months before, he clung to a crate containing mortuary decorations prized from his tomb after the ship, which carried him into exile, had foundered.

In the white and luminous air, he gazes at the package of cigarettes while a gravel of snow clatters softly against the pyramid, the camel, and the palm.

A Telegram Arrives

The Mummy sleeps late and would have gone on sleeping if a knock at the door had not wakened him. Not for refreshment does a mummy sleep, for refreshment is impossible, but to relieve awhile the tedium of incessant thought. He sits on the edge of the bed while shards of past and present circle his mind like pale vegetables in a soup stirred by a slow hand.

Sailboats at Aswan . . . Osiris's floating coffin . . . burning water and a smugglers' launch . . . an obelisk at Memphis in whose shadow the Mummy played with a leather ball . . . a skyscraper in an icy shroud . . . the chambermaid who was kind . . . the cigarette girl with eyes insolent and afraid . . . Tey, the Mummy's wife, whose face he can no longer recall except as a radiant haze.

Knock . . .

In the space between two knocks, he remembers his tomb and how he would rummage there among the tokens of his life: his sword and chariot, a gold cup and plate, a stuffed falcon and a mummified dog, a ball and stick, his library of papyrus scrolls, which he read by sunlight and moonlight entering through a shaft—alms scattered liberally by Ra and Thoth.

Knock.

He opens the door and finds, standing in the hall, a Western Union boy.

"Telegram, mister," he says, eyeing the Mummy with mistrust.

He gives the boy a coin and shuts the door. He opens the yellow envelope, removes the flimsy sheet of paper, and reads:

MAKING MOVIE OF YOUR LIFE—STOP—WANT YOU AS
TECHNICAL ADVISER—STOP—GOLDEN WEST LTD LEAVES
GRAND CENTRAL—STOP—TONIGHT AT 8 O'CLOCK.

TOM LAMAY, DIRECTOR
HOLLYWOOD, CALIF.

A Meditation on Time

The Mummy lies in the close dusk behind a curtain while the train rushes toward the Land of the Dead. He does not sleep in the narrow berth in which he chooses to spend the three-day journey west. Nor can he be said to be awake. Rather, he is in a state of suspension—neither in time entirely nor wholly outside of it, for he cannot enter eternity any more than he can a mortal life.

If one remains housed in the body after death, one needs to vanquish time: the knowledge of its passing, which is, for a mummy as for any other undying thing, slow and harrowing, like the migration of a single grain of sand from one end of the desert to the other. And so the Mummy, who needs none, takes his rest, longing only for Egypt and a cigarette. He lies on his back inside the coffin of his berth, feeling himself to be one with the train, hurtling toward a simulacrum of his life, hoping to put an end to his sorrow.

The Mummy knows what time is better than any living person, or dead one—better than Einstein, whose theories he has absorbed in the same way as Spengler's economics or Cab Calloway's "Minnie the Mooch."

Time is shaped like a pyramid—of this he is certain. Each of us rides its apex a short distance into the future. Moment by moment, do we thus acquire a future (which is formless and not yet an aspect of time) and a past (which is the immense repository of all those who have preceded us). The dead who are rid of the body are oblivious of time and their estrangement from it. Only mummies and other forms of the undead retain an individual consciousness—narcotized by the embalmer's art.

Time is a mummy's tomb. Its weight and solidity are an amber from which he cannot escape, though he can see life passing like a shadow on the other side. Yet that estrangement is nothing next to this the Mummy must endure. Imagine the fly out of its amber and powerless to annoy men or please itself among its kind! To have escaped his time by the intervention of the grave robbers' impious hands, to be dead among the living and a joke—this is the Mummy's bitter and melancholy exile. This is why the Mummy desires nothing more than to return to Egypt and his tomb where he can sink into a waking dream—a sensory twilight easier to endure.

He arrives in Los Angeles the afternoon of the third day and is met by a man in a pearl gray suit and straw hat, whose smile is full of white teeth, between two of which is lodged a sesame seed.

"Mr. Mummy," he says. "Welcome to the Land of Make-Believe!"

"Are you Tom LaMay?" the Mummy asks.

"Jack—his assistant and right-hand man!" His smile with its intrusive seed puts the Mummy in mind of a rat in a granary.

"You'll be staying at the palace," says Jack. "I'll drive you there."

"The palace?"

"Pharaoh's. It's out in the desert. You'll have a room all your own. Here's the script. Mr. LaMay would like you to read it before filming begins tomorrow."

And the right-hand man of Mr. LaMay presses a thick sheaf of papers into the Mummy's hand.

The Mummy's Return to Memphis

The sun is not so hot as that which shone above Egypt three and a half millennia ago, when the Mummy walked the wide, palm-fringed avenues of Memphis. But in all other ways that he can see, the white-walled city that LaMay and his "artists" have caused to be here in the California desert is a perfect facsimile. How often in the distant past did the Mummy pause, here, in the broad late-afternoon shadow cast by Akhenaten's palace's eastern wall over the reflecting pool, to feed the carp, which rose like gold and copper birds to his hand? How many times did he attend the Pharaoh's levee on the royal barge—just there, where the esplanade merges with the Nile's reedy bank (which seems a painted picture)? Once a year, he journeyed from his home near the Nubian border to give an accounting of Pharaoh's subjects under his administration.

The Mummy turns and, shading his eyes with the flat of his

hand, looks out across the desert at the Giza Plateau, where the Sphinx trembles in the heat and the three pyramids stand, companionable and golden in the falling light. He gazes at them as if only miles of sand separate him from the necropolis, not a chasm of time. Suddenly, he is afraid—this living corpse, this undying dead man whose fear the embalmers drained into an iron dish together with all other feeling. Clutching the movie script, he hurries into the palace to his room, which he hopes will be narrow and dim as the familiar and consoling tomb.

Manhattan Mummy

A Photoplay

INTERIOR. A SHAFT INSIDE THE PYRAMID—NIGHT.
Reinhart, Krueger, and Dorfman make their way along a sloping shaft. They carry electric torches in whose yellow lights appear, on the stone walls, cartouches containing symbols of the Egyptian past.

INTERIOR. AT THE DOOR OF THE MUMMY'S TOMB—NIGHT.
Reinhart consults a letter, worn from repeated folding and unfolding. In extreme close-up, we see that the letter is written in German. The men are German and speak with an accent. Reinhart folds the letter and returns it to his pocket.

REINHART: Here is the tomb! We have only to force open the door and carry the sarcophagus outside to the boat. We'll deliver it to the museum, and keep the mummy's treasure for ourselves!

KRUEGER: Is a sarcophagus heavy?

[Reinhart shrugs his shoulders.]

DORFMAN: What will you do with your share of the money, Reinhart?

REINHART: I will buy a small Rhenish castle and invite many beautiful women to visit me there.

KRUEGER: I will buy a pig farm and raise pigs.

[A noise is heard inside the tomb.]

REINHART: What was that noise?

KRUEGER (Nervously): Maybe it was a mouse.

DORFMAN (a laugh of exceptional viciousness): Or a mummy.

REINHART: Let's get to work! We must be far away from here before sunup.

[Reinhart opens a satchel and removes various tools.]

INTERIOR. THE MUMMY'S TOMB—NIGHT.
In the light of the electric torches, we see many fabulous treasures, which would have been buried with a man of importance during the Eighteenth Dynasty. (See Properties List.)

KRUEGER: It looks heavy to me.

REINHART: Stop your whining, Krueger, or I'll leave you here in place of the mummy to keep the rats company!

[Dorfman laughs viciously.]

INTERIOR. THE SHAFT INSIDE THE PYRAMID—NIGHT.
Krueger and Dorfman carry the sarcophagus up the sloping passage that leads from the tomb. They labor beneath its weight. Reinhart follows with a sack stuffed with treasure.

KRUEGER (sweating profusely): I knew it would be heavy.

[Dorfman laughs with pleasure, as if at a good joke. (Of the three, Dorfman is actually the most sensitive.)]

REINHART: Dorfman, did you remember to bring the sandwiches?

EXTERIOR. THE PYRAMID—NIGHT.
The men emerge from the entrance to the pyramid, concealed by a canvas flap painted in trompe l'oeil style to look like stone, which they brought with them for the purpose. The camera should dwell—even at the risk of exasperating the audience!—on various Egyptian splendors, such as the Great Pyramid, the lesser pyramids, the enigmatic Sphinx, the ancient constellations wheeling through the firmament, the mysterious Nile, etc. In the distance, across a moonlit desert, lies Pharaoh's palace, glowing with an eerie light (from who knows what source!).

REINHART: Where's the elephant?

KRUEGER: She's eating dates. I'll go get it.

[The inscrutable Dorfman laughs in a manner that is difficult, if not impossible, to interpret.]

EXTERIOR. THE ESPLANADE—NIGHT.
They sit inside a cabanalike affair on the elephant's back as it crosses the esplanade toward the river, clutching the sarcophagus with its trunk.

DORFMAN (tenderly): The night is very beautiful. On such a night as this, Akhenaten held Nefertiti in his arms.

EXTERIOR. A BOAT ON THE RIVER NILE—NIGHT.
They sit on the sarcophagus while the boat moves down the Nile. There is no other sound than the soft purring of its motor. The camera lingers on the spreading wake (silvery);

then the scene dissolves to the elephant standing forlornly on the riverbank.

INTERIOR. THE MESS ABOARD A FREIGHTER—DAY.
Reinhart and Dorfman play cards at a mess table. Krueger lies in a hammock, sick. Through the portholes, we see the gray ocean rise and fall. Perhaps there is a whale.

DORFMAN: You owe me one thousand marks, Reinhart.

REINHART: When we have delivered the sarcophagus to the museum, I will have a million marks!

DORFMAN (sighs with human feeling): We are in the midst of a worldwide depression. I pity those without our resourcefulness.

REINHART: I will send a whole bag of marks to my mother in Dresden.

EXTERIOR. NEW YORK HARBOR—NIGHT.
The freighter enters the harbor, which is hidden by thick fog. We hear the sound of a foghorn—lonely and sad.

INTERIOR. PILOTHOUSE—NIGHT.
The captain (a Turk or a Greek) is peering through the fog. Suddenly, we hear a fearful noise as the ship collides with a rock, or perhaps a Chinese junk bringing illegal aliens to Chinatown. The captain blows the ship's whistle while shouting in Turkish or Greek down the speaking tube. A great storm begins with terrific thunder and lightning!

EXTERIOR. THE FREIGHTER—NIGHT.
The ship sinks. Fire is spreading on top of the ocean. Reinhart, Dorfman, and Krueger are seen in the act of drowning. Dorfman, who is the last to go under, laughs

mysteriously. The mummy floats into view. The fire has
burned away its bandages. Suddenly, a lightning bolt strikes
the water next to the mummy and we see—in extreme
close-up—its eyes open!

EXTERIOR. A BOOTLEGGERS' LAUNCH—NIGHT.
Some bootleggers also have been in the fog, in a motor
launch loaded with smuggled Canadian whiskey. Rico,
the leader of the bootleggers, sees the naked mummy and
throws it a rope. Helped by one or two other bootleggers,
the wet mummy climbs aboard.

RICO (ironically, to the mummy): Lousy night to be outside
without your pants!

[The other bootleggers laugh and drink whiskey.]

THE MUMMY (with a British accent like Basil Rathbone's):
Are you the god of the Underworld?

RICO (slapping the mummy on the back): That's me all
right!

EXTERIOR. THE DOCK—NIGHT.
The bootleggers load crates of whiskey into an ambulance.

RICO (to the mummy): We'll drop you at the hospital on the
way to our gang's warehouse. Medical science may be able to
make your face look almost human.

INTERIOR. HOSPITAL EXAMINING ROOM—NIGHT.
Dressed in a hospital gown, the mummy lies on an
examining table. A perplexed doctor is listening to its chest
with a stethoscope. Bored, a buxom nurse holds a tray of
surgical instruments. The door is thrown open violently, and
a second doctor rushes in with an X-ray.

SECOND DOCTOR: He's stuffed with old rags!

FIRST DOCTOR (horrified): What's that you say?!

NURSE (drops the tray and screams): It's a mummy!

The Mummy's Second Renunciation

Those scenes of the Mummy's entry into the world of living men, his rescue by bootleggers, and his consignment to the hospital, where he was examined and declared a mummy, are more or less correct. But all that preceded his return to sentience (the result, perhaps, of seawater galvanized by lightning, as the movie suggests) is unknown to him. At that time, he was preoccupied by the memory of Tey's breasts—their divine form and a mathematics to describe it. How he came to be naked and unhoused in a burning sea may well have followed the lines developed in the scenario. How else explain his arrival in Manhattan? But the ensuing scenes—the slaughter of the hospital staff, his wanderings in a labyrinth of sewers, the terrorizing of the corps de ballet, and his hideous revenge on the curator of Antiquities for the Metropolitan Museum of Art—these are fantasies, which the Mummy repudiates with all his heart. His heart remains, although it is a mummified one, incapable of beating, or love.

Mortified, the Mummy goes to the window. Gazing wistfully at the distant Giza Plateau, he yearns for the obscurity of his tomb. He thinks in the morning he will strangle Mr. LaMay and all his company if he does not leave at once—this, the gentlest of men and mummies. He has had enough of life and all those who, for a time, inhabit it as if forever. He steals from the dark palace and, mounting an elephant drowsing under a papier-mâché palm tree, rides toward his pyramid.

On the rim of the world, the pyramids stand clotted with silver. The stone lion crouches warily, confronted by its constellation in the ancient night. Each takes the other's measure;

each is a representation of the same magisterial instinct in a universe fashioned on a principle of absolute hegemony. The Mummy knows his place in it. He is one with the dead and hastens on his elephant to rejoin them—even if this tomb is a plaster replica. As he draws closer, his sempiternal weariness lightens. He will dream again of Tey—her loveliness lost in time to him—without distraction. As if sensing his rising exultancy, the elephant trumpets with a noise that shatters the lunar stillness.

The Mummy is standing before his pyramid, a somnambulist who once heard through thick walls Mark Antony weep with frustrated desire for Cleopatra, and Napoléon rage against Josephine. In a moment, he will climb again onto his stone deathbed and wait for Osiris to raise him—or for the morning, when Reinhart, Krueger, and Dorfman will break open the door of his tomb.

A Theory of Time

For Andrew Comi

1.

    We ride only on the tracks that are orange with the rust of time. How else avoid those other trains criss-crossing a land notable for the variety of its features—observing schedules, answerable to purposes clearly understood by the presidents of railroad companies and their most casual passengers alike? We follow no schedules; and if there is a purpose to our endless divagation, I never knew it. (That the performances might be a figment of my or someone else's imagination is a thought that increasingly occurs to me.) I begin to suspect that we are traveling to no purpose; that the train appeared one day on these rusted rails as if by an act of spontaneous generation such as van Leeuwenhoek claimed to have observed in his retort after the introduction of an electrical current in water.

I do not remember when I first came to be here. Perhaps I, too, unfolded suddenly like a Japanese paper flower in water—like the animalcules in van Leeuwenhoek's laboratory. But something tells me this is not the case: memories, for one thing. I can recall a time when I was not on the train. A boyhood in a town red with brick factories and gray with smoke and dust. And later, life aboard a merchant ship, if the few impressions I have of it can be said to be a life. I seem to have been skillful with a marlin spike; to this day, I can feel in my hand its weight and the rope stiffened by salt water. Of course, they may be someone else's memories. Who is to say that we cannot receive another's recollections like a legacy—an unsuspected inheritance from an uncle who, until the moment when the lawyer informs us that we have come into some money or a property in Ravenna, we never knew existed?

I was the train's brakeman. This much is certain. I remember it in my absent thumb, the pain of its dismemberment. We had stopped for the night in an ancient forest. I would not have been surprised to find Yggdrasil presiding over it—so Germanic the gloom, so primeval the silence. Bewitched into a moment's carelessness, I offered up my finger to the coupling. I feel it still—the pain when finger and bone came away in the train's iron fist. I doubt I would feel it so keenly were it someone else's loss.

In the mirror, I appear to be a man of sixty. But mirrors lie; and on such a train as this, what treachery might not they practice? But let us say sixty, or a little less. I was a young man still when I suffered my mutilation. It has been, then, many years since I have been other than a brakeman. I was not relieved of my occupation because of my accident. I continued for a time after it—of this, too, I am sure. It was for some other reason that I ceased to be a brakeman. My own or some other's.

I am now an assistant to the impresario. I say "an assistant," for I cannot be certain that I am the only one in this capacity, any more than I am sure another brakeman is in the rear of the train, performing my former role. I can only assume that one is: A train must have a brakeman. He may well be asleep at this moment in one of the rear cars set aside for the brakeman—the car I once shared with the flagman, whom I never see anymore. The end of the train is not visible because of the great number of cars, or the frequent turning of the tracks, or the darkness that seems always to be at our rear. As if the train were on the edge of night. The engine and the caboose following immediately behind it are the only cars that have not been tainted yet by that unnatural dark. A premonitory darkness ranged malevolently against us. I feel it just as a gravestone might the pressure of a hand intent on robbing it of its inscription. The engineer maintains that it is only our locomotive's coal smoke blackening the sky.

Nor have I ever seen the impresario. He communicates with me by telegraph, which I can operate and whose language— telegraphy—I understand. Somehow understand, just as I do the many languages in which the telegrams are composed by the impresario, or impresarios; there may be more than one, which would account for the polyglot transmissions: Hungarian, Hebrew, Greek, English, French, German, Italian, Armenian—even ancient and dead languages such as Sanskrit, Phoenician, and Ge'ez. It amazes me how, after a momentary incomprehension, while the receiving key clicks in dots and dashes a communiqué from the last car, suddenly—like a black sky riven by lightning—I understand!

I sit in the chair and take down the impresario's thoughts. They arrive perfectly articulated and composed in logical paragraphs. When the key falls silent, I roll on the chair's oiled castors to the small desk with its typewriter and reproduce the impresario's dictation. In spite of lacking a thumb, my typewriting is infallible. Finished, I proofread the text, enclose it in a manila envelope, then toss it out the window onto the right-of-way. I have no idea whether it is ever found, or read, or set in type and printed. What use the story—the history—of our performances may serve for readers in towns through which we have already passed and to which we will never return—I long ago ceased to speculate. For we never go back, unless it is to hunt for a way forward after having arrived at an impasse. I am ill-suited for my work, yet I manage it well enough and, except for an arthritic condition of my nine remaining fingers, no longer am incommoded by it.

I never leave the caboose or the locomotive's cab. Not now. There is no point. All that concerns me arrives by telegraph, by dots and dashes.

2.

The engineer does not remember a time when he was not an engineer, although there may have been other locomotives in his past besides this one. I seem always, he says, to have been sitting or standing in a cab begrimed with coal dust and ringing with the tumult of history. He wanted to participate in history—this, he recalls as a man does with fondness a boyhood memory, of speckled fish, say, drowsing beneath the scarcely troubled surface of a brook.

"How better to participate in history than to drive an engine through it?" he tells me while we are eating Spanish sardines. "Yet I have seen nothing clearly through the windows, as the train rushes forward or sometimes backward. It is the same when recollecting the body of a lover—all a blur no matter how determined one was in bed to observe this or that part of her."

If ours is its engine, as the engineer claims. I myself have yet to understand how our train stands in relation to history, which appears to eddy all about us as we move within it, on axes of rusted steel, which include surprising switchbacks and spurs, none of which has been set down on any map, at least none in our possession. The train stops arbitrarily, when it does stop at all. More than once the engineer has assured me that the train is obedient to his hand and his alone, although I have seen the sweat start out from his forehead as he tried unsuccessfully to hold the throttle open, or, conversely, to apply the brake against the train's irresistible momentum.

"And did you never walk back to the end of the train?" I ask, daubing at my mustache to rid it of fish oil.

"Never—what for?" he asks, his voice tonic with surprise.

"To see one of the performances!" I cry impatiently.

"When I was young, I may have been interested in performances," he remarks idly while digging with a matchstick the grease from beneath his fingernails. "But no longer—and the end of the train is remote for a man with bad feet."

"So you did see them?" I shout. I do not understand why I am so vexed.

"I seem to remember a very tall man and a bearded lady . . . a trained bear and a juggling act . . . an exhibition of naked female flesh. But I can't be sure that it was at the end of *this* train where I saw them. Doubtless, I was once employed by the Orient Express: I would not picture myself wearing a fez and revolving a string of beads through my fingers otherwise. The women may have belonged to the harem of a sultan."

I want to interrogate him further, but he falls asleep. It is his prerogative; the night is already well advanced, the moon entangled in the trees on the western ridge of the mountain. (I mean the world's natural night, a gift to men and women, not that other.) I climb back into the caboose, leaving the engineer with his hand on the throttle. Whether he is awake or not makes no difference to our progress; the rails rest on sleepers—the tracks are laid to serve the excursions of thought itself. This is not to say that the train is metaphysical: It is real—make no mistake!—and the terrain through which it passes can be analyzed according to theorems of solid geometry. But at times, both train and landscape evade our observation; they become subject to invisible strains, rearrangements effected by unseen forces, and something like transfiguration, though this latter state is rare. We know of its occurrence only by rumor, whispered sometimes late at night by the imps in the firebox.

By "we," I mean the engineer and myself. The impresario confines himself in his telegraphed messages to factual statements concerning the performances, whose history lengthens according to a principle I cannot grasp. How could there have been a demonstration yesterday of lion taming, for example, when, according to the engineer, the train did not stop at all? I grant that a performance is possible within the space of a dream—someone's: the impresario's, perhaps, or the lion's. The engineer is unconcerned, preferring to relate to me the history of the railroad, the invention and technological refinements of the steam locomotive, and to make an inventory of the provisions. Since we never run short of provisions, I tell him there is no need to inventory them. But he enjoys it, he says. Counting the tins, the bottles and mason jars. Whole numbers, he says; whole numbers are comforting.

When the train does stop, the engineer will sometimes climb down from the locomotive and walk into the trees—provided there are trees lining the right-of-way. I follow him with my binoculars until he vanishes among them, absorbed by their entrancing gloom. Invariably, he will return in a radiant frame of mind.

"What do you do in the forest?" I ask him, pulling at his striped trousers' cuff.

"I do what I must," he replies; or "I retrieve lost time," or "I undermine the train—within limits, always within limits!"

"What do you mean?"

But he laughs and will say no more while he opens a tin of sardines or small boiled potatoes.

3.

One day when the train has stopped, the flagman appears from behind the bend ahead of us. Furling his flag and tucking it under his arm, as if it were not a flag but a sergeant major's baton, he climbs onto the locomotive, which I am guarding in the engineer's stead. As is customary when the enterprise comes, for whatever reason, to a standstill, the engineer has disappeared into the trees. I do not fear for the safety of the train, nor has anyone assigned me the role of custodian, but I relish the proximity of the great steam engine, which seems, now that the train lies motionless, a kind of domestic familiar, such as a cat rumbling contentedly on a windowsill. There are also the engineer's calendars stacked in a disused bin—year yielding inevitably to the one before in a recession of time and dishabille. I admit to a sentimental fondness for Robert Giraud's photographs and the naughty etchings of Xavier Sager.

"How is it that you arrived *ahead* of the train?" I ask the flagman, who is preparing an espresso with the aid of the steam boiler. "Unless I'm mistaken, we have yet to make that next turning."

The flagman blows the demitasse's smoking top. "Have you any cinnamon?"

I give him some.

"Do you have a theory of time?" he asks, resting the little cup and saucer on his knee.

"None that I'm aware of. Do you?"

"Time spins like a cyclone; and as it does so, it wobbles—forward, backward, to the right or to the left. Gathering speed or slowing, inching along or making a surprising leap. And all the while, it is gathering up whatever is in its path—jugglers, acrobats, trombonists, anarchists, lions, poets, even elephants. You can easily understand how, sometimes, one may arrive ahead of it."

I lean forward, like a connoisseur suddenly in the presence of the object of his desire. "Are you saying that this train is a *circus train?*"

"It can be—at times, it is. At other times, it isn't; it's something else. You ought to know: You are the train's author."

"But one wishes, for once, to have one's words verified," I remark calmly in a voice that belies my frustration, my anguish.

"To be assured of the truth of what one writes, or its falsity. Besides, I am only an amanuensis, not an author."

"Then why not see for yourself?" He leers.

"I don't seem to be able," I temporize. "I've become sedentary. I write; I seldom go outside. In fact, I never do, except to stretch my legs a little. But I don't go far! Once I went as far as a car full of soldiers. Wounded soldiers. I was attracted by their groaning, their cries. I was frightened and hurried back to the caboose. The next day, I returned with my notebook. To take down their testimony. To record my impressions. To gather background for the writing of a report. But they weren't there—the car was gone. In its place, a wagon of Gypsies. One of them read my palm: She said that my missing thumb would be restored and I would become a brakeman. Ridiculous!"

The flagman shrugs, sips his espresso, looks out the window onto the empty right-of-way, sits the cup and saucer once more on his knee, says, "Time wobbles back and forth and from side to side, picking up this thing and that. Why not Gypsies?"

He seems to fall asleep. I put a recording of *La Sonnambula* on the gramophone, crank its handle; Caruso leaps into the silence—his voice, crackling from out of the tundish. The flagman opens his eyes.

"The 1905 Metropolitan revival was brilliant," he recalls. "A succès d'estime."

I nod. A silence ensues.

"Don't people say that a tornado sounds like a train roaring by?" he asks in an offhanded way, like one setting a trap.

Again, I nod.

"It's the sound time makes as it rushes past. If you put your ear to the rail, you can hear it clearly: the din of history, not to mention the screams."

"Our train, then, is time?" I ask.

"I never said that!" he shouts—whether at me or beyond me through the cab's window is unclear. He is silent a moment, then continues: "We, who ride this train, are aware of our place in time in the same way that the truly giddy are of their place on the turning earth."

"And when, like now, the train is stopped?"

"We've entered the stillness at the center of time—the eye of time's storm. And what better time or place to give a performance?"

"Of what?" I ask, much annoyed by his cheerfulness, which seems misplaced. Irreverent even. Unless it is the gloom, like a yellowish, brownish stain inside the locomotive, which has made me spiteful and afraid. Never in my experience has it dared to invade our precincts, which have been free till now of confusion, but not doubt.

"Of whatever at that moment pleases us most," he replies, taking no notice of my ill will. "Or whatever is most in need of expression. Ours are not ordinary performances: They are desires made visible, not to mention the manifestation of our anxieties, which are desires' accompaniment."

He sets down his demitasse on the iron sill. I observe that the coffee is filled to the brim, though he has been drinking it. Secretly, I preen in my ability to have made so fine an observation in spite of the gloom, which is spreading, and my head, which is swimming.

The flagman polishes his boots with coal soot. Why this, the most ordinary of acts, should cause in me a feeling of terror, I do not know. Whistling a theme from Bellini's opera, he buffs them with an oily rag.

My heart—what's the expression? My heart is in my mouth—and I get ready to eat it.

From the caboose, I hear the telegraph key hiss, in a single angry elision, its magisterial disdain.

"What lies up the track?" I ask nervously.

"*Up, down, sideways*—they have no meaning, for us," he says, admiring boots that might have been glossed by the night itself.

82 *Love Among the Particles & Other Stories*

"What did you see—wherever it was you were—before you came round the bend and saw me?" I shout, my hands at his throat.

Imperturbable, he tears my hands away, coughs, says, "Smoking cities . . . blood-soaked fields . . . endless desert . . . an ice age . . . the aeroplane."

"What's an aeroplane?" I ask, entranced by the word, as if he has pronounced a blessing or a curse on us all.

He smirks, so that I want to fly at him again. Possessed by a sudden listlessness, whose source I cannot identify, however, I remain where I am, inside the iron cab, at the still point. It is as if I and all the world outside the train were drained of potential by a swift plunge of millibars.

"It waits to be discovered or rediscovered, in time, which also has in it forgetting and recollection. This is what is meant by déjà vu. To remember the future."

The recording slows; Caruso's voice drawls, elongates like taffy, metamorphoses into that of an animal and then, attaining at last a mineral modality, falls silent.

"And will time itself stop and, like a spent top, come crashing down or, like a cyclone, peter out?" I loathe this flagman, whom I thought was my friend, unless this flagman and the one whose car I shared are not the same. I loathe him but am helpless against the unfolding of his theory, whose shape reminds me of a portmanteau bag. "For God's sake, finish and be done with it!"

"Time has stopped many times already. Not as this train stops: The train is not time, but rides upon its rails. Of course, this is merely a figure of speech and, like all tropes and metaphors, only partially true. Mostly, I suspect, they lie; but how are we to think about abstractions otherwise?"

I want to know only if the communiqués that I deposit in manila envelopes along the tracks are true. Are we really marionette theater, burlesque house, circus, freak show, music hall,

Grand Guignol, anatomical theater, astronomical observatory, maze of mirrors, botanical garden, inquisition, museum of machines, zoo, waxworks—how is it possible that a single train can be all this and more besides?

He leaves before I can sound him. Perhaps he looked into my mind and read the question there and had no answer (or was sworn to secrecy by the impresario). I watch him walk along the reach of track to the vanishing point. For a moment, there is only his flag to signify his having been, and soon not even that.

4.

A man steps from behind a cairn. Over his shoulder, he carries a portrait camera and tripod. He wears a tweed coat and bowler, spats and gloves, and looks altogether suitable to an upland moor. The train has yielded, temporarily, to a flock of sheep. What seem sheep standing in shadow to the unaided eye become boulders when magnified by my binoculars. Not a flock of boulders, surely! A labor, perhaps, or a team, a mustering, a brood, or an unkindness. But how can I be certain that the optical mechanics of magnification do not transform one thing into another? Or in the time it takes to train and focus the instrument, sheep might not become boulders by some principle of metamorphosis unknown to me? The objects on the tracks do appear to be moving. . . . But boulders, having tumbled down the ravine towering above us, could possess inertia to move them onward—at least for a while. Why not always? Who can say that a thing once set in motion does not continue in some way or another, along unseen paths, by secret and devious passages, in spite of Newton and his apple? If I could magnify time as I do space, mightn't I see even the mountain creep into the valley?

"Hello!" calls the man, teetering on a rail.

"Come up," I reply, eager for company now that the engineer has gone to sleep.

He hands up his camera and tripod, then climbs into the caboose.

"Would you care to have your portrait taken?" he asks after he has settled himself and his equipment within the narrow limits of my domain.

I tell him I would but cannot give him an address where I might receive the developed print. He assures me that it will find me no matter when or where; that we will—my photograph and myself—meet in time.

"By the laws of attraction," he says. "Like to like and likeness to its original. Inevitably."

He asks me my name, and I tell it to him.

"I have read your stories," he says with solemnity, gazing at the typewriter as if it were its stories he meant.

"I have written no stories!" I object rudely.

"No?" he asks, surprised. "Not even one about a hippopotamus bathing in the rank green water along the right-of-way? Or musicians who serenade beneath the balconies of the moon? Or the funeral march of a marionette? Or a talking ape who dueled with a cigar for the love of a woman named Mrs. Willoughby? Or a waxworks in the Belgian Congo? Or the revenge of Hyde? Or the invention of a photographic process by which the invisible is made visible? Or a stenographic exhibition where an amanuensis took dictation from the dead?"

"They are factual accounts of actual performances given at the end of this very train!" I shout. "They were dictated to me by the impresario over *that*!" I point to the telegraph key. (I notice that it is rusty and festooned with a spider's web.)

"Forgive me, sir, I have misunderstood," he says. "I did not understand the nature of the enterprise or your activities therein. One is easily misled. Forgive me."

I am not mollified.

"What has misled you into thinking my reports were anything but the truth of what has occurred? That I am not a chronicler of history? Explain yourself!"

"I have seen several of the performances—"

"You have?" I cry, seizing his wrist with violence enough to make him whelp.

"You're hurting me!"

Smoldering, I let go his wrist, roll back on my chair to put him once more at his ease. Silence reigns briefly, in which I imagine him counting "One . . . two . . . three . . . four," as if exposing a photographic plate in the flash of my anger.

"The performances had been minutely described—by you—in the form of a story—in a book of stories attributed to you—before I ever saw them at the end of this train. You understand me, sir? The enactments follow your account of them."

I think this strange and unlikely but say nothing.

"You did not, by chance, photograph the performances that you saw?" I ask instead.

"Why, yes."

He takes from inside his coat a small album bound in morocco leather. He removes his wire-rim glasses, whose lenses are unusually thick, polishes them on a handkerchief, puts them on again, looping the wire parentheses about his ears. He opens the album. I lean over his shoulder the better to see the photographs.

"They're blurry!" I complain. "I can't make anything out!"

He is incensed. "I assure you they are not! Or if they are slightly out of focus, it is the fault of the subjects. Everything moved. It was beyond the shutter's capacity to stop it."

"This waxwork dummy?" I shout, incredulous. "This poor chained beast? Or this hanged man on a gallows? Surely, he did not move?"

He bangs the album shut; I listen to the volley of his

displeasure inside the rocky defile engulfing us. "The whole earth moves," he says drily, an ear cocked as if to hear it move.

I howl with laughter as the photographer gathers up his belongings and leaves. He goes behind the cairn—to sulk, I imagine. I glare at the typewriter, hating it, feeling in my fingertips a history of pain. The pain of words.

The train begins to move, the deafening roar of its engine drowning all other sounds.

Whether sheep or boulders, it matters not at all. In a geologic age, what might not anything become? The train advances as if nothing at all were there to arrest it. Or what might be, belonged to another time.

5.

We are hurrying through the night. The iron locomotive is cold to the touch, though the boiler blushes with the fury of combustion. The engineer is awake and companionable. He smokes a pipe, which is, in miniature, a firebox ardent with fragrant embers and dreams. Its smoke mimics the immense river of fume endlessly unwinding from out the locomotive's stack—lost now, where all is blackness, in night's vast ocean. The stack, too, resembles the gramophone's tundish; and the rails by day and at night with the locomotive's beam upon them are like a scar upon the body of the earth. It amuses me to consider the correspondences between the similar and the dissimilar by which the world is constituted and made whole.

"It's all an illusion, you know," the engineer says into his pipe, causing a shower of incandescence to erupt from its bowl, the bowl that I have seen him polish on the flanks of his broad nose when he is caught in a dream of who knows what—his other life in the trees, perhaps.

I cast upon him a cunning look of bewilderment; for I do

not trust him, though sometimes—let me admit it now!—I love him. What else is there, here, for me to love?

Removing the pipe stem from between his teeth, he goes on: "What you were thinking just now, it isn't true."

Suddenly, I know what he says to be the case and feel as the condemned man must, hearing the lever yanked, which releases the trapdoor separating his boots from eternity.

The engineer knocks the dottle from his pipe as he gazes through the window at the night's reeling sky. Pointing first to the one, then to the other with the stem, he says, "The Southern Cross and, there, the Great Bear—how is it possible,———?" (He said my name.) His voice is shaken by a profound emotion, which may be fear, or wonder, or something else.

I am moved nearly to tears to hear him say my name, so rarely do I hear it said at all. Except, from time to time, in a dream when a young woman in white speaks it from across the room, in a house between a river and an olive grove. It is always, in the dream, night, with not so much as a cricket to interrupt the stillness, or a firefly to lighten it.

He shovels coal into the firebox; the iron door rings once against the shovel's blade as he roughly closes it. That ghastly sound seems to echo among night's bastions, whose shadows swallow us all.

"A cold night," he says, wiping his hand on his striped mechanic's overalls.

"Do you have a theory of time?" I ask him shyly.

He taps with the toe of his heavy boot the bin in which his calendars accumulate, one year's followed by the next. "Time is as iron and inexorable as this locomotive," he says, "and as cold as tonight. Only in the bodies of women do I find consolation for having been born into it."

"Is that what you find in the trees?" I ask.

In the moonlight streaming though the window, I see the

old man blush. Old, though only yesterday, or the day before, he was no older than I am now.

"We will come soon to an immense desert," he says, gazing sadly at night's falling dominoes. "It will be a long time until we see trees again."

"How do you know when there is no map and we've never before traveled this way?"

I pretend to be calm so that he may let slip some secret of our journey, which is, for me, aimless and obscure. But he says only that an engineer knows such things, that his instincts reveal what is hidden from sight. He uses the word *foretold*, which recalls for me the flagman's theory of time, which I do not understand, though I have thought of it many times over the years.

"You can count them—the calendars . . ." This, my answer to the question of how many years he has been our train's engineer, which once I asked him. The terrain was different from this—a plain, green and limitless, marred by clouds' lumbering shadows. They made me think of buffalo herds slaughtered from a train, which I don't think was this one, but some other. Some other track. Some other time. "You, who like so much to count provisions, could count the calendars in the bin and know then how long you've been here."

He smiles at my innocence, says, "In the beginning, I had no need of calendars. I was happy to give myself completely to time. So counting them now would be inconclusive."

"You never went into the trees then?"

"I tell you there was no need! Life aboard was sufficient. There was no need that was not provided for by the company."

"The company might have had the foresight to include among the rolling stock a car of women—for the coupling of brakemen!" I laugh idiotically. "A rolling brothel." I continue in a voice tinged with weariness and disgust. "We have everything else."

"There is such a car; at least from time to time one appears that answers to its description."

"And you never visited it?"

In spite of myself, I feel my pulse quicken with the voyeur's wild agitation, as if seeing in the mind's eye were enough. And perhaps, for one afflicted with imagination, it is enough.

"Once or twice, no more," he says. "I did not wish to find my pleasure on a manifest among sardine tins, pachyderm, and instruments of torture. It was, as I recall, a performance in which desire was acted out. I left feeling anxious. And appalled."

"What will you do when the desert comes?" I ask uneasily.

"What I have always done," he says.

I study his face: It seems to be that of the moon itself—white, luminous, and cruel.

"Kill myself."

6.

Only once have I seen another train. We arrived together in a narrow valley—our train and some other. The two parallel lines of tracks were forced close together by cliffs on either side of the river, which separated them and the rails. Ours, orange with rust; the other, silver—bright as mirrors in the sun, so that the eyes stared as if stuck open and only by shaking one's head would they close. I looked at our train's reflection in the river, hoping to see its end; but the cars pulled behind the locomotive and caboose were without number.

That train was crowded with passengers. For the space of time we traveled together, side by side, with only the narrow river between us, I could see men and women sitting in their seats, reading newspapers and magazines or sleeping, or else walking up and down the aisles—even passing between swaying cars on their way to their berths, or to dinner, or to the observation car at the end of the train. Although I waved and shouted, they seemed not to notice us. I was close enough to see their faces, their hands in their laps, or in their knitting, or clasped by other hands. These I took to be the hands of lovers, perhaps couples on their honeymoons. At no time in my life have I known anguish to equal this, when I saw those men and women holding hands. So that is love, I said to myself. And again, I tried unsuccessfully to attract their attention.

"They do not see us—not even from the observation car," the engineer said. "We may be traveling side by side, with only a few meters separating us, but we occupy different times. Or if the same time, we are more aware than they of its qualities and aspects, dimensions and liabilities. It is that awareness and not those lovers that cause you anguish. Consciousness is the full awareness of time."

"I would rather be on that other train," I said bitterly.

The engineer said nothing; and in a little while, the mountains fell away behind us, the land broadened, the two tracks veered apart, and I saw neither the train nor its fortunate passengers again.

7.

Just as the engineer foretold, we have come to a desert. There are no trees now where he can take his ease, or practice his subversion, or immerse himself in time's fullness—or escape from it. In the shimmering distance, I see tents, which appear to soar against the unending sands. The tents are colorful and moored by camels and horses, or so it seems from my remote and moving vantage.

العربية

Peering through binoculars, I can see Arab girls dancing at the center of intricate Arabic letters written with silken scarves on the still air. The scarves are rose-colored, pink, orange, blue, and green. At dusk, before night sweeps like a scimitar vanquishing day, the sand will borrow the colors of those numinous scarves; and tiny lights, as if at faraway depots, will mark the place of those mysterious encampments, lost in a vague and noiseless world. A world where time is marked only by the alternation of day and night.

The engineer keeps silent, shut away with his memories perhaps, while the train hurls itself against the desert at an impossible rate of speed, so that the duration of day and night is registered by no more than a flickering light against the neverending rails ahead of us. Or behind us. Or above us, for sometimes we seem to be riding with the sun or moon under our feet, though it may be only the glimmer of the tracks. It must not be forgotten that we are traveling in the land of mirage.

In spite of our velocity, we spend years crossing the desert.

One day it is finished.

Limitless sand gives way to illimitable snow; gold becomes white by a perversion of alchemy. Flatland becomes tundra; and dune, tumulus as the train enters an ice age. The engineer cannot be wakened. It does not matter that he sleeps, except that I feel very much alone. I keep to the caboose, taking no interest in what can be seen through its windows. In London once, I heard Peary address the British Cartographic Society concerning his arctic expedition. He claimed a terrible beauty for the place, but I see only death in it.

I think I am slowly freezing to death.

•   •   •

I hear a clatter on the roof of the car next to mine—not a clatter, a measured, mincing tread amplified by the metal roof but dulled by cold, dead air. A girl climbs down the caboose's ladder. I help her inside. She is wearing only slippers and a kind of corset such as I once saw at the Palais du Trocadero. I think she must be on the verge of extinction to be so scantily attired in this frigid place! I wonder she does not shiver, that her lips are not blue and her fingers black with frostbite.

"I've left my balancing pole on the roof," she says. "Will it be all right, do you think?"

"Who are you?" I cry as one will, finally, who has seen quite enough marvels in his lifetime.

"The tightrope walker," she replies, looking at me with alarm; for I was at that moment tearing at my eyes as if to have them out once and for all.

"Tightrope walker," I say, adding mine to the echoes of what has come and gone or is still to be.

"From the circus. Why are you acting so strangely? Please stop before you hurt yourself!"

"This is, then, a circus train?" I ask, hoping to have found, at last, the ungainsayable truth.

"Yes. What else?"

"And has it always been so?"

"As far as I know."

"How far is that?" I ask, searching her face for signs of treachery.

"For as long as I've lived," she says, much annoyed. "My mother and father performed on the high wire. They fell to their deaths from it."

"But aren't you cold in that costume!" I shout, confused.

"A little, from the wind on the roof. The train's going so fast!"

"You walked all the way from the rear of the train?"

I could love this woman, were there time enough. I could take her in my arms and stop time, though her eyes are not yet shadowed by sorrow.

"Yes, it was very exciting!" she said, clapping her hands like a child.

"Over so very many cars?" I say, amazed.

"Oh, there aren't so many as all that!"

"And what season of the year is it?"

"Summer. July. What is the matter with you?"

"Summer. July. Did the impresario send you?"

"Impresario . . . if you mean the signore, owner of our little circus—yes. He's very angry. Why hasn't the train stopped?"

It has been many years since the train last stopped. Not since the desert—even before that, on a plain in a battle's aftermath. Men lay in a muddy ditch, or hung on wire in attitudes of submission to history and its follies. The sun was eclipsed by cannon smoke. Unless it was the train's own smoke spreading like a canopy overhead as it lost its inertia.

"We ought to have stopped two hours ago! The people were lined up on either side of the track, waiting to welcome us. The engineer did not even sound the whistle! The signore was very angry. He sent me over the roofs to see what was wrong."

"Why didn't he telegraph me?" I ask, turning to the telegraph key. But it is not there. The typewriter is also gone.

She looks at me as if I were something other than I am, or thought myself to be. A thing apart. She climbs into the locomotive to wake the engineer, who is dead. Or revolving through his fingers a *tespyh* while he sits before the Cilician Gates, in the Taurus Mountains, where the Euphrates begins its descent.

"You must stop the train!" she shouts, shaking me like one who is asleep.

"Me? I don't know how!"

The train is hurtling toward destruction, an iconoclasm that will deliver me from all forms and performances, to a forgotten siding where I may rest and dream unmolested a theory of time. I stare, entranced—not afraid in the least that there are neither rails nor ties beneath me.

"But you are the brakeman!" she screams. But already she is fading, like a photograph improperly fixed to resist the seduction of obscurity. It is a great burden to be in time and to know that one is, just as it must be for those giddy ones, who feel always the earth's turning beneath their feet.

Where my thumb was, I feel an itching prelude to growth. My hand is remembering. Soon I will remember myself as brakeman and, perhaps, even as once I was, before I unfolded like a paper flower into time—a young man not on a train and, perhaps, happy.

The Gaiety of Henry James

Dzim trou-la-la boum boum!

1.

Inspiration deserts him, deserts Henry James, by now well along in age, after so many novels, having lingered so long a time in the chaste arms of his muse, the chaste arms of a muse of marble, classically proportioned and cool to the touch. He has been seized by desire and, in his confusion, does not know where to turn to put an end to his suffering. Henry James stops writing. He closes the door to his writing room and, pulling on his gloves, goes out into the street, where he bumps—by a stroke of luck—into Florenz Ziegfeld, who is about to introduce the Follies to New York.

"Ziggy, I'm unhappy."

"I'm hungry!" the impresario answers.

2.

Henry and Ziggy ride the trolley to the Blue Ox. Ziggy wants wurst and sauerkraut. He wants, he tells Henry, to sit in a place that smells like Germany. A young woman walks down the aisle, her left arm lifted so that its hand may take hold, one by one, of the swinging leather straps. Her hips sway beguilingly as the car clicks down the rails, listing left and right, right and left. Henry cannot take his eyes from the girl's white cambric shirtwaist. He traces the curve of her breast with the end of his nose, while Ziggy talks about his latest discovery, a girl from Dubuque "with calves as perfect as if they'd been turned on a lathe." Henry says nothing, his heart in turmoil.

3.

"She comes to me at night," says Henry. "She whispers to me of *la belle époque*. She shows me drawings by Franz von Bayros and sings Mayol's song: '*Les mains de femme / Je le proclame / Sont des bijoux / Dont je suis fou.*' She reads to me from *Story of O.*"

"Who does?"

"A succubus."

Ziggy considers the end of his cigar. "From time to time, I, too, enjoy the attentions of a succubus," he says. "But they cannot compare with those paid by a woman of flesh and blood." He plunges his cigar's burning end into cold sauerkraut, where it hisses. (Like a *fury*, Henry thinks.) "Her name is Esmeralda."

"Mine looks like Edith Wharton," Henry says. "Au naturel."

A barely perceptible shudder passes through Ziggy—less than a shudder: a twitch of an eyelid. He makes a pile of dollar bills on the table, pats his mustache, and pushes back his chair. "I have an audition at two. A girl from Canton."

"China?"

"Ohio. Would you care to come?"

But Henry fears the mere sight of a girl in her shift may unhinge him entirely, sending him out onto Broadway, a lunatic in advance of a tightly laced "camisole." (Who knows the power of suggestion on a man who has dreamed of Edith Wharton naked!)

"I am previously engaged," he says.

4.

Henry visits the zoo, in order to submerge his passion in a "theater of elemental animalism." Finding the big cats too exciting, he studies the passivity of an elephant, whose indolent trunk hangs limply in the summer heat. Henry shuts his eyes, imagining, for a moment, a novel in which a savage man lives in a tree house with a girl named Jane (an idea he will give to Edgar Rice Burroughs, languishing at the moment in Chicago as manager of the Sears, Roebuck and Company stenographic department).

Henry drifts above jungle foliage enameled by the tropic sun and the plumage of birds, one of whose screams wakes him abruptly from his drowse. It is no bird that screamed, but Edith Wharton, in the ardent clutches of an orangutan! Henry rushes to extricate her from the primate's greedy grasp. Extricated, Edith swoons into Henry's arms.

He carries her to the zookeeper's office behind the primate house. While the zookeeper goes for water, Henry regards the unconscious woman. Desire rises up strong in him; and he wonders whether it might be permitted him, for humanitarian reasons, to loosen the novelist's clothes. He has his ungloved hands on the buttons of her blouse when the zookeeper arrives with a bucket. Coloring, Henry removes his hands; and the zookeeper, who seems not to notice Henry's discomfiture, drizzles a little water on the woman. Edith shrugs back into consciousness.

"The beast ate my hat," she says.

"It was the cherries," says the zookeeper, "them that was on the brim. Cecil likes cherries."

Seeing Henry, Edith's indignation turns rancorous: "It's all over town that you entertain me in your dreams!"

Henry sputters an apology and hurries away. He rushes into Central Park to hide his shame among the trees. He plunges headlong through the shrubbery in search of wood nymphs, such is the overheated condition of his fancy. He would not mind in the least being ravaged by a mythological being, so long as she alludes, at least in part, to a woman. He can find no wood nymphs, alas.

5.

Henry receives a telegram from Ziggy: "Going on safari to *la belle époque* to see what women I can capture for the Follies. Care to join me?"

Henry weeps in gratitude.

6.

Henry goes to the haberdashery and purchases, like a bride choosing for her trousseau, the following items: two dozen pairs of silk socks clocked with geometric motifs; two dozen sets of men's undergarments in summer and winter weights; a dozen shirts of the finest linen, one yellow, one pink, one mauve, one robin's egg blue, one of a pale gray reminiscent of smoke—the remainder in shades of white from snow to ecru; six pairs of trousers in wool, linen, and flannel—two yeomanly plain, one charcoal-striped, one tattersall, one checked and verging on the garish (for evenings spent in the demimonde), and one Henry finds irresistible: a mustard color, "which Oscar himself might choose as recherché." In addition, Henry makes extravagant purchases of tweed and linen frockcoats, superbly cut, with impudent silk vests, which would alarm his family and frighten genteel ladies in Philadelphia, New York, or Boston. Hats also does he purchase—a fedora, for preference, named for Sardou's delicious farce, in addition to one of the feathered alpine variety and a cap of a loud and unwholesome plaid.

"Now," he says to himself, "I am ready for *la belle époque*."

7.

New York City
July 21, 1905

Dear Mr. James:

The zookeeper informed me that you were doing something furtive in the vicinity of my bosom. My outrage is boundless, my rage towering. Susan B. Anthony has entered you on her most despised list. Expect a delegation of suffragettes at your door to protest your degenerate condition. I have burned your novels in the incinerator.

Sincerely,

Edith Wharton

8.

Henry's bedroom. Night. The succubus. Her siren song. Henry's lust aroused in sleep. Heated dreams. The succubus undoing her nightdress. Much thrashing about in bed by Henry. Laughter of the succubus. Henry tickled by the succubus. Henry bussed by the succubus. Henry walking above Fifth Avenue on a telegraph wire. Henry crying out. Pedestrians in the street below looking up Henry's nightshirt. Sensations of immodesty and shame. The succubus looking at her watch. The succubus reminded of an appointment in Orange, New Jersey, with Thomas A. Edison. The succubus doing up her nightdress. Henry falling from the wire. The departure of the succubus. Henry waking.

9.

Henry looks at the French postcards left on his bedside table by the succubus.

"Oh, *la belle époque!*" he cries. "I am coming!"

10.

Ziggy stands in the street outside Henry's hotel. "Hurry, Henry!" he shouts, making a megaphone of his hands. "The boat is leaving in thirty minutes."

Henry hurries.

But, as if in a dream, he cannot finish dressing. He puts on first one new shirt and then another; renounces this collar in favor of that, onyx studs for pearl, gray flannel trousers for mustard, diamond-clocked socks for those with interlocking squares; dons the feathered hat, the plaid cap, the fedora—no, no, no! And so it goes until his entire wardrobe is scattered on the bed, the floor, and the chair. Irresolution grips him!

"Good-bye!" Ziggy calls from the departing cab, which rattles down the cobblestones toward the great piers of transatlantic desire and departure.

Henry weeps in frustration and anguished disappointment.

11.

The weather is not so fine now as the week before. The streets are muddied, their curbs and cobbles slick with rain. Outside the hotel, sullen cab horses steam while two ladies, their plumage like drowned birds, hustle their bustles beneath the doorman's streaming umbrella.

Henry's weather is equally dismal.

He visits his brother, the eminent philosopher William

James. "Such maladies as yours originate in a place other than consciousness," he tells Henry in gruff, unbrotherly fashion.

"*La belle époque*," says Henry, "derides consciousness."

"See Freud in Vienna! The unconscious mind is not within my purlieu." William returns to his manuscript and writes: "Within each personal consciousness, thought is sensibly continuous." He puts down his pen and swings round in his chair. "I don't see what's stopping you from going, if you must."

"I need a cicerone," Henry replies. "Someone who knows the way."

"The way lies generally eastward," William says astringently. "The last I heard, *la belle époque* is in France."

"*La belle époque* will not reveal herself to everyone who comes calling," says Henry mournfully. "I publicly abominated modern French literature as 'intolerably unclean.' I decried Zola as 'ignorant and working in the dark.'" Henry sighs. "I might have crept inside while *la belle époque* was seducing Ziegfeld."

"What nonsense!" says William, taking up his pen to scratch another sentence on the page: "Consciousness is nothing jointed . . . it flows."

Henry goes home to bed, to enjoy the consolations of his succubus. But the succubus is in Orange with Edison, listening to his gramophone, and will not come to Henry again!

12.

Henry dreams of a witch. She is nibbling his fingers and toes; she is eating his candied leg. She is biting his neck to suck out the sweetbread. Now she is knocking at his head with her stick. Henry screams and wakes, but the sound of knocking continues on the door to the hall.

Knock, knock.

Henry rising. Henry walking, like a somnambulist, to the vestibule. Henry opening the door. Susan B. Anthony framed in the jambs. Ms. Anthony reading a proclamation. Henry's dream life denounced. Henry kicking Ms. Anthony downstairs. The police summoned. Henry hustled into a van. Charges preferred by Ms. Anthony. Henry before the magistrate. Bruises adduced by Ms. Anthony "in evidence of vile misconduct." Edith Wharton, "surprise witness." The succubus. The zoo. The buttons of her blouse. Sensation in the courtroom. The zookeeper called. Corroboration of Edith's story by the zookeeper. Second sensation in the courtroom. The magistrate outraged. Henry vilified. Henry mobbed by reporters. Henry blinded by photographers' magnesium flash. Henry kicked in the shins by Ms. Anthony. Henry taken roughly to the cells. *Hurrahs*! in the street, from the suffragettes.

Henry composes *In the Slough*, in his head, but will never commit it to paper, having lost the will to write.

13.

At the brink of land and life, Henry hesitates. The rain-vexed river is roiled and oily. The wind has beaten it to foam. Henry admires his pink vest, his soft calfskin boots. Perhaps opium, he thinks, in a Chinese den will make him forget *la belle époque*. He stares, transfixed by the river and by a kind of siren's song played in the sheets of a packet boat docked below.

Ffft! Ffft! Ffft!

The bicycle of a Western Union boy strikes a brick and, wobbling before regaining its plumb, nudges Henry off the pier.

Henry makes an imperfect hole in the water.

Panicked, the Western Union boy flees.

Henry's floating fedora marks his place. Hopefully, he will return to it, after an intermission spent holding his breath.

14.

Henry. The river. The effect of gravity. Influence of displacement. The role of that principle first described by Archimedes. Henry's rapidly depleting reserves of oxygen and its implications for his health. His health's deterioration and also that of his calfskin boots. Approaching loss of consciousness. Speculation on Henry's part as to whether or not there will be a succeeding period, however short-lived, of unconsciousness and what that will be like. A pink area of sensation in which Henry remembers having once observed a girl bathing nude in the river—not this river, but another—while he hid behind a haycock. Henry likening himself to the Shrophire Lad. Henry singing "Rule, Britannia." Henry ruing the day he allowed himself to fall under French influence. *L'art nouveau* excoriated by Henry. Toulouse-Lautrec and the French Revolution decried.

Henry enters the frontier between consciousness and unconsciousness, reciting, from memory, "juicy parts" from *Story of O*.

15.

A gasping Henry regains the surface. His clothes are heavy; his pockets, filled with river. The river seems determined to ravish him—to take him to the silted chambers of its darkest heart. It grasps Henry by the ankles and pulls. He resists but notes, with a novelist's inveterate curiosity, that a particle of himself wishes to drown in order to "know the worst." At least, he thinks, his torment will be at an end.

"Possibly, I'm not the man for *la belle époque*," he tells himself. "Rye, that sturdy brown English town, is better, perhaps, for one such as I, who could, if he chose, write a novel concerning the act of taking off a glove but might expire of apoplexy were he to witness a Parisian striptease."

"*Hallo! Hallo* there—you, the gentleman in the water!"

It is William Vanderbilt, hallowing from the bow of his splendid yacht. "Would you care to come aboard?"

"If you would be so kind," Henry replies, observing, though nearly drowned, a Brahmin's social graces.

A sailor throws Henry a rope and pulls him, dripping, up. A second sailor is waiting with a towel. The steward arrives with a bottle of stout.

"To fortify you," William remarks, accepting a bottle for himself. "To your health!"

"I'm in your debt," Henry replies and drinks, though his teeth chatter against the bottle's glass neck.

"How came you to be in the East River so close to the dinner hour?"

"A boy was careless with his bicycle," Henry replies.

"God damn all boys on bicycles! Might I know your name, sir?"

"Henry James."

"The novelist?"

Henry affirms the eminent yachtsman's surmise with a nod of his wet and hatless head.

"I've got all your things at my Newport cottage. In deluxe editions."

The dinner gong gongs, and William rushes off to the ship's mess.

16.

Henry and William face each other across a pinochle table. William wears a commodore's white flannels and gold-buttoned blazer; Henry, a sailor's summer whites. William withdraws his florid face from a brandy snifter and wrinkles his nose in prelude.

"I'm on my way to race the king of Spain," he tells Henry,

whose underwear clings damply. "Our two yachts. I can set you ashore on the Côte d' Azur. From there, you can take the train to *la belle époque*, though I can't help thinking you are wasting your time. It's a young man's game, and your salad days are well behind you."

"I am grateful, nevertheless."

A girl looks in at the saloon door, winks at William, and disappears.

William rises and wishes Henry a good night. "You can have my cabin," he says. "Tonight, I'll use the hammock, like any simple sailor."

Flowers and boxes of candy have been left for Henry, as if by an act of providence whose workings it is William's pleasure always to emulate. Sucking a pastille, Henry watches the watery light lap at the ceiling. The sea lifts the yacht and lowers it gently. Waves drub the sides, creating in him a somnolence, but also a sensuous appreciation of the bed's luxurious accouterments—satin, cotton, and musky wool. Like a dory whose mooring line is cut, Henry drifts out onto the current of an irresistible tide. He is moving now toward his idée fixe—the object of his desire.

La belle époque!

Henry sleeps as the yacht slips magically across the Atlantic. He will never know whether the crossing was accomplished during a single night or many. Whether William slept in the arms of the pretty girl who had leaned in at the doorway; whether the crew lay all during the voyage tangled in blankets and dreams of barrooms, whiskey, and women.

Ffft! Ffft! Ffft!

Henry starts from sleep. Sunlight streams through the portlights, bringing with it the smell of iodine and cordite. The yacht has been fired upon! A battleship approaches, its iron shadow falling heavily!

17.

Armed with painting knives and etching needles, *l'art nouveau* boards the Vanderbilt yacht. Xavier Sager and Lugné-Poe pinion Henry, while Mademoiselle Lidia, high-wire striptease sensation at the Olympic, tickles him with an ostrich plume. Hector Guimard, whose wriggling wrought-iron entrances to the Paris Métro alarm the impressionable, rebukes Henry "in the name of *la belle époque*."

"You, Monsieur Henry James, are a foe of the unconscious impulse, of strange desire, and forbidden longings. You, monsieur, have proclaimed yourself an enemy of the modern French novel. You, monsieur, have insulted the great Zola! Now that you have come to be, in your old age, a desiccated person, you wish to be rejuvenated with the juice of passion and the renewed secretions of your most secret ducts. Your importunities, monsieur, are unwelcome to *la belle époque*; and we order you to return to Plymouth Rock!"

"Lady and gentlemen of *l'art nouveau* in France," Henry replies. "It is true that I have disparaged those very tendencies of your movement which I now seek. I have suppressed them in my life and work. It is also true that I wish to embrace voluptuousness—the rococo excess and whiplash line typifying the most advanced art of the new century. Humbly, I implore you to grant me asylum in the bosom of *la belle époque*!"

"No."

"But I have purchased a pair of mustard-colored pants!"

Led by M. Guimard, *l'art nouveau* turns smartly on its heels and returns to the gaily painted battleship, which was designed by Antoní Gaudí after his Barcelona apartment building and hardly looks seaworthy.

Henry cries.

William consoles him. "I will run you across to Morocco,"

he says. "Perhaps you will find solace in the perfumed embrace of an odalisque."

18.

Henry in the Kasbah.

A thin music winds like adders through the crooked streets.

The red fezzes.

The Arab women.

The spiced and orangey air.

Henry on the beach. The ocean slides back and forth between Algeria and Spain, rattles over stones, hisses in retreat from the beach, roars down the black jetties. The sun falls behind the rocky hills of Africa.

Henry smokes a cigarette to make a little light in the night.

The beach shines with moon snails, blue and coolly lunar.

Henry stares out to sea.

A light on the water.

A black shape against the lighter night.

A whirring of tiny jeweled gears.

The water rolls forward, seething, and surrounds Henry's boots, which crunch on the gravel. Startled, he drops his cigarette.

A submarine composes itself in monochrome on Henry's field of vision. Jules Verne stands in the open hatch.

"Hello, Henri!" he shouts. "Are you ready to return to France?"

19.

"I mistook you for Matisse," says Jules. "He went ashore on Tuesday to paint harem girls. Do you know Henri, Henry?"

"I've not had that pleasure."

"IIe's a *fauve*—what we call, in France, a 'wild beast.' IIe refuses to be constrained by appearances. That's one of the reasons I'm so fond of him. The other's his women. His women are voluptuous. Would you like something to eat?"

In the submarine's dining room, Henry eats a lobster.

"I'm an old man now," Jules continues over cognac; "but I like voluptuous women." With his hand, the father of science fiction traces, in the air, the symbol for infinity (8). "The curve, Henry, is the archetypal form."

"Perhaps you're the man to take me to *la belle époque!*" exclaims Henry hopefully.

"I would be happy to do so. Would you care to see a risqué moving-picture show made by the Lumière brothers while we make our voyage?"

"Why, yes," says Henry.

"Excellent, my dear sir! You have been overly fond, I think, of the 'virtuous attachment.'"

20.

The voyage. The moving-picture show. Juliette Marval's spectacular "split" at the Tivoli-Vauxhall. Velvet depths. Weird fish observed through the submarine's window. A whirl of batiste underwear at the Moulin Rouge. A monstrous squid. Mademoiselle Bardou's black stockings. A pink sucker groping here and there. Bubu de Montparnasse soliciting in the doorway of the Bal Bullier. *Ffft! Ffft! Ffft!* Rayon d'Or's bare breasts at the Élysee-Montmartre. Lovely sea anemones. Mademoiselle Simier at the Parisot. ("Who will dare to look at her legs!") Gibraltar's limestone thighs. Coral formations of a shocking color. Donkey rides at Barbizon. *Dzim trou-la-la boum boum!* Arlette Dorgère's bloomers at La Cigale. Oh, siren! Traveling down the Seine. Madame Flagel and Miss Birch. Jules reading aloud from his new novel, *Le Phare du bout du monde.* The submarine's motors, like a stringed orchestra. Claudine "unhooked" on the rue de la Gaité. The submarine trembling in response to the galvanic action of seawater. Lidia stripping off on the trapeze. *Trou-la-la!* Henry aroused. *Boum boum!* Henry drinking a third cognac. A sailor dancing for Henry. Henry dancing with the sailor. The red pom-pom on the sailor's hat, the blue on Henry's. Jules beating time with a spoon, singing "*Mettez-y un doigt / Et puis vous verrez. / Vous en mettrez un, après ça deux, après ça trois.*" Henry in abandon. A big thump.

"What was that big thump?" asks Henry.

"Paris," says Jules.

"Ah!"

21.

At last, Henry has her in his arms—*la belle époque!* She is winsome; she is amorous; she is all that his chaste muse is not. He tickles her pink breast with his mustache. The mustache remains on her breast—it is false (the mustache, not the breast, which is ample), but no matter. All is permitted in the boudoir of this, the seductress of France in the nought years of a new century. *La belle époque* contains all that can be said to be of earthly delight. She is, for Henry, food, drink, music, song, and the novel whose writing will elude him; for he is too old now to write of her charms, La Belle's, but not— happily—to enjoy them, here, in her luxurious bed.

"Light, more light!" he says, wanting to see everything, jealous of even the shadow that falls on her from the naughty marble vase by Daum—a column of a bastardized Tuscan order, veined with vines and kissed by a bare-legged maiden very like Isadora Duncan.

Henry turns up the wick, and the flame beats up inside the glass chimney. A yellow light engulfs the room, seeping through the diaphanous bed curtains, and lies against La Belle's unclothed body.

"Oh, but you are bruised!" Henry cries.

"Pablo did it to me."

"The brute!"

"It's only paint," she replies gaily. "Cerulean, this morning; viridian, yesterday. The yellow ocher is from a week ago. Pablo comes every day to destroy me with his art."

"I would thrash him were I younger."

"But it is pleasant to make art."

"I no longer wish it."

"What do you wish?"

"To understand my desire and, having understood it, submit to my fate."

They rise, and together they go to the Eiffel Tower. For only there, at the top of it, can Henry possess what is, in actuality, a city—of desire and indulgence. Paris, in *la belle époque*. (A city and a time doomed by time to become less lovely than they are now at this moment. But neither the city nor the time, nor Henry, knows this.)

Henry looks out at the gray houses, the green parks, the broad avenues, the arching bridges, and the Seine. He imagines women in the houses, letting down cello-colored hair; under trees musical with spring rain; on the avenues and bridges, dizzy with the rolling light. He sees them on the river, indolent in small boats, their faces lifted to receive a benevolent sun and the fathomless longing of men.

He steps from the uppermost landing, prepared to rise into the clear blue Parisian air—upheld by waves of desire, transmitted by M. Eiffel's magic tower like a radio program of boleros. And he does rise—Henry does—in his white sailor suit. Insouciant. Poised. The hollows of his bones buoyant with momentary light. Belle is waving to him, her long scarf tugged by an amorous wind.

Then Henry falls, as he must, all the way back to Rye—there, to live out his life with the memory of this, his life's beautiful epoch. And having suffered desire, to shed words that float like leaves on water stilled after a hectic passage. Henry has come to rest, in Rye, content. He puts down his pen and lets his eyes fall onto the page, onto the last word to be set down there. And the word is *joy*.

Ideas of Space

Found among the papers of Umberto da Silva,
Ravenna, 1761–1833

1.

I had lived always among the trees; and when, at last, I came out onto the plain, my head reeled and I was sick. The uninterrupted light was, in its novelty, nearly fatal—a plague of nettles, a yellow noise, a magisterial voice deaf to all human entreaty. I mean to say that I had not, until that moment, seen the sun whole and undivided. Always, it had hidden behind a screen of foliage or, in winter, bones of twig and fescue. The light was thin and strained. A dusk even at midday. To see it, all at once and of a sudden, was a blow to the senses—not just to my eyes, though they stung and the light turned black within them, but to the other organs of sense through which the world invades and trammels up the mind. I smelled light like a rust or mold, tasted its bitterness, and felt it against my skin—hot and barbed.

Brought to my knees, I wished I had not left the thickset woods to savor distances. What did I know of distance, immensities of space, emptiness, or the vegetable and mineral composition of the world outside the forest? I had heard how, on the plain, one's eyes might rove with nothing to arrest them, that they might sweep in a circuit and encounter nothing but grass and, in the distance, a haze that might be clouds or mountains or—strangest of all—the sea. All of us had listened to stories of a broad river dividing the plain, which appeared in the distance no more than a crooked length of string. We heard how a caravan might toil for days on end and not come to the end of it. I accepted the travelers' accounts without question. I understood that, outside the ancient forest (in which we were born and would one day be no more than dust), people were to the plain as ants are to the forest paths and cramped clearings separating one house from another. But I had not yet felt space as ants must in their unceasing transits. I had no notion then of the dimensions of vastness or the sickness it might cause in me—what bewilderment and fear. Not even from the highest branch could I see anything but trees in an endlessly repeated pattern. The sky itself seemed hemmed in by them, like a piece of blue cloth rucked and snagged by branches. I looked around me with loathing.

In leaving the forest, I had thought to feel space like a wind pleated with flowery airs, its transparent pockets lined with a lint of golden pollen. I had thought to come out onto the plain and be refreshed instantly, as if by cold water. Among the trees, I had begun to imagine that my eyes were "stuck"—that the optical machinery had seized like a lever by rust. To see always only what is in front of one's eyes, to live walled up—what toll might not such a life take? I had imagined my eyes roughly wakened from their myopic trance. The moment, I thought, would arrive like a storm, a catastrophe of light. But I did not allow for the persistence of that engulfment, how it would wrap me in thick cloths of light, blinding and pernicious.

I lay on the ground, face pressed to the cool grass, the colder earth unlike that of the forest floor, which reeks of mold, rotted leaves, and the animal smell of fungi and morels. I shut my eyes to the clamorous light and waited for the earth to stand still and for night to fall.

2.

Supine in the dark, I watched the steep night endlessly receding, its black depths mapped by stars. I remembered how, alone in a narrow forest clearing where onions and turnips grew, I had seen scattered among the trees the solitary lamps of our settlement. I would go there at night to be alone and, in its confinement, imagine a spacious life beyond the farthest tree. I had been no better than a mole! I might have married another mole and fathered mole children to fill my little mole house. I might have done—but always in me was a mutiny against narrowness. I walked as if bearing on my back the weight of the forest. I yearned to walk in a straight line. Such a simple desire—so simple it could hardly be said to be a desire. Distance was coiled up inside me—in the bones and sinews of my legs—the way movement is in a caged animal or flight in the limed bird. I was pilloried, shackled to the trees, which rose up all around us like mute and merciless judges.

I had known time; but it was, like the forest, featureless. Monotonous. It had stagnated in gray pools. It was the color of wash water. It was used up. It suited sleep. I had slept long— we all had. In that twilight, we would be seized suddenly by the need to sleep. And we would sleep dreaming of trees, of the dusky light that sifted down through the leaves or of rain that differed from the gray light only in its being wet. There was no refreshment in either. Mostly, we dreamed bitter dramas set inside the houses we left only when we must, to work in the fields, the mill, the store, the school—the few occupations allowed us by the forest. Time now would be other than I had known it: faster, more varied and complicated. History would involve the plain as it had never done the forest. I understood and braced myself for its onslaught. I imagined a wind, shrill and cold—a hurricane sweeping everything before it like dead leaves. I feared it—what it might pull up by the roots from my dark depths. Already, time was changing. The stars seemed to wheel round the black sky; I saw their fiery tracks instead of the unmoving points of light that had hung above the trees. Watching them in their headlong, I was sick again in the grass and had to shut my eyes. I felt vulnerable—uncovered—exposed to that dangerous light, as if caught in a meteor shower. I lay there, shivering until morning.

3.

"I thought you were dead," he said. I leaned against him as we walked slowly toward the wagon. "You look as if you ought to be."

"I was sick," I said. "I need to get in somewhere."

He helped me onto the wagon seat.

"You slept out all night, then?"

I nodded, saying again, "I need to get inside." I dared not tell him why—this man of the plain, who went without fear of the immensities of distance.

He flicked the reins over the horse's back. The wagon rang with his peddler's wares as it lurched and swayed over the macadam.

"I'm spending the night farther along," the peddler shouted above the crunch of gravel. "Two hours more. You can see it—there." He took both reins in his left hand and pointed with the other.

I could see nothing except gray road and grass. But the river was there, next to the road that followed it. Broad and brown, it was beating against yellow gravel and mud a steady retreat from the mountains behind me to an unseen sea ahead. When I leaned out of the wagon, I saw myself come and go in little bays of quiet water, cut into a shoreline stiff with reeds. The light on the river's back fixed my eyes helplessly in a dazzled stare, freed only when a cloud slid across the face of the sun. But it was the river's music that ravished me—how one moment it might sound like whiskey falling softly in a glass and the next like a rain of hailstones as it sped across a shallows. How could I have failed to hear it during the long night, unless it had been drowned in the noise of stars?

The river was greater even than my idea of it had been. I envied its disdain and the ease of its procession through space. Nothing stood in the way of its ends, which it attained single-mindedly. It spent itself in its solitary bed without love or recompense, obedient to ice and thaw, drought and freshet, indifferent to its own futility. When the sprawling grassland threatened to overcome me, I had only to turn my gaze on the river to quell it.

"What river is this?" I asked the peddler.

"The Po," he answered, surprised. "I did not take you for a stranger."

I would like to have asked him what he saw; I mean to say, how space looked to him and also how it felt as he pushed his way deeper into it. But he would have thought me mad. Is space a dough into which a man might plunge his hands to knead and shape it to his will?

As if he had read my thoughts, the peddler remarked with satisfaction on the plain that lay all round us: "This is mine. For as far as you can see and a little beyond—my territory. Since I was a young man, I've cultivated it, until now I can say it belongs to me by right of possession. They know me—in every village, hamlet, and farm for a hundred miles, they know my name and wares."

"Are there no other peddlers?" I asked.

"No Tubal-cains but me." He noticed my look of incomprehension and, slapping me hard on the back, produced by way of explanation a verse: " '*Sella quoque genuit Tubal-cain qui fuit malleator et faber in cuncta opera aeris et ferri.*' 'Sella also brought forth Tubal-cain, who was a hammerer and artificer in every work of brass and iron.' Genesis four: twenty-two."

His pots and pans chimed an almost musical accompaniment.

"And what are you?" he asked.

I had no answer.

"How do you make your living?"

In the forest, each one did what necessity demanded of him. Because in our occupations we were more or less interchange-able, we seldom thought of ourselves apart from the whole. This is not to say we lived under a tyranny of the collective: The individual will was submerged in a common dreaming, not in an autocracy. To speak of the will is to exalt what was scarcely more than yearning. I wanted no more than what a fly might want, which paces hopelessly the inside of a windowpane: a wider compass. Others may have harbored different long-ings, but none had strength enough to satisfy them. Likewise, dreaming suggests a richness that was not an aspect of our anarchic hours. Our dreams were poor. It was not only their lack of spaciousness that made them so; they seemed rudimen-tary and unformed. We dreamed as children do—no, as people who have all their lives been cloistered or blind.

"It is there for the taking," the peddler said, annexing with his eyes the plain, into which we were venturing like two con-quistadors. "It has made me rich, and I shall be richer still before I'm done." He laughed, but the reason for his laughter was hidden from me.

I stopped at the inn until I became reconciled to space and could walk out on the plain without discomfiture. Even so, it seemed always to recede before me, repulsing my attempts to grapple with it. It was like a painting of a landscape that I tried to enter but could not. My dreams remained closed. In them, I had not yet left the forest.

4.

"My mathematics is helpless against the sea," he said. "But here, it subdues space—vanquishes it—ensnares it in a fine net of coordinates! There is, believe me, no more remarkable occupation than that of land surveyor! Through the sights of my theodolite, I achieve what no rifle or cannon can: dominion—absolute and irrefutable! Only catastrophe—a paroxysm of nature—can annul the results of my triangulation! And we are not in a region liable to earthquake or other subterranean disturbance. Even should drought or fire lay waste the grass, my survey will remain immaculate because it is beyond contingency and accident."

By now, I was used to the surveyor's effusions, having spent three days together traversing the endless grassland. I watched him as he minutely bisected his sandwich, then reduced an apple to meridians of longitude. I wondered why a calculating man should speak with the fervor of an evangelist.

"Were the plain to disappear, we would have its essence—here." He patted his breast pocket, where a leather-bound notebook lay coincidentally near his heart. "In fact, the plain itself is superfluous; what matters is its mathematical representation. It's the same with great paintings: The people who sat for Gainsborough are of no consequence. Who remembers Miss Catherine Tatton or the original Lady in Blue?"

We were making our way slowly across the plain. He carried the Ramsden, I, the rod and chain. The sun beat down, and I wondered what provision his mathematics made for sun or rain or night. Perhaps his maps were like dreams, which were curiously devoid of weather, though there was night.

"What do you dream?" I asked.

"I do not dream!" he replied curtly, as if my question had offended him. "What could a land surveyor do *there*? I detest the very idea of dreaming."

He put down his theodolite and sat on a slight elevation. I sat beside him. Together, we gazed out over the plain while he collected his thoughts, where his anger had dispersed them.

"From what I have heard of dreaming," he said, "it is a lawless and an absurd place."

Again, I noticed how he attributed a space to dreaming; and I thought this justifiable now that my own dreams were becoming more spacious. Each night, I watched myself venture farther out from the end of the trees. My dreaming self looked at the plain through my true eyes, saw what I had already laid eyes on during my journey. How could it be otherwise? Dreams lag always behind the life they comment on, unless one believes in their prophetic quality, which I do not.

"I would not last where all is mutation and caprice, unformed and edged with shadow." He was silent awhile before whispering with childish candor, "I am afraid of the dark."

I patted his boot consolingly.

"Mathematics is incompatible with darkness, which is its opposite," he said earnestly. "The opposite of all that is doubtful and obscure. If there is not light enough to see through my theodolite, I am lost! Can you understand that?"

I told him that I could, and he smiled at me in gratitude.

"The plain is nothing!" he said, returning to an earlier theme. "I would much prefer it if there were none—no land at all. Only the survey, only the mathematics. Nothing but them. Only they are of consequence, are unambiguous and beautiful. I look at what is before us and, shutting my eyes to it, see shining in the darkness of my closed eyes a thousand points of light—a radiant topography—a pure and dazzling topology produced by luminous numbers—inscribed with perfect parabolas and arcs that exist only *here,* in the mind!"

He pressed my hands in his as if to bless me. And then he left me, saying that the remainder of the journey must be made by each one of us alone. He smiled again and, with eyes closed once more, walked into the far distance.

I watched him dwindle until he was no more than a point— not of light, but of darkness against the sunlit plain. And then he vanished in it. How or where he went, I do not know. Perhaps a seam opened in the air or a chasm in the earth. All I know is that he walked out into that green immensity and was seen no more.

Perhaps he is taking the measure of Nothing, I thought; perhaps he is discovering the mathematics of death in order to make a final survey of the afterlife. Or perhaps he has vanished at last inside the dream, which he has all his life been resisting. I stood just as the wind rose and watched it swell and billow in the tall grass all around me. Clouds herded across the sky, dragging their shadows over the plain. The river, which moments before had been glittering as if with the surveyor's thousand points of light, blackened.

I watched, calmly, the earth register its vexations and alarms. I was becoming accustomed to immensity; I was no longer made sick by the blaring sun or the striding moon. I continued along the river, like a prospector determined to stake a claim to the land.

5.

Beyond a reach in the river, I happened on a man asleep in a willow's green shade. Close by, a deep hole had been dug into the riverbank, enclosed by ramparts of dark earth. A ladder led down into the hole, whose bottom and purpose were obscured by darkness. Across the river, another man sat on a rock and smoked.

"Why are you sitting here in the middle of nowhere?" I asked, having crossed over to him on stepping-stones.

He took the pipe from between his teeth and, stabbing at

the air with it, said, "Waiting for the professor to finish with his folly."

"What folly is that?"

"The university sent him to collect broken vases. I bought the deed to this part of the river to build a mill. But the authorities ordered me to desist until every last sliver of antiquity has been mined and cataloged. I'd shoot him, but they would only send someone else to dig in the dirt!"

He had shouted this last sentence, flinging it across the river like a taunt or a challenge sufficiently loud to wake the sleeper.

"Money-grubber!" he shouted in turn. "Philistine!"

"Crackpot!" the would-be miller volleyed. "Dreamer!"

Intrigued, I recrossed the river and, sitting next to the professor, asked him about his dreams.

"I dream of Italy's vanished past," he said, gazing at the plain as if he might find it there. "Of the ancient Villanovans, who crossed the eastern Alps, bringing with them the Iron Age and the practice of cremation. They buried their ashes in funerary urns along the Po. I am looking for them."

"Enemy of progress!" the miller shouted. "Enemy of the living!"

The professor took my arm and led me away from the river, beyond the reach of the miller's denunciations.

"My enemies say I would prefer to live in the past. Not so. What pleases me is to regard the past from the vantage of the present. It is one of history's paradoxes that the past can be possessed—never the present; for the present is occurring and therefore impossible to gauge, and what cannot be gauged cannot be grasped. With each shard, I enlarge my title to the ancient world. With each fact I hold up here"—he tapped with a finger his temple—"I strengthen my claim to it."

"And the plain?" I asked, which was, at this hour, touched with gold.

"I don't understand you."

"What do you see when you look at it?"

"Ancient settlements. Extinct races. The necropolis at Ver-ruchio. All that was on the Adriatic coastal plain—before the Romans, before even the Etruscans. Their light—the light of their skies—is entombed with their dust. If I were to unearth it, what a blinding fulguration there would be!"

"But what is it that you see now—at this moment?" I persisted. I was growing angry, for obscure reasons, which may have had to do with the fugitive beauty of the landscape.

"Nothing. A kind of scab that time has formed over the past, which was vital and alive. Only the past lives, for me," he said gloomily.

His lament was interrupted by a fusillade of stones launched by the miller.

"He prefers millstones," the professor shouted in return. "To make cakes and money with!"

I remembered how, in the forest, I had imagined the plain as a space in which to be in time without encumbrances. To satisfy the desire to walk, coiled in the muscles of the legs. To see the sky disentangled from the oppressive trees, inscribed by the wide flights of birds and luminous traces of the flying stars. I began to understand that space is subjugated to each person. That it is only a screen on which the magic lantern of our thoughts casts the images of our desires. In the forest, we dwelled within; the trees forbade any turning outward to embrace the world—an embrace that inevitably becomes possession, covetousness, and the murder of what we cannot own. Slowly, I was becoming aware that the forest was not so much a place as prelude to self-awareness, a condition of the mind's infancy.

"He tilts at windmills because he is afraid of life!" the miller screamed as he splashed across the shallows, gravel rattling underfoot.

I fled them both as I would a plague. Looking over my

shoulder, I saw them rolling on the ground, hands at each other's throat.

6.

"You are standing in my light!" he said, much annoyed.

Bewildered, I replied that I did not understand.

"You are causing your shadow to fall on the plain—*there.*" He pointed to the darkness that unrolled at my feet. "It is foreign to my picture, which is of this desolate landscape. I wish to paint only what belongs to it. Your shadow does not."

I noticed, then, the palette in his hand.

"So you are a painter!" I said hopefully. Here, I thought, is someone who sees truly what is, who pays so scrupulous an attention to actuality that even an extraneous shadow offends him. Here at last is someone who does not project his own desires onto the world. "I am glad to meet you!" I said, shaking his free hand.

My admiration appeased him.

"You are welcome," he said, wiping his brush with a rag fragrant with linseed oil.

I went round behind the easel and looked at his painting.

"I've nearly captured it," he said smugly. "Only a few more brushstrokes."

"It is beautiful," I conceded.

"Yes."

"Tell me. Does the plain narrow just as you've painted it?" I asked after a moment's study.

"See for yourself!" He pointed with his brush to the far edge of the plain, trembling in the summer's heat. "Space tends toward a vanishing point."

"But is it really like that?" I asked.

"Have you never heard of the rules of perspective?" he said

in a way calculated to belittle me. "Is the name Brunelleschi completely unknown to you? Have you never perused Alberti's treatise *Della Pittura*? We artists employ stratagems—tricks of the eye—to mimic what the eye sees. Art is the skillful rendering of appearances."

"And this elephant-shaped cloud you've drawn . . ."

"You must admit it does resemble an elephant?" he said, looking at the sky, where a grizzled cloud was slowly unraveling.

"To me, it looks like—well, a cloud."

"You lack imagination!" he chided.

"And this purple . . ." I indicated a haze of color on the painted grass.

"A scumble of *Tyrian* purple," he intoned pedantically.

"And if I were to walk out there now, wouldn't the grass be green—as green as that we're standing in?"

"*Verona* green with admixtures of yellow ocher, cerulean blue, and, where the evening sun is transfiguring the horizon, Tyrian purple. Grass is green—any fool knows that! But the eye sees otherwise. I paint what is—for the eye—the truth."

"But what about the truth of the plain?"

"My aim—the aim of all art—is to create beauty. Beauty is a separate category, independent of real objects, to which it alludes."

Not even this man who looked so intently at the plain, who shaded his eyes and squinted as if through cataracts, saw what was really there. He, too, had his own idea of space.

"Do you dream?" I asked slyly. I hoped for a further revelation of his egotism, like a pessimist listening expectantly for overtures of tragedy.

"Constantly!"

"Of what do you dream?"

"Of voluptuous women whose flesh is Tuscan red, Dutch pink, and umber."

I followed the river, which went its own way—telling, in liquid syllables, a story to itself that had nothing to do with men.

7.

               In the forest, we had heard of the balloon; but never could I have imagined what I now saw suspended above the riverbank. In its shape, it recalled a woman's breast; and it was this association that inclined me toward an affection for the thing that was tugging at the rope by which it had been made fast. To say that the balloon was beautiful is only to admit what any eye will readily confirm. It was more, but what that more might be lay between religion and science. The balloon, however, existed only to ascend. As if in scorn of my opinion of it, I heard in the guy rope a strain of opposition and in the wickerwork basket beneath it a whining impatience to be off again.

I was startled by a voice from above. "Are you a Frenchman?" it demanded.

"No!" I shouted at a face overcast by a shako's brim and smudged with a mustache.

"If you were, I would have to drop this bomb on you!"

A hand appeared and menaced me with a dark object.

"Is there war?" The ancient forest kept all but the rumor of war from entering.

"Certainly! With Bonaparte! The Monster of Europe hopes to seize Italy. I am on reconnaissance."

He sounded as if he might be preening in a mirror. He would have minced had there been room enough.

"Can you see the sea?" I called.

"From up there." He pointed at the sky. "The Adriatic is on the other side of the horizon. That way." He pointed east, where grass and sky converged on a dark ribbon of river.

"Can you take me to it?" I asked, never imagining that he

would agree. But he did agree, assuring me that opportunities for reconnaissance were abundant on the coast.

"I shall watch for Napoléon's ships," he said cheerfully. "And if I see one—*boom!*"

He let down a rope ladder; and after having loosed the anchor from a tree root, I climbed quickly aboard the balloon just as it was seized by the wind. In a moment, we were rushing toward the plain's western edge, at an altitude that erased most evidence of man's intervention. Here, I thought, is space unencumbered by others' ideas of it. But my pleasure was cut short when I understood that the aeronaut also conceived of the vast plain unreeling behind us in terms peculiar to his calling.

"It is perfect for a major engagement!" he said, pronouncing his judgment on it. "I can see the formations drawn up on either side of the river—there and there. And *there,* the engineers are throwing a bridge over the river. And where the ground rises to a plateau, I would deploy my artillery. The enemy will be at its mercy! And that narrow defile? What an ambush might be laid in such a place! Not a man would come out of it alive!"

Then he sang an aria of ranks, files, phalanges, ditches, palisades, fortifications, redoubts, breastworks, legions, cohorts, *velites, principes, acies,* maniples, centuries, wedges, squares, quincunxes, tortoises, *enfilades,* and others lost to my ears in the rush of our flight.

I did not need to ask him what he dreamed, but he told me it without my asking. How it was I heard him in the noise of our career above the retreating plain, I did not know, unless the vividness of his reverie, together with his fervent interest in the art of war, communicated itself to me telepathically.

"I dream," he said, "of Titus Labienus's charge and its repulse by Caesar's legions at the foot of Mount Dogandzis and the rout of Pompey's army."

I kept silent—my mind a blank—so as not to encourage

further revelations of his martial fancy. But he was now engaged with a cannoli.

In the trees, war and art, industry and business were unknown. One man might murder another or take what did not belong to him, but there was not the conspiracy of violence that, from time to time, swept the plain. We fought, courted, loved, traded, dug wells, built houses and decorated them with birds' eggs, twigs, stones, and flowers, according to the dimensions of our individual imaginations. We sinned and were virtuous according to our own limited capacities. Our dreams were correspondingly small and somber, always, with the twilight of the forest. Where all was only trees, there was nothing onto which to project our desires, except one another. Our desires were common, in any case. And so I had come out onto the plain to experience space and to alter the aspect of my dreaming self. But I had found only other people's ideas of it, against which I was helpless to propose one of my own. And what of the plain? Ought it not be allowed its own idea of itself and might not this idea be greater than all others and, in the long run, better for us all? For it was to destruction that those others were tending, even the painter's which exalted the facsimile over the plain itself. For in his eyes, the plain could vanish unlamented into oblivion so long as the painting remained.

As if to confirm my fears for the destruction of that space (which must have a form of its own, though it was not mine to grasp), we flew over a makeshift cemetery—remnant of some recent battle with the French.

"See how neatly we have buried them!" the aeronaut shouted into my ear. "Hardly have they finished dying when they are shoveled underground!"

What comedy is this? I wondered, that he should admire the formations of the dead? And then I thought that this, too, was an idea of space imposed on the plain. I shuddered and would have pushed him out of the basket in which we dangled if for no other reason than to mar the deadly order of those earthen ranks.

"How much farther to the sea?" I shouted back at him.

"It comes soon."

Why did I wish for the sea if not in hopes of finding what none could annex?

8.

I had no words with which to tell how it was the sea came upon me, for I did not come upon it, but, rather, found myself there, at the foot of it, as if having wakened from a dream or into one—ankles bound with dirty rags of foam. I say I had not the words: It beggared me. And so I borrowed them from what I had known before laying eyes on it, standing on the beach, with the plain darkening at my back, while the comical balloonist, mustache stiff with ricotta, reconnoitered—his balloon become a comma dragged northward by the mounting wind.

Saturnine, the sea slid down and, turning, folded beneath a contrary motion while waves knotted, wringing out heavy drops of water, only to unknot again, loosening a music made of sighs and seething. I wondered at such sounds, knowing them to be without end since Creation's third day.

Everywhere was sea and only that, and I knew that no one could withstand it—no one could match his mind with its. I wondered what the sea thought as it heaved itself up out of its bed and, shuddering, lay down again, then, without resting, rose and moved restlessly on. If thoughts it had. The sea was without face or features, yet it adjured my eyes to follow it; I could not disenthrall myself. It must be instinct with mind, some capacity of will to bind me to its moving self.

The sea moved in me a sympathetic motion—an emotion that was sadness and pity for everything that was not it and must end. My eyes became wet with it and with tears of self-pity. I was too small to stand against the Absolute. But neither had I wish to return to the plain inscribed by others' desires; and the forest, like childhood, was lost to me.

I felt in my body a will not my own.

I felt the sundering of what bound me to myself.

In my mind, already I had walked into the deepening water. Already, I was letting it into my mouth, tasting salt. In a moment, I would sleep in its wet folds—illusions scattered like paper flowers on the waves. And then I saw out the corner of my eye a woman, standing, like me, on the gray sand with eyes, like mine, gazing out to sea. Her hair was writhing in the wind; her clothes were roughly handled by it. To be so entirely still, I thought, so spellbound by these somber cadences—she, too, must have been brought to the edge of disillusion and found it almost past enduring.

With my eyes, I measured the space between us, calculated how many steps. I almost spoke to her. Muffled like drums in a cortege in which we walked toward our separate ends, hearts (terrified by the sea's indifference to our ideas of it) beat. I almost turned to speak, but what could love—that last illusion—do here? I might have drowned then, and gladly, had not the tide gone out.

The Sleep Institute

For Gordon

I met Myra at the Sleep Institute. She suffered from narcolepsy; I was there for my dreams. Not that my dreams were bad, no; but they were obsessive. They visited me each night with an inevitability that wearied, then rankled, then maddened. Think of watching the same movie night after night: Charlton Heston and Eleanor Parker, for example, overrun by red ants in *The Naked Jungle.* Not that I dreamed of red ants. Thank God I did not! But Africa—always Africa! For five years, the same: Anna surprised by the lion among wild olive trees. Sikh rickshaw drivers and Persian traders languid against a wall in Mombasa. Kemp in the Lorian Swamp, eating a rhinoceros liver. And Kong dressed to kill in tuxedo and top hat, escaping through the topiary with Mrs. Willoughby. Those dreams had nourished my storytelling. But I resolved to quit Africa for good and find another landscape to dwell upon. One closer to home, with taxicabs and all-night movies, and the mild indignities of the street.

"It has rooted in you," the therapist had pronounced after "the incident." "Africa has."

He leaned back in his chair and swiveled toward the window. Outside, a cloud very like a camel was roaming the blue Sahara. (Ha!)

"And may I point out that *your* Africa is not the real Africa."

No . . . but it has been a cherished illusion, dangerous—who knows?—to challenge.

"I would like to dream of other things," I replied after a small silence. "Of Antarctica, snow—of a woman who does not wear a pith helmet. Anna—no, not Anna, or Mrs. Willoughby. Some other woman. Let me please for once fixate on someone new!"

He swung around in his chair to face me.

"I am sending you to the Sleep Institute. There they will change your dreamscape, the pattern of your unconscious life. You will be given a new imagery. Your stories will radically alter and with them your personality, which is odd. Unattractive. The Sleep Institute is the place for you."

"No hydrotherapy! No electroshock! No sheep parts in yogurt!"

I had suffered them in Tunis.

"You must not let yourself become hysterical," he warned.

Hysteria—a major theme in my work.

"I should like to be someone else," I said.

"Who?"

"Someone other than I am."

"Dr. Griffin has a serum."

"Of invisibility?"

The Invisible Man enthralled me, too. But enough of that!

"He has developed a pharmacopoeia of sleep," the therapist said wistfully.

Then he closed his eyes and smiled.

There were six resident patients at the Sleep Institute: an insomniac, a girl with night terrors, a sleepwalker, Myra, a young man also afflicted with narcolepsy, and me. I felt ordinary among such exotic complaints. Mine—I knew—was frivolous. My dreams had come to bore me; they distracted my search for new fictional ground. No more than that. I was never in danger of losing my mind, only my narrative impetus. Having deliberately broken the thread, I was desperate to find another. I had gone to savage lengths for my art—even to having slashed my wrists. (Though I had taken care not to slash too deeply. It was enough that blood flowed, never mind how much.) But my fellow patients suffered keenly, in body and mind. I was like a man who goes for a time to live among lepers with nothing but chapped lips to recommend him.

Gordon came to visit.

"How is it with you, Norman?" he asked.

"I have a sleep disorder. I dream . . . I dream of Africa."

"For you." He presented me with a bottle of gin—Bombay, in honor of my late fiction, which had made much of it.

"The Sapphire bottle!" I cried, kissing his hands. "Thank you, dear Gordon. My thirst—"

"I understand."

He understands everything.

"Is considerable. Is—"

"Your little weakness," he said generously.

I drank—to him, to the Sleep Institute's desirable nursing staff. To Myra, my sweetheart, asleep in the blind-slatted shadows of the solarium. The good Bombay seeped into my consciousness on its way down to my inner being, which thirsted for consolation. For numbing.

"*Seeped* is a good word, I think."

"A very good word, Norman."

I thought of how Africa had seeped into the landscape of my imagination, the rich loam of it, now in need of irrigation. I irrigated it—with the "queen's own."

"All because of Hemingway's lions and the golden beach," I complained. "My youth was spoiled; and now, in middle age, my mind is lost between Nairobi and Mombasa, with blind

Borges for my safari guide." I scolded them and all other writers of fiction whose voices are undeniable.

"You are feverish," said Gordon, laying a rough hand atop my head as if to bless me. "You will make your mark on our national literature," he said affably as he walked to the door. "Never fear."

"Stay with me, Gordon!"

"I have a lecture to deliver at NYU: 'The Art of Fiction.'"

"It is hard to be a writer," I said with unbecoming self-pity.

He turned toward me.

"One needs only to write: one little word followed by another."

He walked two adjoining fingers through the air in demonstration.

"Subject matter eludes," I confessed, much ashamed.

"Pah! You are in the Sleep Institute!"

"I have a sleep disorder!"

I grew defensive. I suspected he understood that I was staying at the institute under false pretenses. I did not want him to despise me. My esteemed editor.

"In just this one room, I see a subject worthy of your fiction."

He glanced slyly at my sweetheart.

"A subject that is also an object—of desire!" he observed.

We walked over to Myra and admired her sleeping body.

"Lovely!" he said, taking off his hat—the one with the pert feather.

"Yes," I agreed, stroking her cheek, the little part of it that was visible beneath her tumbled-down hair.

"Now I really must go."

He returned his hat to his head, opened the solarium door, and left me to my own devices.

"Next time, bring me a cigar!" I shouted after him. "A Monte Cristo!"

I sat and waited for Myra to wake so that we might resume our affair, interrupted by her narcolepsy.

The sapphire light glinting in the gin bottle entranced me!

"Stevens's blue guitar is nothing next to this," I said to myself.

I left Myra's room very late that night. Except for the fluorescent hum, the patients' snores, and the *ping-pong* of Mr. Stanislaw, the Sleep Institute was silent. He was in the recreation room, playing himself. It looked to me a lonely and exhausting way to pass the slow, dull hours till morning. Stosh, as we called him, was then the only insomniac in residence.

"Join me?" he asked with a look of entreaty.

Though I pitied him, I was worn-out. "To a frazzle," as Anne would say. (Forget Anne!) Myra had been awake for a full two hours, and I had made the most of it.

"Another time," I said, and saw the horror in his eyes. The bleared eyes in the gray face. The horror of the perpetually conscious. The terrible burden of lucidity, as Camus would say. (Forget him, too!)

I left the recreation room and tiptoed down the tiled corridor toward my room.

Ping Pong Ping Pong Ping Pong Ping Pong Ping Pong.

"Poor Mr. Stanislaw!"

"Your treatment of Myra's narcolepsy is highly unorthodox," Dr. Griffin said drily. "Not to mention clumsy."

I gave him my most ingenuous look.

"Captured on video," he said with what I considered unprofessional relish. "And now part of the institute's permanent record. You are not a particularly adept lover, Norman."

I accused him of voyeurism. And envy.

"This is a laboratory," he said sternly, "not a love nest! Your behavior is entirely inappropriate for a clinical study. I don't care if the woman *is* asleep more often than she's awake!"

"I don't like that *sneering*," I told him.

"Narcolepsy is a serious disorder," he continued reasonably, if self-importantly. "Under its influence, Myra cannot be said to know her own mind."

I told him we were fond of each other. I told him that our affair, such as it was, did no harm. He accused me of taking unfair advantage of a woman whose mind was, in some measure, disturbed.

"Our patients are unhappy," he said. "Their reason hangs always in the balance."

"Mr. Stanislaw needs another insomniac to keep him company at night."

"I wish you wouldn't meddle in my sleep protocols!" he snapped.

A silence ensued, during which he collected himself.

"It is dangerous, I think, for Mr. Stanislaw to try to play Ping-Pong by himself," I suggested.

"You are a writer?"

"Yes . . ." I said cautiously.

"What do you write?"

"Literature."

"Have you written any literature lately?"

"Not lately, no."

"I have something of possible interest to a writer."

I nodded to show him I was willing to hear more.

"A serum that will enable the user to enter another's dreams. I imagine a writer would find that fruitful of discovery."

"Has it been tested?"

"Not as yet on a human."

"On what?"

"On a dog."

"Did the dog's writing noticeably improve?"

Much annoyed, he pushed back his chair, stood, and paced the consulting room floor. I allowed him this show of displeasure, understanding our human need for drama. I had stung his vanity and must wait patiently for the sting to subside.

"Won't you please try my serum?" he wheedled, having stopped his pacing to beg a favor of me.

"Not until I've had a chance to talk to the dog," I said.

"I dreamed you made me pregnant," said Myra.

I did not much care for her dream, but said nothing and continued to stroke her hair—her very long blond hair.

"We were in the kitchen. I told you the baby was overdone. 'The baby's overdone,' I said. 'It's been in the oven too long.' I opened the oven door and pulled out the baby. It was hard to do: It was a very small oven—a child's play oven—and the baby was tight inside it. I managed to pull it out, but the baby was burned to a crisp. Its head, burned off. I could see the genitals, but I don't remember if it was a boy or a girl."

"That's a strange dream," I said noncommittally.

I wanted nothing more to do with psychoanalysis. Those of you who have read my African fiction know that Sigmund Freud figures prominently among the dramatis personae. He, of course, would have made much of Myra's dream. He would have pounced on it with glee.

Instead, I allowed my hand to slip quietly down from her hair to her breast and take up its stroking once again.

"Dreams mean nothing." I lied.

She smiled a radiant smile, then fell asleep.

I removed the Band-Aid I had stuck over the tiny lens of the surveillance camera, smiled—I hoped winningly—at Dr. Griffin, and left Myra to her dreams.

Ping Pong Ping Pong Ping Pong Ping Pong Ping Pong
Ping Pong Ping Pong Ping Pong Ping Pong Ping Pong
Ping Pong Ping Pong Ping Pong Ping Pong Ping Pong
Ping Pong Ping Pong Ping Pong   Pong Ping Pong
Ping Pong Ping Pong Ping Pong Ping Pong Ping Pong.

"Gordon!"

I had looked up from my book, to see him framed in the doorway of the solarium. (The book? *Cronopios and Famas.* I name it for verisimilitude's sake. It is also true that I happened to be reading this excellent little work of fiction, Cortázar's amusing conceits, before joining my fellow inmates for breakfast.)

Gordon walked robustly toward me, through lozenges of sunlight patterning the golden floor.

"'Golden floor' is good," he said, reading my mind. "'Lozenges of sunlight' is also good. You were wise to resist *splashing*. 'Splashing through lozenges of sunlight' would have been fatally Swinburnian. Hats off to you!"

He doffed his.

"Did you remember my cigar?"

He handed me it. A Monte Cristo.

"I had hoped to see her awake," he said disappointed, nodding at Myra, who was sleeping on the couch, despite the "Havanaise" playing over the institute's PA. "Is she often like this?"

"It is her disorder," I replied—"the reason she's here."

"That is a Stefano Scarampella violin."

Gordon knows *everything*!

The door to the solarium opened once again. A pretty redhead in a black negligee drifted across the room and left by the other door.

"She is sleepwalking," I explained.

"Your fictions are damned attractive!"

"Then this, too, is a fiction?"

I hoped it might be otherwise.

"Norman, all utterance, all perception, is it not all of it a fiction?"

As if to confirm his assertion, Gordon grew vague, by which I mean he faded, by slow degree, until I wondered if life itself must not become untenable in a man so apparently lacking in substance.

(Quite a good-looking man, I thought, even at half strength.)

"Going so soon, Gordon?"

"I am giving a lecture in Terre Haute: 'The Imaginary Self.'"

"Your life is very full," I observed enviously.

"Alas, it is not my own."

"The story of all our lives," I said pithily.

"When may we expect a new piece for *The Quarterly*, Norman?"

"I understood *The Quarterly* to be defunct."

"I am investigating a new publishing method. Dr. Griffin's research into dream transmission is promising."

"A dream magazine . . ."

"No paper, ink—no postage. No inconvenient customs declarations. Nothing between the original thought and the unconscious mind of the subscriber. Think of it, Norman!" He put on his hat. "And now I really must go."

He grew atmospheric. His brain—his *mind* (always subtle!) persisted a moment beyond the body's dissolution—a swarm of radiant particles—until it, too, reached the vanishing point.

"Good-bye, Gordon!" I called into the void, which closed after him with something like a bang.

I began to feel ill at ease.

Myra, wake up! I thought.

She did not.

I repeated it—this time aloud, into her delicately shaped ear. She took no notice.

If this is a fiction, why does she not wake?

"Not every fictional character is answerable to its author, who is, himself, a fictional character," Gordon archly remarked from a lectern in Terra Haute.

Chinese boxes!

Knock knock.

"Who's there?"

On the ledge outside the solarium, five stories up from the street, the sleepwalking redhead was knocking on the window in her filmy black negligee. (Or, better: "in her filmy black negligee roughly handled by the wind.") I opened the window and helped her inside.

"I'm sorry if I woke you," I said, not entirely sure of my responsibility but pleasantly aroused by the pressure of her hand in mine.

"My name is Lulu," she said.

"Of course it is." I smiled, delighted.

Ping . . .

Poor Mr. Stanislaw died of a coronary embolism before reaching the second, ineluctable term in the syllogism. Out of pity, I supplied it for him:

"Pong."

Ping-pong is a syllogism without conclusion, I thought. By its strict, binomial repetition, it generates no new term. In dying, Stosh gave it one.

(Mocking laughter from Terre Haute.)

What of the other residents lodging at the Sleep Institute? Myra, you've met; also Lulu, whom I would have been pleased to know better. But her sleepwalking made me nervous. I did not want her drifting spectrally in and out my consciousness; and the thought of her standing over me during my unconscious hours (with a knife, perhaps, purloined from the kitchen) made me shiver! There is something deranged about a sleepwalker—don't you find it so? Lady Macbeth certainly became one at the end of her life. No, as seductive a young woman as I found Lulu to be (with that coppery hair!), I concentrated my amorous attentions on Myra. (There was another narcoleptic there at the time: a man in his twenties. As I never saw him awake, he plays no part in this story.) I ought, however, to mention the girl with night terrors. But first, I want to tell you about the dog.

The dog's name was Pavlov. It was thought by some to be the canine reincarnation of the great Russian behaviorist himself, whose work had led to the principles of modern advertising as formulated by John Watson in the 1920s. But the real reason the dog was so named was its slobber. Its slobber was ample.

I went to Pavlov's room one afternoon, intending to sound it out on Griffin's dream serum. I had with me a box of liver snaps and the remains of the Bombay gin. (The liver snaps were a conciliatory offering; the gin—well, it was a rainy afternoon, Myra was asleep, and I was melancholy.)

"Can you tell me, please, about your experience with Dr. Griffin's serum?"

"I entered a dream of Dr. Griffin's, which I didn't understand, and then one of a white lab rat, which I didn't understand, either. Then I woke with the disconcerting sensation of not knowing who I was."

"Do you remember anything about the doctor's dream?"

"A bedroom. Lozenges of sunlight and a golden floor. A girl with red hair wobbling across the room on a tightrope. The tightrope suspended above the bed. The girl dressed in a filmy black negligee."

"And the white rat's dream?"

"A black hole. Yogurt. A cigar."

(Howls of laughter from Terre Haute.)

Did I say there was a wing of the institute that was closed to the patients? About which our curiosity was left unsatisfied? I know nothing of what went on there, but I once saw through the wire mesh of the locked door's window a figure of monstrous appearance that seemed to be floating upside down, as if in one of Georg Baselitz's paintings.

"It is the sleep of reason."

"Who said that?"

Anxiously, I looked around me, but the room was empty.

"Is it you, Gordon?"

"No, not Gordon," said the voice.

"Who, then?" I asked again of the engulfing dark, and, receiving no answer, unstoppered the gin, with which to quiet the *ping-ponging* of my heart.

Catherine was fifteen years old, and she had night terrors. One night on my way back from not sleeping with Myra, the door to Catherine's room was flung open by a nurse whose lip was bleeding onto her white uniform. Unnerved by the girl's fury, she asked for my help in restraining her. Her strength amazed me, as did the almost homicidal impulse that seemed to possess her. I remembered *The Exorcist* and half-expected the child to vomit pea soup. The fit passed, and she fell into a deeper sleep. I was impressed by the absolute calm that now inhabited her— all the more so after her recent frenzy.

"I don't like the tone of this at all."

"What's wrong with it, Gordon?"

"It's soporific. Another paragraph and I would have dropped off like Myra into profounds of sleep."

"*Profounds* is good."

"I stole it from Beckett."

"I understand Catherine least," I admitted.

"Because she is a girl or because she is young, and you are neither?"

"Because of her rage, Gordon. I envy her it."

"Her passionate nature."

"How her subconscious must storm! The upheaval and unreason! A lava of thought—hot and unpent. Raw—I would like, Gordon, to be, for once, raw."

"How old are you now?"

"Fifty."

"And a proper grammarian—yes?"

"I hope I am."

"You do not, Norman, have it in you to be raw."

"Still, I should like to know this girl's mind."

"Take the doctor's serum."

"I'm afraid."

"You want to know her dreams. You came here to acquire new images. You want to be raw. Take the serum! Griffin calls it 'dream-walking' by the way. It will do you good to walk out into another's dream."

"And yet . . ."

"What?"

"This *is* all a game."

"And is it not all of it, Norman, a game?"

"One-hundred, ninety-nine, ninety-eight, ninety-seven, ninety-six, ninety-five, ninety-four, ninety-three, ninety-two, ninety-one, ninety, eighty-nine, eight-seven, ninety, eighty-nine, eighty-eight, eighty—"

After injecting me with serum, Dr. Griffin had instructed me to count backward from one hundred. Catherine was asleep in the bed next to mine. The room was dark except for the sickly light of the instruments. I closed my eyes and listened to myself counting in the dark. The fluorescent tubes hummed. An instrument *pinged* like the sonar in every submarine movie

I have ever seen—that climactic moment when the crew holds its breath on the sea bottom, hoping to evade the destroyer and its depth charges. Griffin and his assistant whispered together.

I counted: "Eighty-eight, eighty, seventy-nine, seventy-seven, seventy-seven . . ."

Ping Ping Ping.

Catherine opened her eyes and left the room. I followed—past Griffin and his assistant, who continued to whisper together in the greenish light. The door to the hallway closed silently behind us. We moved through the murky channel of the corridor toward the recreation room.

Ping Pong Ping Pong Ping.

Mr. Stanislaw showed me his heart shaped like a Ping-Pong paddle. I could see the damage death had done it.

"I'm sorry, Stosh," I said. "I cannot play with you."

He bowed his head and wept.

Catherine was far away now, on the river that was salt with Mr. Stanislaw's tears.

"Catherine!" I called, but my voice was drowned in the first explosion.

A dog barked.

I started to run. My feet sank a little into the sand, lifting clouds of silt.

"Catherine!"

The river entered the sea; and in the *pinging* of the sonar, I forgot Catherine. The Destroyer covered me with his shadow; his depth charges rained down on me. Inside the submarine, Griffin made love to Myra, who slept—her white dress torn and spotted with blood. A depth charge exploded, and greenish water flooded the room. I floated grotesquely above the sleeping girl, my mouth clamped to her breast, watched by Griffin through a wire-mesh window.

It's been in the oven too long!

Pulling at her restraints, Catherine was screaming in terror under me.

"She would have bitten through her wrists to wake and have me off of her!"

I shivered with cold. My clothes were wet.

"You slept the sleep of reason," said Gordon, just returned from Terre Haute. "Perhaps, Norman, you are not equal to the game."

I wished now that it were finished.

"It can end only in death," said Gordon, reading my mind. "Ask Stosh. By the way, did the submarine have a name?"

"*Monte Cristo.*"

"I don't understand," Myra tells me.

"I was telling you a story."

"Not a word."

Her look is reproachful—perhaps because of my fascination with Lulu. (I cannot admit even to myself a desire for Catherine!) Myra goes to the dresser. She looks in the mirror. I stand behind her, put my arms around her, and fondle her breasts.

"Stop it; it hurts!"

She opens her blouse and shows me the teeth marks.

I look at them in the mirror. I look and look.

Myra falls asleep.

Love in the Steam Age

For Lee Chapman

1.

I go to the train shed as often as I can find the time. With women whose ardor for modern industrial processes is—I hope—the equal of my own. A woman's frank enjoyment of them is the criterion by which I judge her—the "glass slipper" ensuring our compatibility. And nowhere are industrial processes better displayed than here. The train shed is the quintessence of the age and its sublime expression. I adore the sinuous iron columns, the iron tracery of its vault. I am moved almost to tears by the sooty cloud of accumulated arrivals and departures, nuzzling the mullioned windows high above the platform. I take the undeviating parallelism of its shining tracks as an example, an exhortation, and a moral imperative.

Ernestine and I ought to have gotten on like a pair of locomotives and would have if she had not, in exasperation, railed against the train shed: how bored she was by our daily visits there.

"I'm bored with the train shed!" she whined as I dabbed at her cheek with my handkerchief to rid it of a smudge.

I stopped in mid-dab, horrified by her apostasy.

"It is the cathedral and citadel of civilization!" I cried.

"Wilma's friend takes her to the Botanical Garden."

"The Botanical Garden!" I sputtered in harmony with a

departing express. "People go to the Botanical Garden in order to worship unchecked exuberance," I explained. "They are unsound. They hang landscapes of Provence on their parlor walls and dream of hayricks and threshing parties."

Natural forms are tolerable in iron and plaster—not in nature, where they wither irresistibly toward death.

"Wilma gets kissed among the delphinium," Ernestine replied stubbornly, "and eats ice cream." I cannot swear to you that it was Ernestine, who preferred tenderness and ice cream in the Botanical Garden to civilization's cathedral and citadel; it may have been Caroline, or even Rebecca. I recall Rebecca as a young woman with a tendency to anachronism and friends among the Pre-Raphaelites.

I had broken off at once with Ernestine-Caroline-Rebecca. I had broken off, as well, with Pauline and Sarah and any number of other desirable women who seemed, at first, to be in sympathy with steam and its pent-up ambition to transform the world but, in the end, proved frivolous.

Helen, however, filled me with equal parts of desire and optimism.

"Don't you love the steam-carrousel!" she said as I helped her down from a handsomely gilded horse. "It is tireless in its pursuit of pleasure—a pleasure, I might add, which is all the more piquant for its circularity."

"Would you care to examine the train shed with me tomorrow?" I asked.

"Delighted!" she replied, detaining my hand in hers a moment longer than was necessary.

2.

While I could not offer Helen an ice cream because of the particles of soot, which were general under the great vault, I might kiss her, discreetly, during an escape of

steam from a locomotive. I might even, should I have the au-
dacity, press my hand against her bosom.

"Girls appreciate a bit of *amour*," Willard had said when
I mentioned my high hopes for Helen. Willard was experi-
enced in matters of the heart, having spent a year in Paris at
an impressionable age. "They want fondling—lets them know
they have the power to inflame a man. The face to launch a
thousand ships—hey? That was a Helen, too, though one of
the ancient world."

A thousand *steam*ships! I thought.

"Do you feel as I do?" I ask Helen, having entered the present, where I shall remain. "I mean now, at this moment in time,
standing at what is—for me—the epicenter of our age?"

I have brought her to the center of the train shed—the heroic
bronze Prometheus making man a gift of steam—where innu-
merable vectors of purpose, excitement, and energy converge.
Passengers bustle toward their embarkation, their expressions
commingling solemnity and exultation; the newly arrived
stride toward one of the four magnificent entrances leading to
the city beyond; stalwart men in smocks, carrying toolboxes,
thread their way through the crowd; and the nobility of the
age—the engineers and trainmen, whose authority is unchal-
lenged throughout the empire of tracks and right-of-ways—
pass, indifferent to our admiration. I would have fallen down in
a faint if I had not taken hold of Helen's arm. She interpreted
my having done so as an access of affection and smiled up at
me. (She is a head shorter than I, who am not tall; neither am I
short. I am a man of medium height, build, and intelligence—
neither a nullity nor a paragon; but one who accommodates at
all points the optimum dimensions of his time.)

She smiles up at me and says, "Yes, it is wonderful."

I want her to expand on the wonder that she feels, but refrain
from importuning her for more. I recall Willard's admonition:

"Your enthusiasm for steam is too great, perhaps, for most women. Temper it."

I temper it, contenting myself with an assertion impossible to prove: "What seems to us here anarchic, amid the moving crowd, is not so when seen from *there*." I point to the smutted windows transecting the sky above us—*through* them to a coign of vantage occupied by the Architect of All Things. (Yes, I admit to a *strain* of belief. Although I am sound—a man of scientific bent—there is, I believe, a ghost in the machine impervious to analysis.) "From there, the thousand trajectories inscribed in this perfect space are as intelligible as the grand concourse of the stars." Having her here, I am quite carried away.

"I think so, too," Helen replies charmingly.

Suddenly, a stilled locomotive succumbs to an internal pressure in its boiler, sighs operatically, and emits a white vapor that engulfs us. I seize the moment and, with unaccustomed ardor, press Helen to me. She does not protest.

"Shall we have an espresso?" I ask, picking up my hat, which fell during the embrace.

"Oh, yes—let's!" she replies, straightening hers, which, in its design, alludes to modern industrial forms rather than avian ones.

Arm in arm, we are walking toward the shed's western entrance (decorated with copper repoussé panels depicting the Stations of the Railway in heroic tableaux) when we are arrested by a tremendous shout, resonant in the shed's parabolic vault. Unless you are a contemporary, you cannot know the esteem in which the director of railroads is held. For it is no other than he, who has stepped from a private car onto the platform, to be surrounded instantly by an adoring mob.

"Look!" I shout to Helen. "The director!"

He walks beneath a triumphal arch of red long-stemmed oilers (more fitting than roses!) produced by the mechanics.

"Standing at attention, with right arms upraised, they seem to form the letter *W*," she says.

The director's bearing is magisterial; his self-possession, perfect. He is neither humble nor haughty; neither aristocratic nor common. He bears our homage as priests do, understanding that it is not to them the faithful sing hosannas, but to their God.

For a second time, I might have fainted.

"I shall never forget this day!" I tell Helen.

She presses my hand frankly to her bosom. I take her hand and kiss it—the dainty gloved fingers one by one.

With his retinue of Great Men (though none so great as he!), the director sweeps across the marbled floor, draws to a stop beside the bronze Prometheus, and, stiffening, permits himself to be immortalized in tintype. His image taken, he accepts a key to the city, slices with a gold-plated trowel a track of cake, and doffs his silk hat to the disciples of steam. The ceremony at an end, the director boards his private train in a blizzard of tickets, timetables, and—sown by the mechanics— rubber gaskets. He departs for a city farther up the line—there, to inaugurate yet another epic project in this, the Age of Steam.

I look at Helen—at her eyes—and note with satisfaction that, like mine, they are brimming with tears.

3.

"I'm in love with Helen," I say, setting down my spoon, "and she—I believe—with me."

"You tempered your enthusiasm, then," Willard remarks.

"There was no need," I reply. "Hers, too, verges on intemperance."

"The Queen of Steam."

I solemnly nod.

"A fit consort for the age's most fervent adherent," he states with inoffensive irony as a waiter removes my plate.

Willard unhooks his wire rims, which have steamed over during his attack upon a plate of mussels, and polishes them on the tablecloth's hem. "Will you prosecute the relationship to its ultimate?"

"You mean will I marry her?"

"I mean, my honorable friend, will you sleep with her?"

"I dream of it!"

"For an age of unrelenting actualization, we spend entirely too much time in dreaming. It is the reason so many men go abroad, I think. Or mad."

I sigh; for I, too, have done both on occasion.

"If I were you, I'd sleep with Helen at the earliest opportunity," Willard concludes. "If you insist on discretion, my apartment is at your disposal. I am leaving for Peru in the morning to paint Machu Picchu."

As if to punctuate the news of his departure, a distant blast of dynamite rattles the restaurant's window and causes the silverware on the table to chime.

"What do they hope to accomplish!" I cry.

Willard presses his napkin to his lips and does not answer, his attention riveted by a pair of black wings—or so the empty mussel shell appears to me, who am not, as a rule, artistic.

4.

I send Helen a *pneumatiqué* inviting her to accompany me to the Museum of Steam. It will be a supreme test of her affection, I tell myself as I ride the moving pavement north to that part of the city where the dynamos are in perpetual motion. The Museum of Steam is seldom visited even by aficionados. Admittedly, the entertainment to be found there is not the liveliest, especially as the steam on display is dead.

Helen is waiting on the steps outside the museum as I dismount. I tip my hat. She lifts her veil and gives me her cheek to kiss. I kiss it and, taking her arm, lead her through an iron door ornamented by rivets.

The door shuts behind us, and a folding fan of light leaves the floor in darkness. The floor, like the vestibule's walls and ceiling, is clad in iron. Our shoes ring upon it as we walk to the counter. I ring a bell; and after a moment, a man appears from out the shadows of an adjoining room. He sketches a gesture of welcome in our vicinity and indicates that we should sign the register. We do, and I note that ours are the solitary names inscribed on its yellowing page. Stooped and shuffling, he precedes us into the next room, kept by chance or design in a kind of twilight altogether agreeable to my amorous mood.

He looks to be an old man, though his age may be an illusion created by the dusky light and the vapidity of the displays. Certainly, the skin of his masklike face is minutely lined. His head is hairless—even the eyebrows gone, sacrificed, perhaps, to steam in a livelier form than that captive in the museum he tends. His voice is dry, seeming to issue from an aridity that, like sand, draws all moisture into itself. The dry voice cracks during its recitation as he guides us among the exhibits with the slow and unerring movements of a somnambulist:

"Steam trapped during an eruption of Krakatau.

"Steam abducted from a bathhouse in Istanbul during the Young Turks' uprising of 1908.

"Steam that escaped a rooming house on Cliveden Street, subsequently mangling passersby until it was captured by a resourceful tobacconist in a half-empty jar of Troost Special Cavendish.

"Steam reputed to have heated the private apartments of Gordon Lishkowitz while he composed his 'Ode on Penury.'

"Steam that rose, unbidden, through a heat register, with indecent intent with regard to a young woman's knickers.

"Steam that collected on the bathroom mirror of the notorious Mr. Craig, moments before his dispatching of his mistress with a cutthroat razor.

"Steam arrested, 'in open defiance,' during a railroad workers' strike in Aberdeen.

"Steam seized in a shipment of noodles during the British embargo of Nanking.

"Steam, whose condensation on the lid of a tureen containing a fatal dose of belladonna survived a husband's expiration and his wife's inaugural moments as a widow. Her widowhood was cut short by the blade of the guillotine."

I am, as always, fascinated by the exhibits and press a bill into the cicerone's dry hand in gratitude for his discipleship to civilization's motive power. The museum is not, as Ernestine remarked after having been put to the test, "dull as paint." She and all those others whom I have squired up and down its aisles missed the point: The excitement does not lie in the object (ostensibly an empty bell jar with legend penned in an antique hand), but in the anecdote.

The attendant gives me back the bill, saying that he cannot accept gratuities. I am surprised to see that it is a Peruvian *soles de oro*. How, I wonder, did it happen to come into my possession? I think of Willard; but despite his being in Peru, there is no way to account for a *soles de oro* having come to me—even if pocketed, inadvertently, while I was in his apartment. To my knowledge, Willard has never before been in Peru, nor has he yet returned from there.

My train of thought is derailed by an explosion muffled by the museum walls. Helen and I hurry outside in time to see a mounted policeman charge by. "They've blown up the steam factory!" he shouts.

Helen trembles—in fear, or excitement.

The museum door opens behind us. Our guide stands framed in darkness, his spectacles flaring with late-afternoon sun. Appalled, I seem to see in their twin fires the catastrophe to come. He rubs his hands together and dances—a schottische without partners, round a cast-iron column.

"How very light on his feet he is!" Helen says admiringly.

5.

Helen surprises me with tickets for a performance of the Empire Steam Calliope. Can you guess at my elation when the cab stops beneath the porte cochere of the Hall of Science? Perhaps not. Only one who, like me, has fallen in love in the Age of Steam and who is about to hear an epithalamium on that love, produced by one of the age's foremost musical interpreters, can guess at my joy.

"How did you manage it?" I ask as we take our seats. "The performance has been sold out for months!"

She smiles at me, a smile both charming and inscrutable. I am disquieted, my elation eclipsed, as if a pool's unexpected depths were revealed suddenly by a cloud flying over the face of the sun.

"I hear the machine is quite marvelous!" she says; and I am once again restored to myself and to my desire for her.

"Yes!" I say. "I was disappointed when I could not get tickets."

The lights are lowered, and the evening passes as in a dream. M. Laval achieves on the calliope, whose operation he flawlessly supervises, an ebullition I would not believe possible. The anxiety incited in me by the anarchists and by Helen's ambiguous smile vanishes.

Rapt, I take her hand; insinuating my fingers into the glove, I touch her palm with its significations and mysteries. While the allegretto bubbles and whistles like an exultant teakettle, I am seized by a perfection of form in which my inner life and all that is external to it compose a kind of crystal in the darkness—a darkness whose only relief is the glinting of the calliope's chromium pipes—and all the richer because of it. The music burbles, chirps, and hisses, accompanied by the clanging of cast-iron radiators. The machine gallops to a mad climax, its whirring gears a blur, then, suddenly, ceases. The last mechanical warble wobbles and falls silent. M. Laval's arm drops in exhaustion. The concert ends. And before its recessional's decay among the wavering flames of returning gaslight, Helen and I are rushing in a cab pell-mell for Willard's apartment, beneath the city's myriad of steam pipes and the black, luxurious night.

6.

We undress behind the drawn shade of Willard's bedroom window—our clothing seeming to melt from each other in the heat of our gaze. Naked, we sit in Willard's companionable steam cabinets until our bodies are bathed in desire's rich liqueur, as flammable and intoxicating as brandy. "Blood on the boil," we unyoke our necks from the cabinet lids and fall into each other's arms. Feeling like a live steam pipe about to burst, I pull her onto the bed. She slips from my embrace, landing on the floor. I grapple her up in my two hands and, body pent with steam from the cabinet, allow my piston to range to its maximum ambit, eliciting from her shuddering frame terrific screams. We are both of us soon spent. We lie wordlessly, looking at the ceiling, on which trapezes of dust swing in the warm convection currents engendered by the radiator, intimate altar of the age.

I rise to find a cigarette and trip over a large spool of wire, which has rolled out from under the bed.

"What's this?" I say, surprised, sending with my foot the spool across the floor.

"Wire," says Helen.

"I wonder what Willard wants with wire?"

Helen shrugs and, in shrugging, lets slip the sheet that has demurely hidden her breasts. I look at them and feel again the complicated pneumatic apparatus start up in me. She smiles, and I care not at all that it is ambiguous. I rush at her.

Restored once more to reason and our clothes, we discover one of Willard's inartistic daubs.

"He paints beautifully!" Helen says, turning from it to a mirror in order to arrange her hair.

"It's incomprehensible!" The sight of one of Willard's painted hodgepodges never fails to infuriate me.

"It is absolutely new!" she exclaims, attending now to her hat.

"I don't see anything in it!" I grumble.

"You must learn to see beneath seeming."

"I am no disciple of Swedenborg," I say, answering coldly what seems a rebuke.

She laughs gaily and pushes a last long pin through her hat.

"Shall we go visit the train shed, then?" she asks, taking my arm with an affectionate smile.

7.

In next morning's mail, I receive a note from Willard:

> The "excitement" persists in Peru, where I am now readying myself for a day of pleasure. Do hope you are finding in my rooms reason to be glad. Shall be away for another month, or two.
>
> The ruins are bracing!
>
> W

The postmark, smudged, appears to be that of Lima's. In the envelope is a halftone reproduction purporting to show a disastrous rock slide on the Andean Railroad. I examine the envelope, noting the puckered flap. It has the look, I think, of an envelope that has been steamed open inexpertly. But for what purpose and to what end?

I put the letter in a drawer and write Helen a *pneumatiqué,* inviting her to see the launch this afternoon of a steam-powered sky ship at the military parade grounds. Then I go out to buy a new hat, having left mine at the Hall of Science or in the cab during the ride to Willard's apartment.

When I return to my rooms, a *pneumatiqué* is waiting for me. I unscrew the lid and take out the furled paper. I am seized by horror as I read:

> If you wish to see Helen again, come to 5428 Pearl Street, 2nd floor, at 3 o'clock this afternoon. Deviate from these instructions, or notify the police, or attempt to foil our design, have not the slightest doubt that we will kill her.

The message is unsigned.

8.

I take an omnibus to Pearl Street, hurry on foot past pawnshops, wholesale groceries, and dealers in spurious antiquities to No. 5428. I climb a half-lit staircase to the second floor and find myself in a Turkish bath. A mute attendant gives me a towel and a key to a locker.

The conspirators sit cloaked in steam, which, from time to time, they incite with dippers of water ladled onto rocks. The men, if men they all are, are all but invisible to me.

"What have you done to Helen?" I demand.

A hand appears from out of a cloud and bids me sit. I sit on a stone step and ask again—this time with less force because of the unpleasantness in my chest as the hot, moist air invades my lungs.

"She is well," an invisible provocateur answers. "For the moment."

"Why have you taken her?"

My lungs burn with every breath.

"As surety," he replies. "That you will do what we ask."

"And what is that?"

"Assassinate the director of railroads."

That I, proponent of an age whose chief exponent is he, the director of railroads, should be asked to murder—no, it is too fantastical, too terrible a thought even to entertain! My eyes shut of their own accord; and I become aware of the earth swinging through space, untethered to any sun.

"Does she mean so little to you, then?" A different voice issues from out the steam—one I seem nearly to recognize.

I will myself to consciousness, and the stinging blackness is dispelled. "The director of railroads is—"

"An arrogant autocrat!"

"What is it you anarchists want!" Incensed, I rise and would rush at them, if I were not prevented by a deliberate venting of steam.

The voice of a third saboteur speaks to me now in the moist obscurity: "We want different things. Some believe the world must be rid of steam and its engines in order to make way for the new. Others look back fondly on the naïve technologies of wind and water. We in this room take pleasure in the destruction of forms. We view ourselves not as anarchists but as artists laboring to bring into existence a new aesthetic. I am a composer, but no score or orchestra can accommodate the music I hear inside my head. We seek to intervene in the world, for only the world is large enough to sustain our inventions."

"I do not understand art or artists," I say. "And I do not see what any of this has to do with the director of railroads."

"By killing him, we undermine one of the forms by which

our age is constituted. Lines of powerful influence pass through his hands."

"What proof is there that Helen is in *yours*?" I ask.

A satchel appears from the vapor. I open it and take out a ring, which I remember Helen having worn.

"We are prepared to present you with the finger next."

"I must think!" I tell them.

"By all means," the voice says indulgently. "But if the director does not die tomorrow when he returns to announce an expansion of rail service, Helen will."

9.

I leave the steam room in confusion. Retrieving my clothes from the locker, I find a loaded pistol, which, after a moment's hesitation, I pocket.

On the stairs, I pass someone whose hat and coat conceal any hint of identify. The ruffian forces a handbill on me. Outside on the pavement, I examine it: Except for the letter *M* typeset in a crude variant of the Caslon family, the sheet is empty.

A shadow slips down the street, blackening it as if with sudden rain. It bends sharply and flies up the front of the dye works before vanishing to an accompaniment of a dozen whirring propellers. I look up to see the sky ship pass on its way to the military parade grounds.

Returning home, I find a *pneumatiqué* waiting for me. I unscrew the lid, tip the brass cylinder, and a finger falls into my hand. In its slenderness and in the shapeliness of the lacquered nail, I see a resemblance to Helen's.

That night, I dream I am again in the Turkish bath. I am attracted by the sound of something scratching at the window. The window is obscured by thick steam. I wipe it clean with a towel, and there on the ledge outside is the finger—its red-polished nail scratching at the glass as if wanting to be let in. I run out the door of the steam room, only to find myself on the wing of the great sky ship—its propellers shredding the blue air to ribbons.

10.

In the morning paper, I read an account of the disaster. According to witnesses, a swarm of birds flew into the path of the sky ship, causing it to crash. "They sounded like bagpipes," one witness said. "An infernal racket, though music to some." The birds flew in a formation that reminded witnesses of the letter *M*. When retrieved from the wreck, they proved to be not birds but birdlike machines constructed of an unknown material. "Seen up close, they resemble notes—quavers and semiquavers," a passing musicologist remarked. Inside each is a motor of cunning workmanship, fashioned of a metal so far resistant to analysis. How the motor works, what force propels it, and how the flying objects were controlled with such precision remain a mystery.

I take the crumpled handbill from my pocket and, ironing it against the table with my hand, regard the letter imprinted there. Turning the paper round, the letter form recomposes itself into a *W*.

11.

The pistol is heavy in my pocket. In spite of myself, I take pleasure in its weight and the coolness of the metal against my palm. Although it is Saturday, the train shed is crowded with those who have come to see the director of railroads dedicate the new track. Many have also come to show their detestation for the anarchists, suspected of having authored the recent disaster.

At noon, the band blares our city's anthem into the finely sooted air: "Plunge, Ye Mighty Pistons, Plunge!" A gaily decked train enters the shed; its iron wheels slow, lock, screech, and stop. The locomotive sighs and is enfolded by an immense white plume of steam escaped from its boiler. The director steps from the train's solitary car. He doffs his hat to the crowd. The crowd answers with wild huzzahs, which echo in the vaulted iron heaven of the terminus.

As the crowd surges forward to greet him, I move with it. The director climbs a ladder to a catwalk above the platform. There, he unbuttons his coat, strikes a republican attitude, and prepares to speak. Unnoticed, I take aim and fire. Petals of blood open on his white shirtfront. He stands a moment, looking at his boots, and then falls forward over the railing into the horrified crowd.

12.

My escape was ingenious, involving at its several stages a handcar, hot-air balloon, gondola, and llama. Steam was notably absent during my headlong flight, as one would expect on a route plotted by conspirators pledged against it. When I arrived in Peru, I half-expected Willard to be waiting for me; but he was not. Since then, I have failed to locate him or, indeed, to discover whether he has ever been in the country. Those who might reasonably be expected to have met him during his sojourn here claim never to have heard the name; nor do they betray the least recognition when I show them his photograph. I begin to doubt that Willard has ever been in Peru, although I would not be surprised if, turning a corner on a crowded Lima street or entering a *peña*, I should come face-to-face with my dear friend.

Helen, too, has vanished. I do not know whether she lives or not—I, who purchased her release at the cost of infamy and exile. The consequences of my crime (for crime it is) are all that the conspirators can desire. The Age of Steam is at an end—at least in the nation that was its chief glory; I gave it its quietus. Even in Peru, one hears the most extraordinary news from home: the city in darkness, its public squares broken by plows, streets and boulevards become cattle paths, the Botanical Garden plundered, and the train tracks left to rust.

In Lima, I have made a new life. The steam here is of the first intensity, perhaps because of the purity of the water, or maybe it is the *garua*—the strange mist that falls upon the town from May to October. With several other men of vision, I am building a train shed. When it is finished, the Peruvian Age of Steam will begin in earnest, with myself as architect, evangelist, and prime minister. Already, I have chosen a woman of unusual beauty as consort. Her name is Inez. She believes, like me, that love in an age of steam is incomparable. Were I pardoned, I would not return to the city of my birth—not now that the fires are all but extinguished and the trains have stopped. What is the conspirators' art next to the achievements of industry? What have the anarchists wrought to rival what I—the new Prometheus—plan to bestow?

Ravished by Death

After Alberto Casella

Corrado tightens his gloved hands on the wheel as the Voison leans toward the escarpment that falls precipitously to the ocean. A man who does not allow fear in himself, he knows that if he should let his eyes leave the road for an instant to regard his face in the mirror, he will see something resembling it. A disquiet. Later, at the villa, as he studies with the secret enjoyment of a connoisseur the light caught in the depths of his whiskey, he recalls the sensation in the nearly uncontrollable automobile, when gravity seemed in adjournment and the earth careless of its burden. It was not fear—he tells himself—but an emotion like fear, as if he were possessed suddenly by love. And by love, he means the tender prelude to desire—the exquisite regard he has for Grazia, whose body he cannot imagine abandoned to himself or any other lover. By an effort of his seigniorial will, Corrado has refused the insinuations of carnality, quelled the blood's riot, and made of his finely strung nerves an instrument to hymn her ethereal beauty.

He is unhappy.

He has been visiting a brothel with a regularity that threatens to become habitual. Not a house favored by those of his class, but an ancient hotel near the wharves, in whose rooms the transient and the disreputable lie down by the half hour.

He wonders whether he will be able to abjure the rough pleasure he takes there, in a bed doused with scent, beneath which he searches, with his finely shaped Roman nose, for the odor of other men's sweat.

He turns to Baron Cesarea and attempts to describe again the shadow that appeared out of nothing as the motorcar swung into the final turning in the road before the villa's gates: "It was like smoke. Black. Like soot. But odorless and tasted— if of anything—of almonds. It was like oil, although it was not at all oily. It clung to the road and to the Voison and to us— especially to Grazia. I did not see it cover her; nevertheless, I know that it did. I saw nothing. It covered us only a moment. The time it took for the Voison to slip into the turning and for me to feel the outer tires lift up, then fall. For Father's Ferrari, behind us, to send the flower cart flying into the ditch. It tasted and smelled of almond paste, if of anything at all—the shadow, although it was something more than a shadow. It enveloped us. I could do nothing. I wanted to do nothing. I felt the tires lift, then fall back down onto the road. It could not have been any more than a few seconds. I felt cold—a damp chill. It was more mist than shadow, if a mist could be black."

"It was nothing," says the baron. "Merely the uncertain hour between the evening and the coming of night. It was a trick of light. I tell you it was nothing."

"None of us was hurt in the least. Not even the man on the flower cart, although he flew through the air and landed in the road. His eyes were shut—we thought he must be dead. But he opened them after a moment, and we saw that he wasn't in the least hurt. Not even his mule. Father gave him money."

"The duke is always gracious." The baron stares into his whiskey's depths.

He puts out his hand to steady himself against one of the marble columns that decorate the villa's reception room. The whiskey slips up the side of his glass but does not spill.

Corrado cocks his head as if hearing a tragic overture in the distance.

"It was nothing," says the baron, whose face has paled. "Suddenly, I felt as if the earth had swung free of its orbit. I seemed to hear in the thaw of the whiskey's ice the foundation give way."

The baron said this, or perhaps not. Perhaps it was Corrado, who thought it, mistaking the thought for the baron's voice. Or perhaps another spoke in the sepulchral space of the Villa Felicitá. Death, whose voice entered the room through the French window, ajar in the warm October evening, saying, *Suddenly, you felt as if the earth had swung free of its orbit. You seemed to hear in the thaw of your whiskey's ice the foundation give way.*

Corrado is listening intently, his eyes searching a shadow that might have been cast by one of the moon's mountains as readily as an Etruscan vase.

"Grazia is in the music room," the baron says. "She plays beautifully."

"Yes!" Corrado agrees; for it was *music* that he heard while Cesarea put out his hand—piano music and, at the threshold of audition, the soft crackle of ice as it suffered annihilation in the baron's glass. Those and nothing else.

Corrado forgets the voice (if he has heard it at all). He thinks only of Grazia. The baron has no such distraction. If he heard Death's apostrophe from the garden, where it hides among the lengthening shadows, he pretends otherwise. He concentrates on the music Grazia is playing.

"She plays beautifully."

"Yes!"

The baron turns to the window, which is now black—night having approached the villa from the sea. He shivers and goes to close the window.

"It makes me sad," Corrado says of the music.

"It is always so," Cesarea replies, thinking of the hour—the hour of *tristesse*, when the light is extinguished and the warm Adriatic air turns damp. He would have wept had he been alone. He looks into the whiskey, watered with vanished ice. Its amber light is out. Its little sun. Baron Cesarea finishes the drink, for he cannot go to Grazia and take her in his arms.

"I wish I were a young man," he says, turning to Corrado after both have been silent. But Corrado is looking elsewhere, into the darkness among the columns, which rise archaically from the room's marbled floor. Night has entered unnoticed through the window, powerless to keep it out.

Like a ruin, thinks Corrado, and feels a sudden access of hatred for his father. Or is it for Grazia?

"Fedele!" the baron shouts. "Fedele!"

The duke's man enters from an anteroom, where he has been waiting in another obscurity to perform his role. "Baron?"

"Why have you left us in the dark, Fedele?"

They cannot see one another: Corrado, Cesarea, the duke's man. They are voices in a dark, dimensionless space. The columns are engulfed.

Unrelenting, Grazia plays *Pavane pour une infante défunte*. In her hands, the notes have all turned to lead, to ash. To dead leaves that the wind sweeps—rustling—away.

A wind has risen in the garden, rattles the sash, bends the cypress trees that crowd against the villa's outer walls. Accompanying its mournful music, Death descants, *This melancholy you feel at the coming of night—a sorrow blown by the flying darkness into the duke's magnificent rooms—you have felt it many times before—at this hour, the hour of* tristesse, *when the day is unmade like a bed on which you fear to lie down, in case it should prove to be your last. The bed in which you were born and those vexed by ten thousand nights of sleep and dream, sickness and love. The sheet stinking of birth, of blood, of sweat, of love wound about you at last. But none of this crosses your mind. Only the unaccountable sadness of the hour, which makes you irritable and afraid. So you call for the lights to be lit. You hurriedly dress for dinner and rush out to be among other people, to laugh, to drink, to hear music.*

"Where is Duke Lambert?" Cesarea asks peevishly, because he is afraid.

"In the library," Fedele replies. "Someone arrived a little while ago, wishing to speak to him."

"Who?"

"A stranger."

Corrado goes to the music room to be with Grazia. She is sitting in the dark. For a moment, he thinks that she is weeping, but it is the music—its tragic current. Corrado stands in the doorway, transfixed by absence: His lover seems to have vanished, leaving only rueful notes to mark her place. Not lover—*beloved*. He has yet to measure the length of his body against hers. Their kisses are chaste. He wonders briefly if the unappeased desire aroused in him would be diminished by her surrender—would be erased as completely as her image by the darkness. He shakes his head to rid his mind of an unworthy thought. Hatred steals into his heart, and he turns it on himself like a knife.

"Grazia!"

"I'm here, Corrado."

"Why are you sitting in the dark?"

"It's pleasant to play without seeing."

The wind, which was blowing from the sea, moves on its great hinge, turning against the music room at the opposite side of the villa and scattering the sheet music. It brushes Corrado's face like a papery wing, so that he cries out.

"The wind is strong tonight," she says indifferently.

Strong enough to strip trees of leaves and the sky of all its stars, says Death in a low voice hidden beneath Corrado's footsteps as he rushes to the window.

He shuts the window, but Grazia has stopped playing and

does not resume. She hears Corrado spin the flint wheel of his lighter, smells the fluid's astringency.

"Don't!" she tells him. "My head ached so in the light."

"Did you hurt yourself in the accident?"

He almost touches her face.

"No, it's only a headache."

"I behaved stupidly."

"No, it was wonderful, Corrado! To drive so fast—wonderful! I felt—"

—as if I had been sleeping. A princess in a story—asleep for a hundred years behind thorns, behind glass. Waiting without knowing it. Dreaming of a door through which one day someone will walk. Not a door—a hole in the air—a black emptiness in the gray air, without a particle of light or sound—a rustling of cloth or wings or a murmuring. You drove faster and faster, until I felt something tear—an organ, my heart, a gland whose function has been forgotten, ripped out, ripped. Then blackness and the stinging behind the eyes, and a sickness like rapture.

"The shadow—it seemed to cling to you," says Corrado, who has been listening to Grazia's or to Death's voice in the darkness of the music room.

It seemed to come from inside me, the voice continues, *and when the tires left the road, I was happy. I wanted only to die.*

Again, Corrado spins the lighter's small rough wheel. Its flame trembles in his hand, leafs Grazia's forehead and cheeks with gold, illuminates the line of her jaw, in which an aristocratic nature is wholly revealed. Her eyes are closed. Corrado shakes her more roughly than even his dread can explain. For an instant, he wants to humiliate her; to throw her to the floor and defile her. Grazia has fallen asleep in spite of Corrado's shouting: "Why do you keep me always at a distance? When will you marry me? Why won't you let me close to you?" I hate you, Grazia, for what you make me suffer! I would like to destroy you—your virtue, which is an insult to me, filling me with rage. Why do you make me ashamed? "Wake up, Grazia!"

We had an almost fatal accident, he thinks. I was driving too fast and could not hold the road when we went into the turning. It has made her hysterical. The effect of encountering, perhaps for the first time, a force she cannot command. Powerlessness before an uncontrollable event. I may also be hysterical. Because of how close we came to it. Death. It is only natural that tonight we should not be ourselves. Tomorrow, we will be restored. After we have slept. Grazia can't keep her eyes open. Mine, too, want to close. I thought it was the whiskey. The baron is right: It was nothing—the shadow. A trick of light.

Grazia's arm falls across the piano keys, sounding a discordant finale to Corrado's meditation—her lovely white arm, on which she rests her head.

Fedele enters the music room, obedient to the will of others. It is the will of Duke Lambert that Grazia and Corrado come at once to the reception room. Prince Sirki has arrived, the duke's friend. Fedele turns on the lights. (Why didn't Corrado, who knows the location of the light switch in this, his father's house and his?) Gently, Corrado lays his hand on Grazia's bare shoulder. Despite himself, he hears desire whisper its insinuations. Grazia shrugs into consciousness. She lifts her face; a strand of hair falls, and she pushes it away. She lifts her arm from the piano, and a second confused chord rumbles. Corrado helps her stand. Neither of them knows that Grazia was dead—had gone a little way into Death's kingdom. It clings to her now the way salt does a swimmer who has set out into the sea, only to repent and return to shore. If Corrado looked into her eyes, he would know that she has just returned from an immense journey. But he does not look. This man, whose eyes seldom leave Grazia when she is near, does not look at her at all. He is looking at nothing, or rather, at a seam of darkness lying somberly within the fold of a drape or the peculiar vacancy of the window, which, in its utter blackness, neither reveals anything of the outside nor reflects anything inside the lighted room. Could glass be said to have died, this glass is dead. Corrado does not remark on these uncanny effects. He does not even consider them as effects (which would lead him to ask himself, Of what?); he does not notice them. His eyes are ravished by darkness.

He leads Grazia into the salon and to Prince Sirki. The prince, Duke Lambert, and his guests would wonder at the young man's haste if they saw him enter, but they do not see him. They form a tableau: Prince Sirki, standing by the French window, with the darkness of the garden at his back; the others facing him—Lambert in front, the apex of a triangle of bodies in postures of obeisance. Princess Maria, Grazia's mother, indicates a curtsey: She is Sirki's titular equal and need do no more. Alda, the contessa de Parma, is seen in an attitude of homage, which would strike Corrado as charming rather than abject. But he sees only Prince Sirki. The prince is dressed in the white dress uniform of his Balkan country. The jacket blossoms with rosettes and decorations. His black hair gleams with the light of the chandelier. Although he is aware of Corrado standing at the entrance, he has not acknowledged him—pleased by the scene of welcome before him. Corrado takes a step into the room, drawing behind him Grazia, who seems to be sleepwalking. Sirki now turns—not to Corrado, whose eyes are transfixed by the glint of light cast by the prince's monocle, but to Grazia, in whose eyes he sees a languor irresistible to him. He walks toward her in his high, polished boots, dispersing Lambert and the others. The prince smiles. Corrado is swept aside by his indifference. Sirki marches on Grazia as if she were a town to be taken. He stops in front of her, hesitates, does not take her hand to kiss. Having cast off sleep and the remnant of whatever it was she dreamed there, she begins to fold like a flower at the coming of night. But the prince prevents her from completing this gesture of submission, which he has allowed—accepted as his right—from the others.

"It is I who should bow to you," he says, and does. "Your beauty."

He is—there is no one word to tell what Sirki is or why he has moved Grazia. He is neither charming nor courtly, for they require insouciance he lacks, nor does he have the equanimity of a Don Juan. He is possessed of an absolute authority and behaves as one used to obedience. Yet Sirki wishes to be liked in spite of the militancy with which he confronts the duke, his wife, Stephanie, and their guests. His severity of dress and manner distances him from them. Sirki wants to be admired—no, *received* as one of them. But they cannot receive him. He is cold: His presence in the room chills them. Lambert almost calls Fedele to close the windows, but the windows are closed; and besides, the night is not unpleasant. It is a warm autumn night; and while the summer blooms are past, the grass and leaves are green. But the chill inside the villa is undeniable, and Princess Maria shivers. Or is it that the prince is looking at her daughter with such intensity and she, having raised her head, is looking at him with equal interest? Interest scarcely describes the quality of her gaze, which, perhaps, alarms the princess. She is not the only one who registers disturbing sensations. Each of them is disconcerted by the prince, although none could tell, if asked, what it is about Sirki that dismays them. For *dismay,* more than any other word, most aptly describes the emotion predominant in the room. Except for Corrado, who is angry because of the way the prince is looking at Grazia. She returns his gaze without blushing—or flinching; for there is something painful in that gaze. To suffer it is almost to die. Aware of the young man's hostility, the prince turns to him. Sirki's eyes having left Grazia's, she is like one who has wakened suddenly: She starts and nearly cries out. She shuts her eyes and opens them—her pale eyes no longer in thrall. She watches Corrado fall back before the prince's stare. The young man has the look of someone about to be destroyed. Now it is Grazia's turn to shiver—with cold or fear. She saves Corrado without knowing it.

"Corrado, I'm cold; please get my shawl. I left it in the music room."

Prince Sirki lowers his eyes from Corrado's, permits him to leave the room in order to bring Grazia her shawl. The young man goes without a word. Perhaps he knows how close he came to death. Perhaps not. Lambert's guests are reminded that they, too, are cold and ask the duke if a fire cannot be made up in the great hearth. Duke Lambert pulls a sash; and a bell rings in a distant room in the villa, summoning Fedele, who arrives within moments, his face a mask showing neither irritation nor servility.

"Make up the fire, Fedele," the duke says with the air of one who asks the impossible, because he alone understands that the room is not cold; or if it is, no fire can warm it.

Fedele bows and does as he is bidden.

Released, Grazia goes to her mother. They withdraw to a corner of the salon that puts them at the farthest remove from Sirki. The others also seek—consciously or not—to separate themselves from the prince, who stands isolated and for-lorn. He is like a boy abandoned by his friends, who go off by themselves, heads together in conspiracies of mirth. Sirki is offended. Only the duke understands their danger—how cruel the prince's rage is likely to be. (Even Lambert cannot know the extent of it. How—with a single terrible look—the prince can stop the heart of each, stop light from entering their eyes and sensations from knitting themselves into thoughts on the mind's dark loom.) The duke herds—like a shepherd his scattered flock—his wife and guests to the center of the room, dogging them with whispered reminders of their obligation to make welcome his eminent guest. They assemble once more in a tableau of respect. Lambert implores the prince with his eyes not to give way to rage. Sirki glares in answer, reminding him with a magisterial look of their agreement and the consequences of its violation. The duke lowers his head as if to ask that the prince's wrath fall on his alone. The others are silent, sensing in the tension between them a crisis that concerns them all. (All but Fedele, who has fallen asleep with the fire tongs in his hand. He has been neither more nor less reserved toward the prince than toward the other guests.) It is the moment when the executioner's ax is gathering to itself the weight of finality. The air between the blade and the neck of the condemned becomes electric with an insuperable attraction. No one dares enter its dangerous current. The moment is being swiftly drained of potential. In seconds, actuality will succeed inevitability; and the ax will begin a descent that neither a king's pardon nor the executioner's remorse can stop. Corrado enters with Grazia's shawl. The interruption is in time. The accumulating charge dissipates; the ax is lowered harmlessly. Prince Sirki relents. Grazia smiles. Duke Lambert takes out his cigarette case. Fedele wakes. The guests move about the room as if nothing has happened.

"Thank you," says Grazia after Corrado wraps her white shoulders.

"Come with me into the garden!" he begs. "The moon is bloodred tonight, and nothing seems to sleep. The larks and the nightingales are singing in the trees."

She looks toward the windows, but they are still dead, revealing nothing outside, reflecting nothing within. She shivers and closes herself within the shawl.

"I am very tired, Corrado. I must go home to bed."

"But, Grazia —"

"She had a fright this afternoon in the automobile," says the baron, who has been drawn irresistibly to the young woman because of her beauty or for another reason he himself does not know. "It's tired her."

"We must be leaving now," says Princess Maria, who senses that her daughter has stepped, without knowing it, into a current against which she is too weak to swim. Maria only senses it; for the dread with which she beholds her daughter standing inside the shadow of Prince Sirki remains a nameless one.

The prince's anger overtakes them like an early frost. "They are leaving?" He looks to Lambert for an explanation.

"They did not plan to stay, Your Grace."

Only Lambert knows the cost to them all should the prince be made to feel that he is other than what he seems.

"Believe me, Your Grace—they did not mean to stay!" Lambert pleads; and in his pleading, his son perceives an abjectness, which rankles him. Shame for his father's humiliation and for his own before Grazia incites Corrado to act. He moves against Sirki, intending to fling an insult and a challenge at him, then halts. There is an inviolable zone around a monarch none may enter, upon pain of sovereign displeasure. It is a realm in miniature, whose borders are secured against trespass. That surrounding the prince is mined with destruction. Duke Lambert seizes his son's arm roughly.

"Prince Sirki is my guest!"

"He insults us by his presence!" Corrado shouts, his voice tremulous with indignation and fear. "I demand that he leave at once!"

"What is this insolence, Lambert?" Sirki's voice tolls a warning.

"Forgive him, Prince—his youth!" The duke pulls his son from the brink. "He doesn't know what he is saying. Forgive a young man his folly!"

Corrado allows himself to be led from the room. He does not admit his terror, telling himself that he withdraws in deference to his father's wishes. Could Lambert see him, he would be struck by a face emptied of blood. If he looked closely, he would note a wildness in his son's eyes and a twitch in one eyelid. But the corridor leading to the music room is dimly lit.

"You must not provoke him, Corrado! He is more dangerous than you suppose."

Feeling himself safe, the young man answers with bravado: "You should have let me slap his face for the insults he has given you."

"It would have been the last thing you ever did on earth," Lambert says with a solemnity that stops Corrado in mid-step.

"I thought he was your friend," he says.

"I met him for the first time tonight."

"Then he is not Prince Sirki?"

The duke does not reply.

"Who is he, Father? I demand to know!"

"It is enough for you to know that he is a most powerful prince who can, if he pleases, bring your life—all our lives—to an end."

"One man—"

"He can strike us without raising a hand."

Corrado shivers, as if the cold emanating from Sirki has pursued him. "What does he want?"

"To study us."

Corrado is bewildered.

"Our fear."

"I don't understand you."

"For all our sakes, Corrado, don't meddle in this! And unless you want to bring catastrophe to this house, treat Prince Sirki as you would any man."

"For how long?"

"Until tomorrow night. Now I must see to the others. Your room is the safest place for you."

"I'm not afraid."

"Be afraid, Corrado; be very much afraid."

Duke Lambert returns to the salon. His wife and guests are as he left them. They stand with heads bowed before the prince, who also has not moved. They are not, as Fedele appeared to be, asleep. Seeing them now so immobile, Lambert imagines that it is he and not Prince Sirki who directs the action; his consciousness, which contains them all. They are like characters in a play, who, their parts having been performed, go backstage to smoke a cigarette, embrace, or read the newspaper while their fictional lives are in suspension. Their most dramatic selves. Are Stephanie, Alda, Rhoda, Eric, Cesarea—even the prince— waiting for him to set them going again? A pretty delusion! Sirki turns to Lambert, and the others are immediately disenthralled. The duke quails as Sirki faces him. But the prince is smiling and so, too, are the others.

"I have had a most enjoyable evening," he says.

Lambert staggers, as if felled.

"I look forward to tomorrow," Sirki continues with the savoir faire of a courtier, which he has acquired during Corrado's retreat.

"Where are Grazia and Princess Maria?" the duke asks.

"Gone home to their beds," Sirki replies.

Lambert's face registers minutely his relief. It does not escape the prince, who says, "They will be back tomorrow night for my farewell party. Grazia will be unable to resist."

The guests are laughing. The bond, which joined them with a force stronger than their wills, is dissolved. Each is free to move about the room with another whose interest is, for the moment, mutual. Baron Cesarea and Eric stand by the hearth, smoking cigars. Alda and Rhoda sit on a banquette, vying in their fascination for the prince—all fear of him forgotten. Stephanie goes to her husband to ask what has happened to Corrado. Fedele enters with a tray of brandies. As if the house were his, Prince Sirki proposes, "To the pleasant dreams of my guests." His toast strikes all but Duke Lambert as presumptuous. Even so, they drink to those dreams, which are theirs—having felt, perhaps, misgivings about the coming night, when they would each leave the shore and drift out onto the black ocean alone.

Already, Grazia is drifting. She and Princess Maria travel in reverse the road that brought them earlier from Ravenna to the Villa Felicitá; but they are not menaced by shadow, and the sedan presses against the curves in the road almost amorously. Maria watches as the sea (the Adriatic, not the figurative one on which Grazia has set out) approaches and recedes according to the road's caprice. Entranced by the wind's mussing the water silver, she thinks of nothing, nor does she wish to ask her daughter how she has answered Corrado's proposal of marriage or what she thinks of the irascible prince. She herself does not wish to think of him at all. His impertinent gaze disturbed her—how it bore into one! After the driver has brought the automobile to a stop in front of the palazzo, Princess Maria nearly orders him to drive on through the night, the next day and night, until he has traveled the length of Italy, to Otranto, where she and her daughter can board a ship to Africa, to China, to someplace far from the Villa Felicitá and the prince. But she does not give the order, and the driver is now opening the door for her. Maria shakes Grazia awake, gently; for she is not yet so far from shore that she cannot return.

Prince Sirki rests—he who is never tired; wills himself to sleep, who has never slept. To understand men, he must know the life they lead asleep. He has visited them so often in their beds, but never slept. He has entered their final dreams as easily as one might put a hand through a pane of water and has watched there enactments of human desire and fear—fear of Death, fear of him. Desire, too, for him. But he has never dreamed. He has listened to the cries of passion and distress, the shouts, whispers, riddling speeches concealing so much of interest to occultists and psychiatrists but not to him. Until today, when curiosity for once overcame him—curiosity concerning men:

why they should claim to fear him and yet do so much in his service. For his approval and—who knows?—love.

In the Great War, men showed a genius for the invention of new forms of extermination. No longer indifferent, Death hastened from muddy ditch to the garlands of twisted wire, to flaming oil spreading mortally on the waves, to the burning cages in which men were hurtled, like angels, from the heavens to a blasted, unlovely earth. On earth, in air, water, and in fire—there was not an element in which men did not bring forth some novelty to enliven the history of slaughter. He was astounded by the eagerness of their complicity and enraptured by the sight of so many caught in attitudes of submission. For him, a death has no moral quality, although it does possess an aesthetic one. Sensuality is his only human aspect. It has enabled him to make of Grazia an object of desire. Her beauty, however, is not a sufficient explanation for his fascination. If beauty were enough, Sirki would be attracted to Countess Alda or the American girl, Rhoda. No, Grazia must possess a fatality—must be in love with Death without knowing it. Perhaps this adoration compels her each morning to pray to the Virgin—not to be delivered from it, as she believes, but *unto* it; for who among women is more qualified to be Death's intercessor than she who gave birth to man's deliverance from it? Her lassitude, her remoteness—what are they but warrants of Grazia's willingness to be taken? In dreams from which she wakes at once troubled and exultant, like a wife remembering a lover's embrace—she is ravished by Death.

In her bedroom in the palazzo, she is dreaming of the prince. She sees him as the medieval allegorists painted Death: faceless, cloaked in darkness, carrying a scythe and an hourglass. She knows, in her dream, that Prince Sirki and Death are one and the same. She is afraid of neither. He comes to her where she lies beneath an azure canopy embroidered in gold thread with astrological signs. She does not find him ridiculous; she does not feel revulsion at his touch. He puts aside the scythe and the glass, removes his cloak as a lover would, and lies beside her. He is a void. An emptiness. Nothing. And like nothing, immensely potent. He ravishes her. She need not part her lips or open her legs to let in her death: It enters as easily as a man does water. Only it is Grazia who drowns. Prince Sirki sleeps— he who has never slept—and dreams this while Grazia rests in his dream, smiles in its sway to be possessed by Death. To be loved by him. To be adored. In the morning, she dresses like a bride and returns to the Villa Felicitá—unable to resist.

The Love of Stanley Marvel & Claire Moon

For Philip Roth

1916

It was the day of the boat races, and Stanley Marvel and his friend Rolly were there, sitting on a grassy bank overlooking the river. The river was brown. On it sped the thin, bright shells of the rowing teams. Red, blue, green, and yellow boats coasted over the river. In the stern of each boat, a coxswain rocked, urging his team on through a megaphone strapped to his head. Neither friend could hear what the coxswain said to inspire the oarsmen in their furious paces, but Stanley Marvel secretly believed it was dirty stories.

Stanley and Rolly were alumni of one of the colleges whose boat crew raced toward the yellow rope stretched between two boats downriver. They were members of the class of '15. It was Skimmer, an annual college spectacle, which had brought them to sit on the grass.

Haberdashery

Rolly wore a striped jacket, boiled white shirt and collar. His school tie waved in the breeze from the river. Stanley Marvel wore his varsity sweater, emblazoned with a capital *P*. Both men wore straw hats with round, flat brims, known as straw boaters or skimmers, white duck trousers, and pearl gray spats. Both sported pencil-thin mustaches and gold pocket watches fastened to their waists by fobs and chains. Both wore hair oil, which trickled down their collars in the summer heat.

From time to time, they took swigs from flat silver pocket flasks. Between races, they read newspaper accounts of the game played the day before between the New York Giants and the Boston Braves.

Conversation on the Bank

They had little to say to each other.

But suddenly Rolly said, "There's some loveliness over there by the *pro bonum publico*."

Stanley Marvel turned down a corner of the paper and looked.

"That is a very accurate observation: There is certainly loveliness over there. And I think I shall go speak to it."

"You go, and I will see what happens."

Claire Moon: An Inventory

    white linen pleated dress
    white high-necked shirtwaist
    white chemise ("shimmy") w/pink ribbons
    black cotton stockings
    black kid boots
    black wide-brimmed hat
    a string of dime-store pearls (Woolworth, 79¢)
    strawberry-blond hair
    green eyes w/gold flecks ("pretty eyes")
    upturned nose
    small mouth
    small breasts w/large, pink aureoles
    slender ("waspish") waist

narrow hips
a beauty mark on the inside of the left thigh
2 legs
2 arms
2 feet
10 fingers
10 toes
32 teeth

Claire Moon: Health

"Corn-fed."

Her Statement

"I was riding the trolley car on my way home from Gimbals. I'm a salesgirl there, in lingerie. Today was my Saturday to work. I sat on the river side like I always do to look at the boats. And it looked so cool there by the river. So when the trolley stopped to give the horses a drink, I thought I'd just get off and have a nice cold drink of water from the fountain by the horse trough and then go and have a look at the boats."

They Meet Watching Boats

Stanley looked up from the newspaper. A lovely girl leaned over the stone trough and filled a tin cup. She had removed her hat and with a dampened handkerchief was mopping her forehead and neck. Her forehead was high and wide, her eyes set rather far apart.

He went to her.

He tipped his skimmer and said, "Hello. My name is Stanley Marvel."

She said nothing, but instead looked away to where a shell from the Vesper Boat Club sliced through the river.

"Do you like the races?" he asked. He was confident with shopgirls.

"Yes," she offered.

"Those boats there, with the crimson-and-blue bands slanting diagonally on their hulls, represent my alma mater."

"Oh, you're a university man!"

He pointed to the capital *P* made of thick felt sewn onto the chest of his college sweater.

"Would you care for a lemonade?"

"That would be nice," she said.

They bought lemonade and cakes in the basement of one of the boathouses. Then they went and strolled along the pavement that followed the river and looked at the boats sliding crisply through the dark river as the sun dropped behind the heroic statue of the Union soldier on horseback.

Fireworks

And then all was dark.

Stanley held Claire Moon's hand in the darkness.

There were around them little fires where the racing crews and their girls cooked hot dogs.

Someone played "Where the Mountains Meet the Moon" on a ukulele.

Suddenly fireworks. Over the black river. Showers of bright sparks. Pinwheels of flame. *Whoosh*. In the light of the fireworks, they could see boat crews putting their boats away in the boathouses. *Bang*. Claire Moon moved into Stanley Marvel's arms and was enfolded there.

Conversation in the Dark on Boathouse Row

"I am a rising young man. I have my own business—the butter and egg business. I have a truck, and there are not many men in the butter and egg business who have a truck.

"Would you care to take a ride? I have a can of milk that should still be nice and cool. You could drink milk and ride in the truck. I'll drive you home."

Riding Through the City at Night

Stanley Marvel guided his butter and egg truck through the park and into the street. On Dauphin Street, Negroes sat on steps, drinking and laughing. Under a streetlamp, a man was retching.

Stanley Marvel: "We have given them a part of the city in which to live. They should not soil it with the way they live."

Proposal of Marriage

"And why not marriage between you and me?"

The Wedding Day: 9:00 A.M., His Toilet

He scraped his cheeks with the Gillette and then swished it in the gray shaving water. The Gillette was heavy in his hand. Tiny whiskers marked where the shaving water lapped against the porcelain sink. They showed the high-water mark made each time the Gillette displaced its equal volume in water.

Bay rum on his cheeks, neck, the back of the neck, just where the hair begins, brushed into his hair with his fingers.

He brushed his hair with a pair of tortoiseshell military brushes. Hair oil. A rakish sweep of dark hair over his forehead achieved with a comb.

"I want a girl just like the girl . . ."

Then he gargled thoroughly with Listerine.

9:25

Rolly was downstairs. He wanted to take Stanley downtown to a taproom where he knew some girls, so he would forget all about this wedding business. But Stanley wouldn't let him upstairs. Rolly left.

10:00 A.M.

And then Stanley rode to the grocer's and bought two wooden boxes of big strawberries. He put these in the icebox of their new house. He also put a bottle of champagne on ice.

The Wedding

Stanley Marvel: "It was over before I knew what happened. The organist played the Purcell thing, and then next thing I knew I was knocking rice out of my hat. I wanted to walk out with Claire on my arm with a certain . . . dignity, like I was used to all the fanfare; but I forgot all about it. I may have shuffled out."

Rolly: "He shuffled out, the chump."

The Recessional

Leaving the church, Stanley noticed his friend Rolly at the back. He was standing with some colored people. They were dressed flamboyantly. They each had one of the woven straw (rattan?) fans that had been donated to the church by a neighborhood funeral parlor. It was hot. Rolly and the colored people stole the fans.

Leaving the Church

Rolly had tied the butter and egg truck to an orange fireplug. When Stanley and Claire pulled away from the church, waving to family and friends, the truck yanked the hydrant out of the pavement like a tooth. Water burst from the stump and fountained into the blue air.

Several well-wishers were soaked through to the skin. Stanley Marvel's mother dropped her flowers onto the pavement. They lay there, pink and white carnations, in a puddle.

Rolly: "I did it because I wanted to marry Claire Moon myself. I'll break up this marriage yet."

Changing Clothes

They drove to their new house and parked the butter and egg truck outside. Stanley carried Claire inside and kissed her. They sat in the kitchen, eating strawberries and drinking champagne. Then they went upstairs and changed from their wedding clothes into their traveling clothes.

"Not yet, Stanley," said Claire as she went into the bathroom.

His Poem

Stanley read Claire a poem through the bathroom door. The poem was called "A Vow," by Edgar Guest. It goes like this:

> I might not ever scale the mountain heights
> Where all the great men stand in glory now;
> I may not ever gain the world's delights
> Or win a wreath of laurel for my brow;
> I may not gain the victories that men
> Are fighting for, nor do a thing to boast of;
> I may not get a fortune here, but then,
> The little that I have I'll make the most of.

Honeymoon

They stopped at Haddon Hall in Atlantic City. There was a white bar of Clover Leaf soap in the soap dish on the Belgian marble-topped sink. There was a clean water tumbler. There was a small brownish bouquet of roses with a little card: *From the Management.*

"How thoughtful!" said Claire.

She went into the bathroom to change. She wore a robe that reached to the floor. She wore underpants with lace edging for her bridal night. She sat before the mirror and combed her hair one hundred times. Stanley marveled at its length and shininess. He bent and sniffed it.

"It smells like lilac, your hair does."

Claire smiled secretly. Then she unstoppered the bottle of Thelma, "Queen of Perfumes," her sister had given her for a wedding present. Claire moistened the heel of her hand with Thelma and dabbed the sweet fragrance onto her neck and temples.

Claire Moon's Portrait (I)

She left school after the tenth grade. She worked for a while as a filing clerk in the Contagious Hospital. In those days, there were lepers behind high stone walls. She worked next in a downtown department store as a salesgirl.

Occasionally, she bought fancy underdrawers. She was a virgin until her wedding night, although she once permitted John Grabowski, an orderly in the Contagious Hospital, to put his hand under her shimmy.

She wanted several things in life:

1. to be married
2. to have a motorcar
3. to ride in an airplane

Stanley Marvel promised her all three.

The Air Circus

They went to the Air Circus outside Atlantic City. They drank a mixture of lemonade and beer and ate hot dogs while they looked at the sky. It was a cloudless day. Red, blue, green, and yellow biplanes purred and putted above them. The airplanes banked and turned and dived at the grandstand and buzzed the fairgrounds. Clowns rode on the bottom wings, holding on to the struts.

Claire admired the dashing aviators. They had little mustaches, leather jackets and helmets, and long white scarves, which snapped behind them as they bounced down the field and took off.

After the show, Stanley Marvel gave one of the aviators two dollars to take Claire and him up. They rode in a big circle. At one point, they could see Haddon Hall Hotel with its red tile roofs and green awnings and, behind it, the Atlantic Ocean. The ocean looked blue and flat. As the aviator turned his airplane toward the field, Stanley looked at the people milling about below him. From where he sat, all the derbies looked like periods.

Claire Moon's Thoughts in the Airplane

When the plane went up, I felt this feeling between my legs; it tickled me and made me want to wet, like on the roller coaster. Suddenly, we were in the air, and I had another peculiar sensation. I was excited. My nipples got hard and the rough cotton of my shimmy rubbed against them. In the wind, I felt like I was tugged at. I turned around, and the pilot winked at me—I'm sure he did. His mustache was blond. His eyes were blue as the ocean. When we turned around to land, I felt like all the men on the ground were looking up my dress.

Claire Moon's Portrait (II)

1. There is always the possibility that everything in her first portrait is false.
2. This possibility may mean Claire is more complex than we at first thought.

Hotel Breakfast

Stanley and Claire went downstairs to breakfast. Breakfast at Haddon Hall was a high-class affair. A waiter with black morning coat and velvet collar, waxed mustaches, and hair oiled to the top of his head showed them to their table. On the table were a white linen cloth, two white linen napkins rolled inside rings, a bowl of fruit, a cut-glass vase of pinks, and a card. On the card someone had written in calligraphy with India ink: *Mr. & Mrs. Stanley Marvel.*

A string quartet played chamber music in the drawing room, through the double doors.

From where Stanley and Claire sat, they could see the ocean. Bright parasols paraded on the yellow boardwalk, escorted by bobbing skimmers. Prams and bicycles rattled over the boards. Kites with rag tails flew from the beach over the ocean; and just beyond the white-edged surf, small boats drifted at anchor while men in derbies and skimmers and ladies with parasols fished for the delicate white-fleshed weakfish.

A waiter brought them ice water, silver, and the menu.

MENU

orange juice

buttered toast

eggs (shirred, fried or scrambled)

bacon

sausage

or Philadelphia scrapple

baked scrod

fried potatoes

& coffee or tea

As they ate, they listened to the string quartet; admired the quiet precision of the black-coated and oiled waiters moving among the tables with deference and the assuredness of people who know how to behave in opulent surroundings; watched the men and women promenade on the boardwalk; watched the boats at anchor lift and settle on the ocean's heave, the sudden bounding of a sailboat; and caught the occasional flash of sun against a fish's belly as it was reeled in and netted.

Stanley Marvel looked up from his eggs and started. Rolly stood over them, tall and blond, elegant in white linen suit and pink tie.

Disruption of the Breakfast Airs of Morning

Stanley Marvel was not pleased to see his friend Rolly, who dragged a chair over to the table and sat without waiting to be asked.

1. He hadn't forgiven him for tying his Ford truck to the fireplug.
2. He resented his attempts to lure him to a taproom and an easy girl on his wedding day.
3. He was shocked that Rolly had brought colored people to the Presbyterian church and had stolen the fans.
4. He wanted to be alone with Claire.

5. He secretly feared Rolly's power over women.
6. He hated Rolly's pink tie.

"I would be pleased if you'd leave immediately," Stanley said.

Rolly drew on the white linen cloth with a fingernail, looking all the while at Claire. Claire blushed deeply at the throat and looked at Stanley. Rolly pushed back his chair and stood up.

"All right. But I promise you this: I will take Claire one of these days, and I'll kill you, Stanley Marvel, if you try to stop me."

Stanley knew Rolly was capable of killing him.

Rolly: A Portrait

Rolly came from a big stone house. There was a gravel drive in the shape of a half-moon in front of the house, and automobiles were always parked there. Not black Fords, but red Double Berlines, cream Renault Petit Ducs with green trim, yellow Rolland-Pilains, and white Peugeot Double Phaetons with red leather seats.

There were servants, and Rolly would sleep with one of the maids when he came home for vacation.

He loved to hunt. He and his father had gone shooting out west with Teddy Roosevelt when Rolly was a boy. He liked the company of violent men. He boxed and fenced at the university. He flew his own airplane. His father had taught him to shoot a dueling pistol with deadly skill. His father had killed two men. Rolly loved his father.

Rolly was cruel to women: He had beaten a girl in his rooms, but his father prevented the incident from becoming a scandal by making a large endowment to the university. The Modern Language Building bears his name.

Rolly dressed in flashy clothes, enjoyed appearing in bad taste. He wore French cologne. His underwear was monogrammed, and women loved him.

The Call-up: 1916

Luckily for Stanley, there was a war. Rolly enlisted in the Army Air Corps. A few months later, Stanley Marvel was drafted into the Signal Corps. He trained at Fort Lee, Virginia, and was sent from there directly to France without leave and without a great coat. He received his great coat when he disembarked from the troopship, in New York City, in 1918.

Stanley Marvel at War

"It's a heck of a war!"

Postcard from the Front

Dear Claire,

We are in the Argonne Forest. I am in a rest area, so do not worry. The sergeant says there's nothing to it, and we'll be home by Christmas. I saw some very fine French cows this morning on a little farm. It made me think of the butter and egg business. I hope you are well and getting out once in a while with friends. I miss you.

Love,

Your husband Stanley

Stanley Marvel: A Portrait

Stanley Marvel was over six feet tall. His father was an ingot straightener in a steel town, and Stanley had won a scholarship because of the things he could do with basketballs. He liked to be cheered by the crowd more than he liked basketball.

He was someone who needed to be liked. He hated unpleasantness. He didn't understand why Rolly was making things unpleasant for him.

He didn't know how to fight and, if left to himself, would

have guided the enemy's bayonet for him into his own vitals. Luckily for him, he never got near a German.

He loved girls and still believed a beautiful girl was the source of all art and was the song of the world. He would have groveled at Claire's feet to have something to worship and to prove that she, as a woman, was worthy of adoration.

While Stanley Marvel Was in a Trench . . .

Stanley Marvel sat in a trench, quaking. He sat on a board to keep the seat of his pants dry. His feet were in the mud. It was raining. His shoes were wet. His puttees were wet and unraveled. The blanket he had around him was wet. It smelled like a wet blanket. Stanley hadn't had a change of clothes for three weeks and so his clothes smelled, too.

He was quaking because he was wet and cold and because of the aerial bombardment. The aerial bombardment had been going on for three days without stop. It had finally gotten on Stanley's nerves. Bad nerves made him quake with each concussion. He could feel each concussion in his ears. They hurt him, but he let them hurt. He could not keep his ears covered anymore. His nerves were bad, and he just sat there on his piece of board, in the mud, wet and quaking.

He thought he would like to have a cigar.

He thought the sight of the aerial bombardment was very pretty. He thought it looked just like the fireworks over the river the night he had met Claire Moon.

I'll put electricity in the house when I get home, he thought.

Claire Was at a Party . . .

While Stanley Marvel sat in his trench and quaked, Claire was at a party. She wore a pink summer dress and low white shoes. Her strawberry-blond hair was unraveling from its knot on her head. She looked very pretty. Her white gloves were in her purse; and she was drinking champagne cocktails, one after another. She scandalized her friends by coming to the party in a motorcar with a handsome slacker, who was a floorwalker in a furniture department.

"I want to have some fun," she said.

And Rolly Was in the Air

While Stanley Marvel sat in his trench and quaked and Claire was at a party with a slacker, having fun, Rolly was in a Jenny going loop-the-loop to escape the German triwing on his tail. There was very little night flying done then, but Rolly was doing it.

The struts hummed, and Rolly's white silk scarf crackled.

I will get Claire as soon as I get home, he thought. I will spread her delicious white limbs on my bed and get her.

Then Rolly crashed.

Then Rolly was sent to the field hospital.

Then Rolly's left arm was amputated.

Then Rolly's left sleeve was pinned up.

And after a time, he went home.

Armistice

And then the war was over.

Demobilization

Stanley Marvel was put in a troopship and sent home. After crossing the Atlantic in eight days, he was put off the ship at New York Harbor. The ship bumped against the dock. They gave him a great coat. It was brand-new. He wore his great coat as he marched to the Armory. It was summer. Then he was mustered out.

Reunion

Stanley Marvel went home to Philadelphia. He came by train and walked along Broad Street in his uniform and great coat. People were sick of seeing soldiers.

"Hey, buddy, the war is over!" they yelled.

"Get a job!" they yelled.

He stood in the living room of his house and said, "Is anybody home?"

Claire was at the movies with the handsome slacker, who was no longer a slacker now that the war was over. He was manager of the furniture department.

Abduction

Several weeks later, Rolly forced his way into Stanley Marvel's house and shot Stanley in the knee with an army pistol.

"That's for you," he said.

"And you're for me," he said to Claire.

He took Claire outside and pushed her into a motorcar driven by a confederate he had engaged while in the army hospital. The confederate had his right arm pinned up, and together they drove the motorcar to the airfield.

Rolly and Claire were flying to Canada in Rolly's airplane when the accident occurred.

Strange Accident

August 29. One of the strangest accidents known to aviation caused the deaths of Rolly Wincapaw, well-known playboy and flying ace, and Claire Moon Marvel of Philadelphia. Wincapaw was piloting his Fokker T-2 over Lake George when a gust of wind wrapped the lady's skirt around the "joystick," or control column. Frantic efforts to disentangle it failed, and in a wild swoop the airplane struck the water with terrific impulse. A sliver from a wing strut pierced the pilot's skull, and the unconscious Mrs. Marvel was drowned.

Conclusion (I)

Claire made no resistance during Rolly's abduction of her, and was secretly glad.

Conclusion (II)

Claire made heroic resistance against her abductor and entangled the joystick with her dress rather than dishonor her husband.

Who's to say?

To Each According to His Sentence

Words create out of silence and nothing everything we know.
—Alessandro Comi

1.

I have not read Gaston Leroux's 1909 novel, *The Phantom of the Opera*. Like many others, I know the story by its cinematic adaptations: the 1925 silent film with Lon Chaney as the Phantom and the 1943 version starring Claude Rains. (There are newer treatments.) I do not wish to read the novel, nor is reading it in any way essential to my purpose, which is to re-create *The Phantom of the Opera*. You will be led, inevitably, to think of Borges; but believe me, I am not such a fool as to attempt what he has done! In any case, his intention, if it can ever be said to be known, is not mine. Mine is to build an edifice of prose in which to hide. What drink had done, words will now do. According to commentaries I have read, the 1925 film version is more faithful to the novel than the 1943 variant, although the former omits much of the original. Neither version contains what in the original is for me of principal interest: that the Phantom was an architect employed in the construction of the opera's cellars. This detail in the Phantom's background suggested to me a possible way out of an increasingly impossible détente with—I leave it to you to say what.

My first impulse was to create anew—that is, to write a story in which to achieve my end. I struggled for months, however, without discovering a narrative structure with a mise-en-scène so richly provided with hiding places as the Phantom's. (Not even in Borges do we find Leroux's gothic elaboration of the principle of concealment, perhaps because the Frenchman had, in aid of his imagination, the actual Paris opera house.) At last I determined to follow the example of the hermit crab and borrow another's construction: Leroux's novel and its cinematic equivalents. I would appropriate the story as I knew it (a conflation of sources). Having found a form to inhabit, there remained the problem of how to insert myself into it.

2.

In the Phantom's rooms far below the Paris Opera, there are two mirrors: one in which the silvering behind the glass has tarnished, making all that is reflected in it obscure, and another, which presents to each thing seen within it its likeness. At times the Phantom wishes to see himself as he is—in all his ugliness—and will gaze hours on end in the second mirror. For a while he will be a tragic figure, a Werther doomed to a life underground, despised, shunned—a castaway deprived of hope and love. He will revel in an austere pathos, making it his meat and drink—his tainted meat and bitter drink—until pathos, drained of tragic feeling, becomes maudlin. He will long then for the sentimentalities of song and beauty—that of a woman, young and virtuous, whose chaste lips taste of violet pastilles, a woman altogether worthy of his abasement. He will weep luxuriously. He will become drunk. He will submit himself to the engines and instruments of torture installed in the opera's cellars during the second revolution. He will compose for the organ Romantic rhapsodies. At other times, however, the Phantom is impelled to gaze at himself in the tarnished mirror (the one the world calls kind). Touching his disfigured face, he becomes a grim Realist, who understands that what can be seen of the world is not in any case the truth. It is then he is most to be feared, for he will wish nothing more than to destroy beauty, to remove its pleasing mask—even with a knife.

THE PHANTOM: I have not left the opera house since escaping Devil's Island [or overseeing the construction of the opera's cellars, depending on one's source material] and taking refuge underground. But I go out on the roof at night when moved by the music and sit atop the statue of the winged figure above the frieze of grotesques.

3.

Neither was I attracted to the Phantom's suffering (sumptuous though it may be) nor did I pity him his agony or the hell in which fate—say, rather, accident (of birth or engraver's acid)—had consigned him. No, the solitariness of his life in the cellars of the opera house drew me to his story—this and his having been the architect of his own prison. That a man's search for privacy should have been abetted by a genius (however perverse) for form—this I, a writer dismayed by the presence of others, found attractive. How I came to this extremity of reserve, I do not know. Whether by a sudden contract with sobriety, made in a hospital emergency room, or the result of something less apocalyptic—all I do know is that I lacked a necessary defense against the world and could not—cannot—endure it.

THE PHANTOM: Consider what it means to have been shut away in a cell beneath the opera house—there to be subjected to torments unknown even by the damned, whose chief desire is to die. Like them to pray daily to be dead and to curse God at finding oneself yet alive; to say endless rosaries of suffering and to endure savage martyrdoms; to undergo incomparable mortifications and to invent anew the theorems of annihilation and remain, in spite of all, caged inside one's own hated self—hated because it insists on sovereignty over death and will not, will not even in hell's fifth cellar, let go of life! Think further of this same animal (for he cannot be said any longer to be a man) cornered by walls, which to gnaw on is to break even rats' teeth, released into the open air at last, only to be delivered into another hell—a flowery, tropical vacation hell where all that is rots and rot is all there is. They set me down among lepers and the mad and would have fed my corpse to shark or crocodile or the accommodating mire! Devil's Island. No place more aptly named! No place in the history of torment better equipped to hollow out a man and fill the cavity with gall! Having suffered this (you cannot know all that "this" entails) and having borne it, or not borne it, accompanied by such a disfigurement as mine—do you wonder I am cruel, that I can be moved swiftly to murder? Wonder, instead, how I could not be otherwise. I ought to be dead, wanting nothing else; but denied that balm and deliverance, I am and can be no other than a malignant rage.

Unlike the Phantom, I am not disfigured, deformed, or solitary. At least in none of the visible dimensions. I am of ordinary appearance and possessed of a wife, two grown children, and a sufficiency of friends (meaning enough to appease a small appetite for society but not so many as to make writing impossible). I am, as I said, embarrassed by the presence of others outside that little circle of intimate relations; racked by self-consciousness; encumbered by the obligation to converse with strangers so as not to be considered strange. The truth is, I wish to be thought of not at all—neither looked at nor discussed, nor weighed and found wanting. I wish to be invisible like him, like the Phantom, and to be left alone to do my work. We are creative men, whose joy is only in creation; both bedeviled by an unopposable need to invent forms. His genius was to have designed a structure (the labyrinthine cellars beneath the opera house) that concealed him and modeled his unconscious mind. (If the mollusk has a mind, might not its thoughts be deduced from the topology of its shell?) My intention in these pages is to follow the Phantom's example (and also, perhaps, the mollusk's): to devise a form in which I can disappear.

THE PHANTOM: I might have been content to remain as I am, where I am, if it were not for ambition, which gnaws me, and love in which I burn—skin, hair on fire, eyes scalded, a human torch not to be put out even in death. I might have been content to be master of all I survey, lord of the underworld, making a royal progress daily through the five cellars of hell, whose rooms and passages multiply in a lunatic arithmetic beyond the knowledge of their architect. There are worse than I put away, deformities greater than mine shut up in more grievous confinement than this. I tell you I would have been content—more than content: happy!—to have found myself in this meager granary provided, nevertheless, with enough to nourish dreaming. Does a rat not dream even of its sewer, and is not the sewer, being all there is, not a sufficient condition for a rat's happiness? Or have you never given thought to a rat—you in your wider, sunnier world? The companionable rats dream as do I—of walls of brick, stone, and earth, of the black lake that laps the foundations of the Paris opera house and makes a not unmusical sound in the sluices like the flushing all at once of a thousand water closets. And do you think that rats do not apprehend music of a mineral modality, whose timbre is an oozing and whose dynamic sotto voce? I have seen them transfixed by sounds at audition's furthermost limit, like Elijah in his cave by the voice of the Almighty. And if a rat can be so enthralled, how much, then, the man who hears for the first time an angelic voice? And if that man is I and the voice that of Christine Daaé—how can I do otherwise than burn?

4.

Charles Garnier designed the visible Opéra National de Paris. By "visible," I mean that which can be observed either above the street or below it. The Phantom's engagement with the complex structure is illusory. Allow me to retract: The Phantom's design for the tortuous cellars beneath the fifteen-thousand-square-meter building is real insofar as it was conceived in the imagination of Gaston Leroux, author of *The Phantom of the Opera*, and of its malevolent central figure. To say that Garnier's subterranean construction is "more real" (or less) than Leroux's (or the Phantom's) is to become embroiled in a philosophical controversy for which I am not trained. (Leroux's opera house does stand and impresses us greatly.) I am equally unwilling to conduct a stale inquiry into fiction as a valid model—or even a substitute for—the verifiable realm of fact. Suffice it to say that Garnier created his opera house in a traditional Italian style inspired by the Grand Théâtre in Bordeaux, built by Victor Louis in 1780, and by the Italian and French villas of the seventeenth and eighteenth centuries. Leroux's was influenced by Garnier's, and the Phantom's cellars by the topology of his own imagination, his disfigurement, or both.

Two events (one geological, the other political) impeded the building's construction: discovery of a lake far below the building site and the 1870 Franco-Prussian War, with the ensuing siege and reduction of the Paris Commune. The latter not only halted construction but resulted in the Phantom's incarceration in the fifth cellar. Time emptied the dungeons of their prisoners and rid them of the tangible apparatus of torture. (They continued in the Phantom's mind.) Engineering raised a massive concrete well to carry the opera's immense stage and fly tower and flooded the well to counter the pressure of the underground lake (thus, overcoming the geological impediment). The Black Lake, as it is called by Leroux, on which the opera's stage can be said to "float," is—for me—the novel's principal topographical feature. Indeed, my interest in the opera house's architecture centers not on Garnier's grandiose achievement aboveground but on the Phantom's cellars (or Leroux's, if you insist on making the usual distinction between a novelist and his character. Both men having been architects of an identical space, I do not—in this case—make the distinction). In fact, my optimism concerning my relocation to the cellars lies here: If Leroux could build his underground out of nothing but words and attribute its design to his character the Phantom, I, too, can build the cellar in my own century and with my own words, out of my own nothing. And in building it, I will become—like the Phantom—a character inside it.

THE PHANTOM: Lately I feel the presence of an interloper. At first I believed it was the Persian, who lurks in the opera's dim corners to spy on me. Or Christine's lover, Raoul, or his brother, Philippe, the comte de Chagny. Or the secret policeman—or someone employed by the opera's managers after I had purloined their wine and left them my ultimatum regarding Christine and the fate of La Carlotta, should she fail to yield to her young rival the role of Margarita. If my threats are not taken seriously, let the catastrophe be on their heads! How can they fail to prefer Christine, whose reach, tone, clarity, and declamatory power are superior to Carlotta's? Who better than I can judge her absolute authority of voice? Not these vermin! Christine is an object of constant obsession. The desideratum. My devotion to her voice, her career, and to her sweet self is single-minded. And yet . . . something there is that gets into my mind of late—interfering and disturbing. The voice of a man—not sweet, not melodious, not even French—whose quality is a querulousness I consider inane. What is his tribulation against my own? I feel him hunting the margins of my story, probing for a way inside.

5.

From his apartments in the fifth cellar, the Phantom can enter, by means of subterranean ways and secret passages, rooms in the opera house itself. He comes and goes, freely and undetected, through panels cunningly concealed in the wainscoting, trapdoors, and the full-length mirrors in the performers' dressing rooms. He persuades Christine Daaé to follow him below by passing from her room's mirror to one of the two mirrors in his. (I am inclined toward Professor Lishkovitz's view that the passage is psychical and that the mirror in which the Phantom gazes—and draws Christine to himself by his gaze—will determine whether he appears to her as a sentimental lover enamored of her voice or as a homicidal maniac incited by desire.)

Yesterday, my therapist wondered—provocatively—if I could be content, hiding within an "edifice of prose," were I no longer able to write and, should I be able, to what degree my happiness depends on publishing the results. I must admit that my happiness is dependent on both conditions being met and am optimistic that a way will be found for me to do both, as a fiction within a fiction. One can write anywhere! Publishing is, of course, problematic. Within all but the most scrupulously objective narratives, however, there is a general telepathy; my hope is that I can use it to "send" my work out into the world. I will look to the Phantom for whatever technical facilities may be required. He will not deny me what services he is, by nature, equipped to provide!

A fiction within a fiction? Surely I can be nothing else, once ensconced inside the Phantom's story! Unless being conscious of my self (of my being Norman Lock) is sufficient to satisfy actuality's minimum requirement; in which case, I will be an actual presence inside Leroux's own edifice of prose. (In what way and to what degree I may alter Leroux's original structure by the "spaciousness" of an existence no matter how seemingly cramped, I leave to poststructuralists.) I assume—I can do nothing else!—that I will receive by the grace and power of the imagination (the Phantom's or those who will subsequently encounter me in reading or by other mechanical means) raiment—that is to say, flesh or flesh's simulacrum. I shall not be a ghost. Whether I will, in time, be bewitched by Christine (if we do indeed come to inhabit the same story), whether or not I will, like Erik, love her and, unlike him, consummate that love—all this remains to be seen. I do believe that the present inadequacies of my personality will vanish when I have disappeared inside *The Phantom of the Opera.*

THE PHANTOM: Ambition, too, goads me. The gala when Christine, as Margarita, swept La Carlotta into the dustbin, in the prison scene and final trio of *Faust*—that night Gounod conducted his "Funeral March of a Marionette," Reyer his overture to *Siguar,* Massenet a Hungarian march, Guiraud his *Carnaval,* Saint-Saëns the *Danse Macabre* and a "Reverie orientale." I ought to have been among them, smirking at the mob as it surged forward on the ballet foyer! If I were not . . . unprepossessing. Ha! I exceed all definitions of ugliness!

Quasimodo's is nothing next to mine. Esmeralda would not have given *me* water. I am grotesque like the opera gargoyles in whose company I indulge in nocturnal rages at the City of Light. I am more animal than man, more mineral than animal—scoria, slag of the Beast's foundry, lava of Vesuvius, cinder of a burnt offering. To see me is to be turned to salt, to stone; is to gain admission in an instant to Charenton Asylum; is to be struck deaf, dumb, and blind. God knows I am repulsive! But if I were not, my genius would be proclaimed, my music famous, my face adored. I would be illustrious, and Christine would not have swooned at the sight of me.

6.

To enter Leroux's edifice, I must first become prose. Only as words can matter and its energy exist among other words. I sometimes think that when the last word is spoken or set down—at the moment utterance ceases—all that is will vanish, will become again the aboriginal thought. The film will run in reverse through recorded and unrecorded time all the way back to Nothing. (I believe that a case can be made for everything that is as being only words—knowable by words, invoked by words, and created by them. But I will not make it here.) And when I have entered *The Phantom of the Opera,* will I—like Wells's Martian machines—perish by a germ endemic to melodrama, or will I—a foreign body—carry off the Phantom?

The fifth cellar incorporates the principal features of an eighteenth-century pleasure park. There are a room of mirrors, a chamber of horrors, a maze, and boats moving silently through a flooded grotto. None was in Garnier's original plan or in Leroux's projection of it onto the fictional space of *The Phantom of the Opera.* These are elaborations made by the Phantom, who as a child was captivated by holiday visits to the Tivoli Gardens in Copenhagen and the Prater in Vienna. (Theories of the novel aside, you must grant me that a character will sometimes take on a life of its own, seemingly independent of its author's conception. What else can we mean when, in the presence of remarkable fiction, we say that a character lives and continues to do so after we have closed the book on its recounted history? And to live is to change, at least subtly, the surrounding world.) Reminded of my own novel *The Long Rowing unto Morning*, I thought that, in the submerged channels spreading like black lace beneath the opera house, I might insert myself—as prose—into Leroux's novel and the Phantom's actualization of it. I have already constructed—in words—an eminently stable and watertight boat and demonstrated—in words—that I know how to set it going. I will, then, row my way inside the edifice! It requires only a single sentence, ostensibly written by Leroux (and rendered into English)—perhaps in an early draft of his novel, suppressed or forgotten until now: *The oar blades dipped and rose, scattering garnets and rubies in profusion in the fitful light of* flambeaux, *which, at regular intervals, relieved the grotto's otherwise-absolute dark, as M. Lock entered the Black Lake.*

THE PHANTOM: The intuition that a person extraneous, adventitious, alien to my world has been probing the margin for a way inside is now a certainty. He has come by boat: I have heard the oarlocks creak in the brick vaults and the rats' alarms. I am used to intruders and know how to scare them off. Those that won't scare, I murder. As architect of the mise-en-scène, the advantage is always mine. But against this infiltrator, I have none; he knows what I know—every secret passage, trapdoor, and sluice. If all that I know can be told in words, he has imagined them. If every brick is a word and every drape in whose folds I can hide is, too, those words are also his. I am bound to him and he to me by a paradigm established elsewhere. Call it my sentence. My only hope to escape it is to act arbitrarily. Only in the principle by which rooms and corridors propagate and mirrors unfold unplotted spaces can I be free of an invisible dependency. The Persian, Raoul, Philippe, the secret policeman, the opera's managers and minions—they want to put an end to my incursions into the upper world, from which I am banished. They want to be rid of me as you would a rat. I understand them—their repugnance. But this other who inserts himself into my realm—what can he want? Certainly he does not mean to befriend me, obtain for me justice, or restore me to the podiums of the great orchestras of Europe. He can have come only to harm me, kill me, expel me from the only place in which I exist: this story, these words of Gaston Leroux's, surrounding and defining me, which I enlarge according to my capacity and will. Do not ask how I know! I do as the sluice does the pressure of water or the lightning rod the electric current's heat. I know it the way an actor would if something not written were introduced into the play. My antagonist is rowing upon the Black Lake. I might release the pent water that acts as counterpressure to the lake on which the stage floats; it would be a second Deluge. Would he drown in his boat, or has he foreseen my hands on the massive valves? I ought to put on my cloak and hurry into the passages to seek in the opera's foundations that part built according to an irrational design. If I could chance upon a moment of expansion when time stretches like an elastic, the cramped view enlarges to a panorama, the space between atoms yawns—if I could only! But I am weary suddenly of the game in which I have been made to play. Leroux! It would have been better had I been left ignorant of my author; better yet if I had never been. I wish you had been run down by a carriage, carried off by fever, or had written instead about the man in the moon! I feel the other's presence like a microbe and am made sick to death! I will not join the rats tumbling pell-mell over the Turkish carpet. I will play Bach—*Passacaglia and Fugue*—and wait.

7.

I tie the boat to a heavy ring and climb stone stairs slippery with ooze. Light from a pair of smoking torches trembles on the black water. The air is foul. A rat climbs over another, then falls into the sluice. On the other side of the iron door, the Phantom plays Bach's *Passacaglia and Fugue*. The playing is manic, portentous, doom-cadenced; and I am aware suddenly of what I risk by my intercalation—the danger in hoping to lose myself in another's story. But my abnegation has been thorough; already I have acquired something of a character's insubstantiality. The Phantom has his cloak, his mask, and his scars with which to imprint another's memory, while my face in its bland ordinariness has nothing to commend it. I had intended to keep out of his way, haunting the opera house's labyrinthine passages, listening to music and silence. But the story's magnetism drew me at once to its center. The boat fetched up at the Phantom's door.

Anna Karenina, Marguerite Gautier, Lear, Kurtz—what was death for them? Is there pain in the words of pain's depiction? Is death no more than an end to words? If I should, while writing this sentence, stop, never to begin again, is that death? When the Phantom kills me (he must, for there is room only for a single tragic destiny in Leroux's conception), will I become the word *corpse*, left to lie where it fell upon the page like cigar ash, which the reader in his headlong flight will forget? Or will I simply enter the white space where writing does not exist? And is this not what I wanted?

THE PHANTOM: By a moment's inattention, I may unbind myself from the one on the other side of the door, from Leroux's nightmare, from the rack of my special destiny. It needs only art—a momentary bending of its rigor. If in the twentieth and final variation I transpose certain of the notes or depart briefly the key signature or linger overlong on the pedal, it will be enough, perhaps, to disenthrall me. By error I may escape my assassin and the mob whose own destiny it is to harry me tonight into the Seine! I may escape, as well, Christine, who is bound to the bed of my desire by Leroux's rope and whose mouth is muted with his handkerchief. I will rise from the organ, which will have ceased intoning another's music, put on my cloak and hat, and walk out of the opera house into a soft Parisian night—handsome and free of the thralldom of art. And should a reader turn anew to Leroux's story, it will not be I buried beneath the opera house, but another delivered up according to his sentence.

Tango in Amsterdam

For Marco & Marian

It is raining. I am tempted to elaborate, to compose a striking literary trope. So that you will know—know with whom you are dealing. What quality of author. But I like this, a plain statement such as anyone might make and does make, standing in the doorway of his house and, perhaps, putting his hand outside to confirm the truth of his eyes: *It is raining.* In Holland—a land famous for dampness as much as for tulips, which are at the moment bending, if not actually bent, beneath it. The Dutch rain. Which is falling, falling on the blades of charming windmills, on the Zuiderzee, and on B. Street, too, where Karin is at this moment worrying about Peter. Where is Peter, the wandering husband, tennis player, and actor in minor roles in the Dutch film industry?

He is in Cannes, walking the streets beneath the fine, high, blue Mediterranean sky. This is the Côte d'Azur after all! Peter is walking with the director of *Tango in Amsterdam*, an exciting new film; and they are wondering, each to himself, how they will act if it should receive this year's Palme d'Or. Peter hopes he will be composed. He may, he thinks, appear to be even a little weary of celebrity, although—to tell the truth—Peter's role in *Tango* is small. He plays a man in a bar who puts his hand on the breasts of a beautiful woman of the demimonde. One breast—but it is a firm and shapely one. Peter was secretly thrilled to be touching it, although he could not, of course, show it. Instead, he pretended to be weary of the world and its dissipations. A jaded and phlegmatic Dutchman. That is how I shall behave when we are awarded the Palme d'Or, he thinks to himself. I shall remember how it was I pretended to feel when I touched Margot's breast.

He thinks again of the secret pleasure he felt—in his very loins!—when he did touch it. And then he is ashamed, remembering Karin in Papendrecht—how sad she must be to hear the rain on the roof of their little house. For Peter knows of the torrents descending on his homeland.

Karin is sad. The rain rains. Peter walks up and down, looking in the windows of the chic shops of Cannes and dreaming of secret pleasures, of applause. And I? I sit and write yet another story of my friends Peter and Karin K., who are real and imaginary at the same time.

And Maus the dog?

Maus hides under the bed because of the rain beating on the roof and because he knows what neither Peter nor Karin does (nor I myself knew until a moment ago): The Merwede is rising! It is about to breach the banks, spill into the streets of Papendrecht, and, within hours, submerge the town to its second-story windowsills!

How is it that Maus knows before I, the author, do? I do not have an answer for you; but I suspect that there are areas of consciousness, even that attributed to dogs, which withhold themselves from my interventions in the world. Yes, yes!— Maus is a creature of my imagination; but he is also a real dog that barks at the postman, likes to gnaw at Peter's boot, and will, when alarmed by presentiments beyond my ken, crawl under the bed.

But for the moment, Karin and Maus are safe while the riverbank holds its own against the turbid Merwede—a river, by the way, that begins as the Waal and ends in the Noordzee at Hollands Diep. It is a gray river, Karin says, except at the beltmill, when it becomes "an exotic, deep blue."

Why not, dear reader (I do not know if you are a gentle one)—why not learn some geography while you are beguiling yourself with this story, which I shall call "Tango in Amsterdam," although it has nothing to do with dancing or Amsterdam. Are you beguiled? How should I know? I can read the minds of only Peter and his Karin and also of their Maus—and with only partial success because of my limited omniscience. Yours, reader, is entirely unknown to me.

Karin stops worrying about Peter long enough to fall asleep. The rain—the rain—the rain! It makes one sleepy.

Would you care to know what it is that Karin is dreaming? Windmills.

Always, she dreams of windmills when it is raining.

I have written already of Karin's fascination for them, these Dutch icons. You know it has been her dream and Peter's (and—for all I know—Maus's) to live in a refurbished windmill. People do do that, in the same way that people live in train stations, schoolhouses, and churches once the buildings have lost their original intention. This is interesting, I think: how something can stop meaning one thing and start meaning something else entirely.

Like *Tango in Amsterdam*—a real Dutch film.

I would like a drink but decide against it for now. Today is my birthday. I think I can be forgiven this personal note in a narrative that is, admittedly, slow to develop. I am today fifty-two and am thinking maybe it is time to do something about my drinking. Oh, gin—I could compose an ode on you, especially Bombay or the excellent blue Sapphire! Beer is also good, if not for the body, for the soul, the spirituality of man, which is constituted, in part, of Fuggle hops—of this I am sure!

On! as Beckett would say, exhorting his characters as they flounder in a swamp or mud or in their own mired minds.

Mud. The Merwede has breached the banks of Papendrecht and is now turning its paths to mud. See how the water swells and sweeps its wet hem across the soccer field where Peter will sometimes kick the ball to Maus on a summer morning.

Maus. Is he still under the bed, do you think?

No, he has gone to the bedroom window to bark at the rising water.

Woef, woef! Wat doet dat water in de straat? Kijk daar, Karin, een eend zwemt voorbij!—which is Dutch for "Woof, woof! What is all that water doing in the street? And look there, Karin, a duck swimming by!"

Don't be surprised that Maus understands that the proper place for ducks is in the pond or in the canal but—please!— not in the middle of B. Street. He is an unusually intelligent animal.

(Have you never heard of the Dutchman Jakob Boehme? He believed that Adam spoke to Eve, when he spoke to her at all, in the language of animals. Boehme wrote that we will speak this "natural" language once again when we enter Paradise. When we no longer have need of words. I think this language may well sound like Dutch to unaccustomed ears.)

Karin's anxiety has been mounting with the water. She remembers well the stories her mother used to tell her of the terrible flood of '53, which wrought so much devastation in the Netherlands. But I must leave Karin a moment to answer an e-mail from a man perplexed in Pasadena:

What do you mean by writing such things as these Peter and Karin stories? (Stories?!) They are even worse than your so-called histories of the imagination. They eat themselves up as they go along, like a snake that swallows its own tail. For your own good, pal— give it up!

Indignant in Pasadena

Dear Pasadena:

What you say is true: My stories do devour themselves on the way to being told. They do so to achieve a kind of lightness—the lightness praised by Calvino and also by Ionesco, who wrote: "I feel I am invaded by heavy forces." I am worn out by gravity. Or maybe it is that I do not know yet how to tell a story?

N.

Dear N:

If you don't know how to write stories, you have no business taking up a person's valuable time. I'm surprised you got this crap into a magazine in the first place. Who'd you have to pay off and how much?

Infuriated in Pasadena

Infuriated:

Perhaps if I explain myself: I am, in these stories, proposing myself as a subject of fiction in the same way that Peter and Karin are both real and fictional. Again, in the interests of weakening the gravitational attraction that binds me to what I am.

N.

Nuts to you, Lock! And who wants to hear about your drinking problem!

Pissed off in Pasadena

Instead of e-mails—let's make them telegrams to delay the narrative time so that Karin may devise a plan to escape her bedroom, now that the river has surrounded her little house.

Singing telegrams delivered by a charming chanteuse named Amelia, who is studying opera at the university. She sings sweetly to my ears. (Sorry, I have not the skill to reproduce the melody.) She is attractive in her official Western Union uniform but refuses each time to have a drink with me. An honest young woman, although I am disappointed she is not so convivial as she is lyrical. It is better not to drink alone, as anyone will tell you.

Karin has once more fallen asleep.

"Wake up, Karin!" I shout, as if my unaided voice could make itself heard from New Jersey!

Wake up, Karin! I type peremptorily.

She opens an eye, then closes it, preferring unconsciousness to the experience of drowning.

Maus begins to lick Karin's face. And she wakes.

Outside, the sky is gray. The water is gray. The houses are gray. It is grayly raining. Gray is the color of herring, which the Dutch love to eat. The duck was nicely yellow but is nowhere now to be seen. The telegrams were blue. E-mails are colorless and inhuman. I wonder if one day there will be no more stamps in the world, when things are finally and completely electronic? Think of the loss—not only to philatelists but also to the ordinary man or woman who is charmed by the colors and images on stamps. I have a number of lovely ones from Holland, snipped from envelopes bearing greetings and little gifts from my two friends there.

(What now? I wish, for once, something could happen on its own!)

Karin takes a telescope from her desk and, standing by the window, examines the submerged streets and the rooftops of Papendrecht. Thank you, Karin, for showing initiative! And thank you, Hans Lippershey, the Dutchman who invented the instrument in 1608. Where would Galileo have been without the Dutch? A serious consideration! The Dutch have done much for civilization besides: such as putting mayonnaise on french fries.

Can Karin see the sea from her window? I don't know. But if she could, she would see Peter sailing bravely to rescue his little family in a yacht stolen from the quay at Cannes.

Ha, dear reader, I have played an excellent trick on you, I think! While I have been going on, digressively, about the Dutch and their place in history, the story has been advancing! Digression is the soul of my art.

On the Riviera, Peter held a gun to the captain's head and was fully prepared to use it. But it was unnecessary; for while studying philosophy at the Sorbonne, the captain had written his dissertation on Erasmus and wished to visit Rotterdam— a short train ride from Papendrecht. He never wanted to be the captain of a yacht but was compelled by circumstances. He had gotten a linguist pregnant in the spring of 1968, when all the world went mad. But that—as they like to say—is another story. (What isn't?)

Let me describe, instead, the coming of Peter across the Polderland, now flooded by the North Sea.

The dark sea is etched by wind. The yacht is knotted up in waves as it plunges from one sliding trough to the next. The salt sea scours its decks, which are empty in this storm; the elemental wind lashes the yacht's bright pennants. Birds wheel in the confused air, screeching a guttural Dutch translation of a poem by Edgar Allan Poe. (Well, why not!) Titanic forces are loosed upon the world. It is all very thrilling; and despite his anxiety, Peter is happy to be in it. He stands in the pilothouse, beside the captain. They are singing—some song or other. A sea shanty, "I'm Ahab the Sailor Man!"—some lively maritime air. They are snug inside peacoats and wear, for preference, sailor's hats in the French style, with red pom-poms stuck on the top. Peter and the captain have grown by several feet since leaving Gibraltar, to achieve heroic stature. Their penises, which are in the classical mold, bring to mind Michelangelo's *David;* but they remain limply buttoned up inside their naval bell-bottoms. Peter and the captain are friends, but not overly friendly. (I resist the impulse to have them dance a tango in the pilothouse, however much a bravura moment it might be.)

Karin spies the yacht now through her telescope. She paints a picture of it in watercolors. (She, too, is an artist and must grapple with her art, no matter how dire the straits.) It turns out to be a fine picture and will, in years to come, hang in the Papendrecht town hall to commemorate this dramatic event in the unofficial history of the nation.

And Maus?

Running in circles round the room in anticipation of rescue and of reunion with his beloved master, Peter.

The yacht stops outside the house. The anchor drops onto

Love Among the Particles & Other Stories

the street below. Peter breaks a window with an ax and climbs into the bedroom. He embraces Karin and pats Maus affectionately on the head. Thus Odysseus, returning at last to his Penelope, must have greeted his dog before slaying the suitors. Peter wonders if there is time to make love to Karin, who has never looked so desirable. He feels—how does Eliot phrase it in *The Waste Land?* "Memory and desire, stirring / Dull roots with spring rain. . . ." Yes, Peter feels his own dull root now stirring inside his bell-bottoms. But no—he decides against it. For the river has risen to an inch below the windowsill; and the captain, who has shut his eyes shyly, is honking his yacht horn!

Hurry!

Peter hands Karin over to the captain, and Maus, in his arms, jumps onto the yacht as the house begins to uproot, like a tooth loosening in the gum.

No, let's leave the house where it is. Let us, in fact, leave all the houses intact so that when the Merwede recedes next week, their owners can return and live in them again without so much as a muddy rug to mark the river's ever having left its bed. Not one teacup shall have been broken during this latest intervention, not one antimacassar soiled—this, good people of Papendrecht, I promise you!

Peter and Karin are cruising to the Canaries, those "Fortunate Islands" ravaged by the Dutch in 1599. The Dutch couple is below, in the master stateroom, folded together sweetly, while the Indian Ocean drums the hull. Maus sits at the captain's feet as he steers for Tenerife. A parrot sits companionably on the captain's shoulder. All is as it ought to be. The sky, yellow like an egg yolk, leaks into the water rimming the horizon—the water strewn with orchids, red and blue. Big beams of orange light fall against the yacht. The yacht flies a flag emblazoned with the Palme d'Or. The parrot speaks Parrot; the captain sings; Peter and Karin kiss and cuddle; Maus hopes there will be a Canary Island bitch to keep him company.

I turn off the machine and go upstairs in search of my wife to see what comfort we might offer each other in the gathering New Jersey dusk. Whether we might not speak a little the sensual language admired by Jakob Boehme. And should Helen withhold comfort (for reasons known only to women), there are gin and a tin of herring to see me into night. And beyond that, who can say?

The Brothers Ascend

For Kathryn Rantala

1.

Finally, we went to Madame Sosostris, the clairvoyante, because of the darkness—the darkness that was now general over Dayton. We were anxious, of course, and mystified as to its meaning. Its meaning escaped us, although we pondered it ceaselessly—in private and in public assemblies at the town hall.

"I'm sorry," she said, spreading her hands in helplessness. "The glass is clouded."

"Ah!" we cried in our desperate desire to know.

"I'm sorry," she repeated sincerely. Having fled Tereu in panic, she had made Dayton her home; and the darkness that lay like a hand upon the heart unnerved her, too.

She covered the glass with a purple cloth.

"Would you like tea?" she asked gravely, embarrassed at having failed us.

We shook our heads and trooped out the door, pausing on the sidewalk a moment to tip our hats to Wilbur and Orville, who did not tip theirs in return or make any other sign of acknowledgment. We were not offended, knowing their minds were preoccupied with gravity.

Buttoned up in long black coats, Wilbur and Orville walked past, derbies plumb on their high foreheads, behind which filaments of science and intuition knit into shining ideas, which could not, however, illuminate the unnatural night. Inseparable, the brothers communed with each other silently, in an immaculate exchange of thought.

Some boys appeared, offering to sell us torches. Most of our deputation bought them; but I would not, preferring the dark as I made my way down Dayton's empty streets, which bristled with iron railings and wooden palings, to Stella's.

2.

"I'm afraid," Stella whispered in the darkness of her little room.

"It is nothing," I said, unbuttoning my shirt.

"Nothing?"

"A phenomenon—meteorological or hysterical; nothing more."

"Still . . ."

The ellipsis was audible; it plashed upon the silence. In it I detected something other than her uncertainty. I detected her dread. Not of the darkness but of what it augured. I sought to calm her—sought her hand and stroked it.

"Night—real or imagined," I said soothingly. "Only night."

"Night that never ends." She shuddered.

"An endless time in which to make love," I said, loosening her hair.

"But the sun doesn't rise!"

"Perhaps it does, but we can't see it rise."

My hands trembled at her blouse's buttons.

"But why?"

I shrugged—not knowing, not caring at the moment. Wanting her. Letting my hands behave rudely. Their fingers made a kind of twittering song inside her chemise. The fingers of the hands: They had their way. There was nothing I could do to stop them.

"I'll bet the brothers know," she said, sulking.

Perhaps.

"Wilbur and Orville . . . Orville and Wilbur," she continued uncertainly.

They were, after all, indistinguishable.

"Ask them!" she entreated.

"The brothers are busy."

"Do you believe in the aeroplane?" she asked after a moment's hesitation.

I wasn't sure. I cranked the gramophone.

How lovely the music coming out of the dark! And the woman in it!

3.

Shall I describe to you Dayton? An American town, in southwest Ohio, where the Great Miami River joins the Stillwater. There, the brothers had a bicycle shop. Once I had worked for them, oiling chains and tightening spokes. Dayton had been a pleasant town dreaming slow river dreams in unending sunshine. Before the sun disappeared from the sky. I rode now on my Wright brothers bicycle to the river, to listen to it sing among the stones, and saw Huck and Jim fetch up in a raft.

You shout, Liar! Theirs was the Mississippi River, which is not in Ohio!

I reply imperturbably, Maybe not in any geography book. But the Mississippi that runs through mythology, the Mississippi of the imagination—that river lapped the green shores of Dayton. Was beaten into foam by the brightly painted paddle wheels of steamers. Was—after years of naïve sunshine—surprised at the sudden dark.

You say, Was?

I reply, Until what was hiding in the night, what is meant by the dark, jumped out to scare us beyond hope. *Was*—I repeat—and is, alas, no longer.

"Hello," said Huck.

"Hello," said Jim.

"Hello," I said, turning my bicycle lantern on them. "How is the journey?"

"Finished," said Huck, coming up the bank toward me. "Is it always so dark?"

"Lately."

"Dark as the inside of Becky's cave. Dark as old Jim here."

Jim joined us in the little spill of light. Like Huck, he had grown noticeably older with each step taken away from the river. The river, which lay down in its bed like a man sunk in dreams of a woman glimpsed once on the street, a woman whose head he had not the power to turn.

"It's technically unexplainable," I said, gesturing at the dark all around us; "though personally, I think it signifies the end of childhood."

"The end of innocence at any rate," said Jim. He lit a cigar, smoked a moment in silent contemplation of its own radiant end, then continued: "The mythology of light has, in this place, bumped up against the mythology of darkness—and sunk."

Huck whistled in admiration. "I never knowed you to be so eloquent, Jim!"

"I'm free now," said Jim. He said it simply, but I heard the pleasure he took in saying it. A man free of mythic obligations. A man free of lies.

He tossed his cigar into the invisible river. We listened to its quick hiss.

"I'm glad to be off the river," said Jim. "I'd like to see what the night has in store for me."

"I would like a beer, a bath, and a woman," said Huck, whose thoughts were now centered on Dayton and the actualization of his grown-up desires.

"I would like one of these curious two-wheeled contraptions," said Jim.

"You can have mine. I can always get another; bicycles are easily gotten in Dayton."

Jim mounted the machine and, in an instant, was sailing down the levee into obscurity—that of a man savoring his release from fame.

You ask skeptically, How, since he had never before ridden a bicycle?

I reply, Some of his mythic life must have clung to him still.

I watched the bicycle disappear and then the lamp, like a firefly extinguished by the dark.

4.

Wilbur and Orville walked to the river, turned, and walked back to town. Deep in thought, they did not see Huck pass on his way to the Dayton Arms Hotel, Jim and his bicycle vanish down the levee, or the Mississippi turn back into the ordinary Great Miami River, which has never, to my knowledge, figured in myth.

"The brothers are thinking," I said to the weeping willow whose long whips brushed my face. "It is somehow important that they do."

A night bird shook itself free of the branches.

I remembered Stella's hair—how, after I had unpinned it, she would shake it down over her lovely white shoulders.

5.

A woman stepped from an alley and accosted me: "Do you know Wilbur and Orville Wright?"

"In Dayton who does not?" I replied truthfully.

She laid a gloved hand on my sleeve. I lit a match to see her better and saw that she was beautiful.

"I'm a stranger in town," she said. "My name is Mata Hari."

I apologized for the universal murk.

"Oh, I adore the dark! One can move about so freely."

"Yes," I said, and thought of Stella, who waited anxiously for me.

"I want to speak to them."

"Them?"

"Wilbur and Orville . . . Orville and Wilbur."

"That is difficult," I said, shaking my head.

And then, as if ready to prove me right, the brothers passed along the opposite sidewalk. They were, of course, silent.

Mata Hari stepped toward them. They instantly changed direction, as birds do, with unerring precision and unity of mind, and vanished into a side street, their hands deep in the pockets of their overcoats, their heads bowed in thought. Whether their evasion was an act of will or a tropism protecting fragile thought from fatal interruption is impossible to tell.

"The brothers are absorbed by their invention," I said to mitigate the effect of their discourtesy.

"They are a strange pair."

"They are geniuses."

"But it is essential that I talk to them about their aeroplane."

"Do you believe in the aeroplane?" I asked.

6.

At that time in Dayton, belief in the aeroplane was very like belief in God: An ungainsayable article of faith for most, it was denied by many. As the weeks passed, all concluded that the existence (or nonexistence) of the aeroplane was in some way linked to the darkness that had be fallen us.

"It's a punishment because of our trespass on divine pre rogative," the righteous declared.

"Because of your benighted attitude toward progress!" the enlightened maintained.

They were the believers. Those who doubted the existence of the aeroplane ascribed the darkness to their "despair of ever believing in anything that is not verifiable." They were desper ate for amazement, but black was the color of their thought.

We urged them to make the leap beyond reason—to take the jump, as it was called—but they refused, tearfully, and would not join us in transcendence.

Schism for the first time beset our town, enacted outside the brothers' house by contentious ideologues demanding they be shown "the evidence," so that the aeroplane might be affirmed or negated once and for all.

Increasingly, I feared for the brothers' safety.

7.

"Where have you been?" asked Stella.

"I lost my bicycle and had to walk home."

"I dreamed you were lost in a maze of dark streets and alleys. I could see you but not the way out."

"My desire is like a thread from your body to mine. I would have only to follow it."

She enclosed me in an embrace, which excluded darkness, nightmare—everything that lay in wait outside her room.

"I dreamed I went outside and walked to the brothers' house at the top of the hill," she recited in the remotest of voices. "I walked so very slowly—my legs like iron!—weighed down by gravity. Their front door opened. I went in. The room was empty; the furniture, shrouded against the dust. Trapezes of dust swung from the ceiling. Everything was silent. And then the brothers floated down a great staircase in their long coats and derby hats, floated down, shoulder-to-shoulder, and came to rest lightly on the landing. They cocked their heads at me looking, looking at me with their heads cocked like a pair of owls. I told them you were lost, in Dayton, and could not find your way to me. I wanted them to find you in their aeroplane. It was on the lawn—a beautiful machine! Its wings painted yellow and blue—I saw the bright colors no matter the darkness. Orville went outside and sat in it—a big grandfather's clock lying open in the grass. I shut my eyes a moment, then looked once more into the ticking dark at Orville—or maybe it was Wilbur—sitting now in a coffin. Then I woke with the sheet twisted round me and the pillow wet."

"So you do believe in the aeroplane?"

"In my dream, it was real."

She stood at the window with her hand on the heavy curtains, as if to open them and look outside, a thing she had not done since night descended on Dayton. (And now it was always night, and we did not know when to sleep.) She stood at the window for a long time, but in the end she kept the curtains closed.

"Won't you let me take you outside today?" I asked softly.

She shook her head. The gas bloomed above the mantel; a bluish yellow light throbbed. I touched her thickly plaited hair and remembered how I had climbed it into the very lap of desire.

I cranked the gramophone.

"Dance with me," I said, holding out my arms to her.

Stella danced with me in the narrow room, dreaming of Sousa's men in the band shell beside the river wrinkling with light.

You ask, incensed, How could you know her dream without her telling it!

You shout, All lies, all!

You say warily, wearily, I do not believe a word you say.

I answer you: True, I am only partially omniscient. But I have learned a thing or two about mind reading at the Institute for Psychical Research.

8.

There was a third faction in Dayton: those who believed the aeroplane to be a dream object. I, myself, was inclined toward this view.

9.

The brothers glided silently down the dark streets. Behind them, just outside their field of awareness (which was small, because of their introversion), Mata Hari skulked. And behind her stalked Huck Finn Indian-style from elm tree to alleyway.

"I'm in love with Mata Hari," he later confided in the barroom of the Dayton Arms Hotel.

"She has an unnatural interest in the brothers," I said suspiciously.

"I want to sleep with her."

"Sex may be dangerous for one who was, until recently, a mythical character."

"It's true I have no experience with women," he said after a brief silence. "I was in timeless suspension on a raft during my adolescence."

How quickly he's lost the vernacular! I thought to myself, marveling once more at civilization's transforming power.

"Find out what she wants," I urged him. "And remember, Huck: Wilbur and Orville are more important than the gratification of any one person."

"Because there are two of them?"

"Because of their influence on our possible future."

Huck drained his beer mug, wiped his foamy lips with the back of his hand, and said, "I still want to sleep with Mata Hari."

10.

"It is good to sleep with a woman," I said.

"For a man, maybe," said Stella. "Is it still night?"

"Yes."

"I think I want to kill myself."

"I wouldn't just yet," I said. "I think something is about to happen."

"What?"

"I don't know."

"I dreamed the end of the world . . ."

"It is your nerves," I said. "Nothing more."

"A flash of light. A terrible explosion. The earth lifted and was swept away in a great wind."

"Your nerves," I repeated. "A bad case of the vapors."

11.

I went to the brothers' house and knocked. No one answered. I beat on the door with the flat of my hand. I hammered on it with my fists.

"Wilbur, Orville—come out. I want to talk to you!" I shouted.

No answer.

And then I cursed the brothers—a thing no one, to my knowledge, had ever done. Heaped imprecations on them, execrated and damned them! For I was now certain that they had brought the darkness on us. Had brought dear Stella to the brink of suicide. Had brought Huck to Dayton and corrupted him.

"Orville, Wilbur—come out!" I thundered.

I went round back to the barn where they worked on their inventions. The door was locked; the windows were painted over. I listened intently. I heard my own heart beat in my ears and, from inside the barn, a hooting of owls.

I was afraid and ashamed, too, for I had loved the brothers.

A bell rang twice as a Wright brothers bicycle crunched to a halt on the driveway.

"Telegram for you, sir."

It was Horatio Alger, who doffed his cap and handed me a telegram. He shone a light so that I might read it. He was a type of ambitious young man who would make his mark.

The telegram came from H.G.

August 19

Dear N.:

Understand you are once again in the metaphysical swamp. Darkness in Dayton: It is your Black Cloud. Too much Bombay gin! Am sending T.T. to advise. He has seen the future, and it scares him. Remember me to Mrs. Willoughby should you see her again. All is forgiven.

Wells
xoxo

"Thank you, Horatio."

Pocketing the coin I had tipped him, he swung up onto his bicycle and pedaled off through a wobbling funnel of light until I could see him no more.

And who, I wondered, is T.T.?

12.

"She wants the plans of their aeroplane," said Huck. We were sitting on a divan in the parlor of what was affectionately known as "the House." "And she wants me to help her get them."

"Why?" I asked, uncoiling a feather boa from my neck, left there by Lily, the mulatto girl, a special favorite of the gentlemen who called regularly at the House.

"She's a spy," said Huck. "For the German army. I wish Tom was here; he loves skullduggery!"

"Of what possible use is an aeroplane to an army?"

And then, as if to provide us with an answer, the Time Traveler slowly materialized in the middle of the parlor, astride his fantastic machine—all gleaming dials and crystal, ivory and burnished metal.

"T. T.!" I said, remembering Wells's telegram.

"Hello!" he said, brushing his time-stained clothes with his hand. "I have a warning for you concerning the future."

"Are you with a carnival, mister?" asked an astonished Huck.

"I am the Time Traveler, lately of Mr. H. G. Wells's remarkable first novel."

He bowed his head suavely, having retained his Victorian manners despite the future's rough-and-tumble.

"He's nothing but a fiction!" sneered Huck, who seemed not at all aware of the inappropriateness of his remark.

"If one is prepared to take the long view, there is no difference between fact and fiction," reasoned Jim, who had come into the parlor. "All of us are fictions. We make each other up— we make *ourselves* up."

"What brings you back to Dayton?" I asked, surprised.

"Leaving here, it seems, is impossible." Jim sank wearily onto the divan. "I pedaled fast and furious but could not escape Dayton's irresistible gravity."

"Only the brothers can," the madam declared loyally.

"That's why I've come," said the Time Traveler, posing like a pugilist on the Turkish rug. "The brothers must withdraw their invention."

"Withdraw it?" I was growing nervous, and my head—which had to contain all this extravagant burlesque—hurt.

"Their aeroplane will evolve into a flying warship whose single discharge will raze a city: the *Enola Gay*."

"Why, that's *my* name!" the madam exclaimed.

"And that warship will evolve into far more monstrous machines." He sat, exhausted. It was getting very uncomfortable on the divan. "I have seen the end of the world. *'The sky was absolutely black.'* The darkness all about you is its foreshadowing."

Then the aeroplane does exist! And how right Stella is to fear the dark!

"What proof is there that you have visited the future?" demanded Huck.

The Time Traveler took from his pocket two withered flowers, which until that moment had been unknown on earth.

"A girl of the far-distant future, Weena, gave them to me."

Madam Gay, an amateur botanist, pronounced them "unique!" She sniffed them as if to savor the highly exotic odor of futurity. "Incomparable!"

"Will the brothers withdraw their invention?" demanded the Time Traveler.

"I suggest we adjourn to their house and ask them," Jim replied.

13.

We battered down the barn door and surprised the brothers, who were polishing the wings of their aeroplane. It shone in the gloomy barn like an iridescent insect, a dragonfly gilded with forgotten summer light—an, as yet, undiscovered specimen that had more to do with the landscape of desire and of the mind than nature. They stopped their polishing and looked at us in disbelief, chamois rags limp in their hands.

Conscious of a gross affront, I hung back in the shadows, determined that the "fictional characters" should conduct the brothers' inquisition.

"This gentleman has been on an excursion whose last stop was the end of the world," Huck began, indicating the Time Traveler. "He tells us that the only hope for the future—and the only way we'll again see daylight—is for you to withdraw your invention."

Acting for the defense, Jim objected: "An invention cannot be withdrawn any more than an idea can. Once thought, the idea exists and does so forever. Once created, the invention cannot be uncreated. So the brothers' answer—yes or no—is irrelevant to these proceedings."

Huck challenged: "If we set fire to the aeroplane, it will no longer exist."

Jim retorted, "But the brothers exist—or would you set fire to them, too?"

Huck temporized: "I'm sure it won't come to that. . . ."

Jim: "Whether you murder them or not cannot change the fact that the idea of the aeroplane is now in the world, and the world will not be rid of it —"

Huck: "—until the world explodes because of that idea!"

Jim: "There is no proven link between the aeroplane and Apocalypse!"

Huck: "We have seen Weena's flowers!"

Jim: "I don't dispute the Time Traveler's claim to have seen the end of the world, only that it is in any way the result of Wilbur and Orville's invention!"

(Silence.)

The brothers had not moved or opened their mouths to speak. They stood, shoulder-to-shoulder, chamois cloths clenched in their hands, their gazes fixed on something beyond us and the walls of the workshop. They, too, saw the future. Whether it was the Time Traveler's, I do not know: The brothers' minds were impenetrable to me.

"Will you renounce your invention?" Huck shouted, maddened by their indifference.

And they answered him: "No." That one word and no other. They would not recant.

"Though it leads to catastrophe?"

They would not.

"You can't make a man unsee what he has seen," said Jim.

"Death to them, then!" Huck shrieked.

"Death to them!" the citizens of Dayton seconded from the field outside. "So that the sun will shine once more on our fair city."

A rope was produced. A noose knotted. A rafter chosen. They would be hanged as they had lived and worked . . . in close-knit partnership.

"Stop!" Mata Hari stepped out of the shadows. Behind her, a German U-boat crew armed and guttural. "The brothers are coming with us," she announced, "to the Fatherland, in our submarine."

I wondered idly down what river the submarine had sailed into Dayton—the Great Miami or the mythical Mississippi.

Without ceremony, the brothers were taken outside— chamois, luminous with bluish yellow dust, still crumpled in their hands.

"Give us back the brothers!" the mob screamed (so that it might hang them or enthrone them in its heart again). "Wilbur and Orville . . . Orville and Wilbur!"

At last, the brothers spoke. Not with their mouths but with

their minds in what the Time Traveler later called "thought projection"—common practice in the future.

We only wished to make something beautiful, they thought. Not for you—not even for us. But so that it might take its place in the world among other beautiful things. Now that it has done so, we cannot undo it or take it back. We no longer have the power to intervene in its progress or in its degradation. For us it is finished. We're sorry, and we hope your future will be a different one than the Time Traveler describes. Good-bye.

The brothers projected their final adieux, which fell benevolently on us like a gentle rain; and then, slowly, in defiance of gravity and in accord with the prerogatives of the imagination, they began their ascent into the pitch-black sky. We fell back amazed. Slowly, the darkness lifted, the night rolled away like smoke, and the light appeared. The brothers had vanished— dissolved into higher mathematics, or into Paradise, wearing raiment of light in perfect self-effacement. Or more likely, into Dayton—the actual Dayton of commerce and industry, where the Great Miami River joins the Stillwater, beyond the force of *my* invention—there to build aeroplanes.

Inside the barn, the brothers' machine, expectant wings tense with desiring, was transformed by spontaneous combustion into a cone of white ash. Only this was left of their enterprise—and a pair of lavender suspenders no one could explain. (Not even I, whose story this is—my invention, which cannot be renounced.) Neither do I know if the Time Traveler will be upheld in his desperate vision, nor if the brothers will precipitate the final night of the world. Only time will tell.

I laid Weena's flowers beside the white cone, in homage, and mounted my bicycle.

14.

I pedaled back to town and untangled Stella from sleep, drew the curtains, and showed her the risen sun.

"Is it real?"

I shrugged uncertainly, though the sun stung my eyes. I drew out the long pins, and Stella shook down her hair for me. I climbed it into a further mystery: a tower besieged by necessity and reason against the mind's play.

Yes, yes, I admit it!—admit to my helplessness before life. To my unfitness for it and my utter dependency on art and on the artifice I have made of women. I am a fool who much prefers his dreams. Who, though he saw it, is not entirely sure that the aeroplane is not a dream object after all.

The Broken Man's Complaint

For Edward Renn

Love Among the Particles

1. My Metamorphosis

I may never know why I have changed. Perhaps I'm being punished in a classical style. Or it may be that I became entangled in an astronomical event or a caprice of weather. Whatever the reason, on a morning unremarkable except for a cloud edged strangely by phosphorescence in an otherwise-ordinary summer sky, I was transformed from a man in his middle age with a mustache, slouch, and an awkward gait to a collation of sentient particles of uncertain age that move with the genius possessed by all gregarious flying things to rise, turn, and settle as one.

I was anxious but had only to recall metamorphoses recounted by Bulfinch and Kafka to console myself. In truth, I had much rather be what I have become than an ass or a cockroach, regardless of its adoring sister. Such calm acceptance is uncharacteristic of a man whose personality was liable to shatter under stress like a Raku bowl or—if you prefer a metaphor drawn from the musical world—to crack like a Stradivarius sat on by an elephant. In a past as recent as the night before my metamorphosis, Bombay gin in the sapphire bottle favored by connoisseurs was my stay against nervous collapse. I have often wondered if an excess of that imperial distillate might not have encouraged my dissolution. (But how very lovely the world looked through the gin's empty blue bottle!) However the thing was done, I, who was always nervous and afraid, now approach my life with insouciance. To be frank, my carelessness may be the result of inhabiting a life-form immune to injury and the ordinary frustrations of men and women. What does a swarm of particles as impressive as a cloud of gnats know of your kind's tribulation and discontent? Oh, I, too, am human! But my humanity is of another order than yours. And much more ancient.

2. Developing a Theory of the Self

My wife—yes, until that summer morning, I had a wife—was on her knees among the phlox, singing earnest hymns to fertility, as is the prerogative of women. I don't mean modern women: My gaze is a backward one, suitable to a consciousness not exclusively animal. Regardless, it was with a sensation of, of—well, I cannot tell how it felt to look at her through the kitchen's mullioned windows, where on so many tranquil afternoons hummingbirds were to be seen gorging their jeweled throats with sugar water. As I took a last look at this kind and gentle consort of my youth and middle age, I thought in every particle of my being that she belonged now and henceforth in the life of some other man. Perhaps the man I had been before my transformation, who, for all I know, may continue in my stead. I wished her well and, bidding a mute farewell to the row of liquor bottles sparkling in a slant of morning light, drifted like a river of birds straggling above a freshly harrowed field, under the back door and out on into the new day. In time, I would learn that walls cannot discommode me: My particles pass through them and much else besides. And if in your opinion my imagery runs to extravagant lengths, it is—in *my* opinion!—appropriate to an essay in the marvelous.

In the garden, I was moved by the sight and sound of a swarm of bees, which had made their hive inside a rotted post of the grape arbor, whose fruit was, at this season, hard and bitter. They lived, I supposed, in anticipation, as did I now. I thought we had much in common and wondered if I could pass among them, unnoticed and unharmed. And by such speculations—some tested, others not—I assessed my new world and place within it. I was not unhappy with—let me call it my existence, in case you doubt my life. No, I was not unhappy then, as the sweet airs of morning swept lightly the garden paths and ruffled the pond with its brightly colored koi.

Indolent and with a native buoyancy enjoyed by fish, my particles had dispersed so far that I began to lose the sensation of my extremities, by which I mean the ambit or furthest limits of my self. To this day, I maintain that I have a self, if by self we mean an intelligence to regard space and to know one's place within it. Despite my present atomized condition, the world is apparent to me as I move through its four, five, or twenty-six dimensions, depending on whether you parse it according to Minkowski, Kaluza-Klein, or the string theorists. Held together by the strong force, my particles are in no danger of catastrophic divorce; however, they are subject to varying degrees of estrangement within the space of their mutual attraction. The separation is useful, but I suffer by it. At their furthest remove from one other, the communal intelligence is weakest. It is then the broken self is most vulnerable. Until I learned to keep a grip on my constituency, I was liable to become confused by the slightest movement of air or lapse in attention. Later on, when I had become master of my self and its motions, total disintegration—that is, annihilation—was no longer a concern: I could maintain a shape such as bees, birds, or fish compose in their congregations. Aware, suddenly, that I was adrift (a "wisp" of neutrinos was oscillating painfully among the roses), I intensified the strong force and succeeded in withdrawing my straying quarks and leptons from the backyard's perimeter, described by an electric wire to keep the rat terrier out of the phlox. (A dollop of my dark matter having brushed against the wire, its rude charge had no effect on me.)

Having come as close to my wife as I dared, I delighted in a sensation of fullness and in a strength that I would have called virility had I been a man in the ordinary sense. My wife rose from the flower bed with the intention of harrying me out the front door, for the time had come and gone when I should have left for work.

3. In Praise of the Digital Age

I never intended that this account of my life after the disaster that befell it should be in any way comic. To be emasculated— no, for what happened to me is worse! To be the abstract of a man, to have been reduced to bits of elemental stuff is no joking matter; it has not even the black humor of dark matter to recommend it. I am bodiless and yet not a ghost. Of this world but not in any appreciable sense. To write my story, I thought, will confirm my existence. Had I been living in the Mechanical Age, I could not have done so, lacking means to depress a typewriter's keys. But in the Digital Age, one need not be substantial to make a mark: One has only to enter a word processor via its data port and *think*. Don't ask how the trick was accomplished, but I found that I was able to think my words into the machine in which I—let's say "sat" so as not to be vague. It's all *data*, after all—words, speech, thoughts— just so many units of information waiting to ride the lightning bolt, like bodies queuing up for a roller coaster. I would shake my shoulders and crack my knuckles (figuratively speaking) and wait for my muse, clad in brightly colored data like a video image pixilated by solar flares. And when at last she had come to me, I would think and my words would stream into the processor along streets of circuitry and become the flesh of our time—immaculate, spelled-checked, and laid away in dust-scented files. Yes, even a computer's innards are prey to dust—the cloak and calling card of time.

    I was not alone there. Bits of a pornographic novel, Steampunk stories, love letters, iTunes, and erotic poems kept me company in the phosphorescent dark—artifacts of the computer's owner, who was a writer, of sorts. After I had (so to speak) banged out a couple pages (how colorful the language of the Mechanical Age!), I would leave the machine the way I had come and then linger, phantomlike, in a corner of the room while the writer smoked and typed and paced and furiously compressed his hard copy into a tight ball to hurl against the corkboard, where it made only the slightest sound in evidence of his self-disgust. He was often frustrated in pursuit of his muse. But I remained in the room with him, not to distill a sympathy in which he might take comfort, but to bathe—selfishly, indulgently—in the rich and penetrating odor of his cigarette's smoke. How fortunate to be alive (if alive I am) in the Digital Age *and* to share it with someone who has not renounced tobacco! All the nearly numberless particles of which I am comprised relished that smoke—inhaled (as it were) and drew it into their lungs and breathed deeply their sighs of relief.

Smoking was not the sole pleasure in which I luxuriated while the writer struggled to write—his computer piercing the gloom with its intense bluish rays. When the work was going badly, or not at all, he would drag out a bottle of single malt from the closet and pour liberally into a heavy glass a drink whose delicious fumes drew me from my corner to the very surface of the smoky decoction. There, I would allow myself—that is to say, my particles—to dissolve into the whiskey as if it were a stoup of holy water. I would have much preferred the "queen's own gin," but beggars can't be choosers. And what am I now if not the most arrant beggar who ever existed? Always, we would become ecstatic, many times slipping carelessly down the man's throat with his last swallow—so utter was our communal oblivion. And when we had reassembled into me, my self, I was delighted to find that the euphoria persisted for days.

4. Circulating Through Space and Time

To talk of days or hours or any other of time's denominations is a convenience only, for time is not for me as it is for you. Mine cannot be regulated or metered by any clock. It is— how do I say what time is for me? Like an ocean—vast and seemingly shoreless, deep and subject, like the ocean itself, to storms and confusions. I am in time as swimmers are in their element, crawling easily across its tranquil surface or near to drowning in its uproar. When it comes to time, you and I are on different wavelengths (to continue in the pelagic metaphor, which is apt). Once, unable to shake off the melancholy that more and more beset me, I collected myself and, mustering the intelligence by which the collective is governed, drifted across the city, from the writer's apartment to the house in which my wife and I had lived together. To call the movement by which I transit space (and, as you shall soon see, time) *drifting* is also a convenience, for there is nothing at all slow or peaceable about it. It is, rather, a disturbance at the subatomic level—fierce and nearly reckless in its energy—directed by some lower drawer or subdirectory of that intelligence, whose operation eludes my understanding. That it does elude it is no doubt better; better that it should be "automatic" and second nature to me.

I traveled across town with astounding rapidity, very near the speed of light; yet because I experience time as an elastic and unpredictable construct like the Möbius strip or one of Oscar Reutersvärd's impossible objects, I did not arrive at the house instantaneously. I wobbled "awhile" in the space-time continuum. When I finally passed through the wall into those familiar rooms, my wife and dog were gone; outside, the phlox had perished and the beds were bricked over by the new house-holder. Glancing at a calendar on the pantry door, I realized that twenty years and more had gone by since that summer morning. But for me, it seemed no longer than a month or two since I had last seen my wife making her determined way over the flagstones to roust me from sleep.

5. "Cogito Ergo Sum," *Et Cetera*

What does it mean to be human? Is it merely to act as humans act, to do what they do—good or bad? I smoke cigarettes (after a fashion), I drink scotch (after a fashion), I move and sleep and dream and grow steadily toward loneliness in a way that can be said to resemble how it was for me before my breakdown (to speak of a condition with which you may be familiar). In my way, I am in the world. I perceive it, though without organs of perception. Somehow I see, hear, touch, taste, smell what surrounds me, although—I have come to realize—I do so without clarity, recognition, savor, or delight. (Scotch and cigarettes aside.☺) My being is too radically dispersed, I suppose, for meaningful contact. It was little better when I was all of a piece. And yet I am human if for no other reason than I am able to think and to remember and to suffer.

6. *The Past and How I Got There*

Space—other places—had done nothing to lessen my solitude. I visited all of them I had wished to see when I was whole—no, I am whole even now! Nothing essential has been lost of what I used to be: I have merely suffered a change in—in format, in resolution. If a person is a unit of information, as has been said, I am that unit digitized and processed for some purpose—a design and reason unknown to me. My dispersal is a kind of distraction, nothing more.

I went first to Tahiti to look for what Gauguin had painted, then to Arles, where van Gogh had been driven mad by the color and fierce light of Provence, then to Seville to listen in the torrid darkness to water chattering in the Moorish fountains, then to Venice to smell its stink and ride in a gondola rowed by a man with a monkey, striped jersey, and sneer, through fetid canals overlooked by rotting palaces. I went to Egypt to watch the ibis, sacred to Thoth, wade in the Nile on stiff legs and to the Argentine plains to see a red horse, head lifted to the sun. I went elsewhere—to Tunis and to Kampala to see where the lion had surprised Mrs. Willoughby in an olive grove and even to the roof of the world, where the ice is melting. I could feel sorrow, regret, nostalgia, but not cold or heat. I could fear the lion but feel not at all its ravening claws, which passed through me as if I were made of air. Everywhere I went was the same: One place was as good or as bad as another.

And having had my fill of the present and fearing the future, I went into the past. You don't believe me? I tell you for a man to travel in time is no more impossible for him than to be changed into a congeries of elementary particles, endued with intelligence, sensitivity, and (after a fashion) a sense of humor, however much it is dwindling. If time can be stretched—if it will, on occasion, shorten or ruck, knot or twist like a rope, then one can be displaced (or misplaced) in it. For that matter, one can find (or lose) oneself in other dimensions. I have often thought that when my wife pulled off her soiled gardening gloves, wiped her feet on the back-door mat, and went inside to hurry me up, she found me standing by the kitchen window, coffee cup raised to my lips, dressed for work, and waiting only for her customary kiss to send me on my way. She and I may be living still in that house with its dusty shelves and sparkling liquor bottles, its flagstone path and flower beds harried by a rat terrier named Malcolm. (Bodies in space and time, separated by space and time—sing it as you will.) In spite of all, I would like to see them again but know in my soul (to speak nostalgically) that I will not. No, not in this life or in any other. Alive or dead, they inhabit realms from which I am forever banished. What I begin to fear more than death is immortality. If, as I think, I am indestructible, how, then, will I die? If everything is possible for me, then life without end is possible. But how am I to endure it?

But you want to know how I managed it—how I traveled the rails of time into the past and what I did there among the dead. I packed myself—my particles—into a photon of light as you would throw clothes into a suitcase. Light is the conveyance, the superconductor, the carrier of time—streaming, in particles suspended in a wave, from the past of our universe into its future. And by mingling my particles with light's own as it passed nearby on its outbound journey into space, I rode at light's speed to a planet hidden within a Magellanic Cloud— the large one called by the Arabs al-Bakr, "the Sheep." There I found—not Paradise, not even Eden's fallen and corrupted east, but ruins and a prison that might have been drawn by Piranesi and inscribed by pantograph on that fantastically distant remove. Three centuries earlier, they had been carried there (unless I brought with me—in whatever part of myself that holds memory—those sinister dreams). And what did I find wandering among tumbled columns, clinging to iron ladders and catwalks, gnashing teeth in bleakest jails? Images. Phantoms. Specters. Things even less substantial than I! I would have been better off mingling my atoms with the bees where they swarmed under the grape arbor of my house all those— what? Years, decades, centuries ago? Or has it been only days since my self-imposed exile from the garden? I cannot tell the time—do not know anymore what to make of it. There was nothing on that inhospitable rock for me, and, suspecting that anywhere else I traveled in the fields of night would be just as vacant, I boarded a wave of earthbound light and fled back among the living (though they do not live for me).

7. Painful Acknowledgments

Once again on earth's surface, which was no longer mine to speak of as firm or blessed (not now that I no longer stand upon it), I went to the apartment where I had enjoyed the company of the writer, insofar as I could enjoy what I could not touch or speak with. The writer had fallen into the hands of mystics! With unkempt gray hair and long beard, he looked like Tolstoy. Just as before, he paced the room. But he no longer smoked, and having sent a scouting party of free quarks through the closet door, I determined that he did not drink. He appeared to have relinquished his vices, and in place of pornographic and Steampunk fiction digitized within his word processor, I found moral tracts and maxims and downloads of Arvo Pärt and Philip Glass. He still paced disconsolately, and he still wadded up his hard copy into paper balls, although instead of throwing them against the corkboard, he set them alight on a small brazier as though burnt offerings to his new muse, who was, presumably, one of the Hindu gods. My eyes (to speak familiarly) smarted, and I knew that whatever consolation was his was too narrow to share in. I spun round in space like a dervish, feeling myself shunned by even this meager, unsatisfactory society. I longed to look into the mirror and see myself there, even if my hair had turned white and I was no longer young. I wished to have an identity! But only those fated to pass away in time are granted it—or so it seemed to me as I gathered myself together and prepared to take my leave of someone who did not know that I was there.

What began as a comedy has become a fable or farce of a self pulled to pieces by strong forces and dark matters whose cause and meaning are incomprehensible. Why have I lost my composure so completely as to be no more than a cloaking mist or a dirty cloud of dust raised by a truck lumbering over an excavation site? Excavating what? Precious metals? Antiquities? Or nothing more fabulous than broken terra-cotta pipes of an ancient sewer?

In panic (call it "agitation" to remind you of my particulate state), I fled the writer's apartment by the window (open or shut, it does not matter) and hurried to the office building where I had passed so many years of my working life. On the twelfth floor, I entered the labyrinth of cubicles, illuminated at this late hour only by the tiny green and blue lights of electronic equipment—silent in their sleep mode, except for the intermittent muffled noises of background processing or the suppression of rogue data. In one cubicle, I had racked my brains at a computer monitor for headlines with which to sell all manner of useless trash. Was it this, I wonder, that had broken me? I roamed the office's subdivisions, recalling this man and that woman and seeing clearly—for the first time—how they had eluded me. I had passed among them as if I were made of air. We had spoken and, at times, touched; but of mutual contact at the depths of our separate beings, there had been none. Was it this that smashed me to smithereens, that confirmed my estrangement in space and in time past all hope of rescue? Or was it so that I might be given a second chance? How given and why, I could not even begin to imagine.

8. Consulting the Oracles

Inside a computer at a branch of the New York Public Library, I searched the Internet in order to illuminate my condition. Elementary Particles, Behavior of the Strong Force, Quantum Chromodynamics, Condensed Matter Physics, Electromagnetic Radiation, Fundamental Forces, Higgs Boson, Antiparticles, Muon and Tau, Supersymmetry, Kaluza-Klein Towers of Particles—I surfed as if on waves of light the data streams of the World Wide Web, consulting Wikipedia as in the ancient world victims of a tragic fate had consulted oracles. Many times, I was attacked by interceptors and antivirus mechanisms that sought, like antibodies, to annihilate me. The digital world is also cruel to interlopers. Whether an existence as refined and fundamental as my own can be destroyed has yet to be tested. In my despair of a possible life without end, I may have yearned to be no more; but I do not want to die at the foot of a firewall, coughing up dark matter and bitter squarks.

I no longer needed a word processor to record my story: I could think words into being without intermediary, imprinting them onto the electromagnetic field that is, I suspect, my consciousness. Saved in my own random access memory, thoughts—dark as clots or colorful as jelly beans—can be accessed whenever I wish. I can project them, at will, into another's data cloud. The gist of what you are reading here was imprinted on the mind of Norman Lock, who believes himself sole author of this eventful history. During my wanderings in space and in time (unfixed, capricious, and circular), I rested—unknown to Lock—among the Edwardian railroad timetables he collects, in order to slow the wild arrhythmia of my heart (to speak hopefully). I had overtaxed my particles in the Tierra del Fuego archipelago during a failed experiment in romance.

9. *Sleeping Among Tortoises*

I had gone to the Galápagos Islands to think about time in time's stillest backwater. There, among giant tortoises whose species' evolutionary history spanned five million years or more and whose individual histories, a century, I roved the desolate beaches. The ancient tortoises were like objects left over from the past: To wander among them was to feel time—know it intimately—as you might a rock that has lain in the hot sun of a garden or scarcely visible under snow: a thing familiar to your eyes and touch and smell and (should you be imaginative) to your taste; for we can, some of us, imagine the taste of rock—the very different tastes of granite, soapstone, basalt, and marble. And for me, who had been given the power of empathy raised to an extraordinary degree, my experience of time under the volcanoes on those fabulous islands was . . . immense. I'm sorry to be vague. But how can I be otherwise, speaking as I am trying to do of a subject forever beyond our grasp? I empathized with the tortoises, which are wise. If anything can lay claim to wisdom, it must be they. I mingled my atoms with theirs and apprehended, by sensations rich and various, what it means to be a tortoise and, therefore, what time must be—its qualities and flavors. Physicists speak of elementary particles as having flavor, although they mean by it something other than the taste of a thing in one's mouth.

I remembered how, in the middle of the night, I would wake. Perhaps the moon had come riding into the window, splashing its garish light over the room, or maybe my wife had been startled by something monstrous in her dreaming. Awake, I remembered that I must die—in time—and grew, after so many nights of waking in the dark, to fear time and to hate it. Now that I am mired inextricably in its morass, I feared death's opposite—seeing in it only an ultimate intensification of my loneliness. Stroking a tortoise's shell (the color of smoke and nothingness), I spoke to it in Tortoise (why not?) of my longing to escape time and be no more. Despondent, I wound myself into an empty chambered-nautilus shell to be reminded of what it had been like to sleep in a narrow space, pressed against another's sleeping body. Afterward, I dreamed. And of what might a swarm of particles dream? Of an orchestra playing on the sea a serenade for strings from the deck of a ship—its portholes blazing white light onto the black water, like pinpoints of illumination cast by electronic devices in a dark room. By this simile, I acknowledge—as I must—that all things have been annexed to the digital world. The night and the harrowingly beautiful music invaded the shell's small rooms and seemed to dispel, for the moment, time's appalling mystery and give me peace.

I inhabited the shell (for a moment or an age) as the mind does the inside of a skull—my thoughts' data streaming like luminous ribbons far and wide: to the cold ends of the universe as they are known to me, who is—in his makeup—their comrade and who had—as a householder and husband—watched in fascination science documentaries broadcast by PBS (and, with equally rapt attention, *The Adventures of Buckaroo Banzai*). Was it for this, I wondered, that I had been re-formed and reformatted as a swarm of particles? Was it for this that I had traveled to one of the ends of the earth to sleep among giant tortoises, where Darwin had landed and dreamed, too, in his time, about time—its grand recessional, whose origin is a protein compound in "a warm little pond"? Or was it (to speak sentimentally) to meet Marie Risset, who, like me, had been reduced to fermions, bosons, and assorted hypothetical particles whose existence (like ours) is yet to be (dis)proved?

10. Dance of the Particles (in 4/4 Time)

Commingled with the flavors of that remote place (tang of brine, pungency of tortoise and guano, the charcoal and tannin of red mangrove, the tartness of prickly pear cactus favored by iguana and tortoise) was the unique flavor of what I knew at once to be a woman. I insist that Marie Risset is a woman still! I promptly emptied the nautilus shell of my agitated particles, attracted by the intense flavor of her subatomic structure. Marie had been particularized beneath the Franco-Swiss border near Geneva, at the Large Hadron Collider while inspecting one of its superconducting magnets. (The cup of French roast she had held in her hand lent its own stimulating flavor notes to her altogether-delightful ensemble.) An immensely energetic particle beam on the order of 3.5 TeV had derailed in her vicinity. (She maintains that the accident was the result of a "magnet quench incident," subsequently covered up by CERN.) I wondered how she had managed to arrive in the Galápagos. Her answer pleased me by its frankness and by the compliment it paid to my own flavors—let me call it sex appeal for old time's sake. Not that I had possessed it. On the contrary, I was a dull and plodding lover, inclined to fall asleep during foreplay. But I now imagined myself quite other than I had been then, in this novel shape and form purged of gross matter—the "fat" of a previous sedentary life.

"I felt your attraction," she said to me in French, "across the distances of space and time."

Doubtless, you are ready to protest. And you would be right in thinking that I know no French and she, not a word of English. "Furthermore," I hear you demand of me, "how could two discrete swarms of particles—however they might be favorably disposed—converse?"

I would answer you thus: "Among the particles that comprised and created us were other energies obedient to their own rigorous constitution and government. I am speaking of letters of the alphabet—French and English, both—which constitute words governed by syntax. Parts of matter and its energies . . . parts of speech—the same, in that worlds may be constructed of them!"

"But you don't speak French!" you shout, your willing suspension of disbelief at an end.

I shrug my shoulders and would remind you that not everything can be explained.

So it was that Marie and I exchanged information (to speak in the new style), talking together—shyly at first—of this and that:

"These tortoises . . ."

"Yes?" I said.

"They live to a great age."

I agreed.

"Like rocks, they seem to evolve not at all."

"Evolution," I said stupidly, "is one of the grandest of ideas."

"I have been thinking," she said after a pause that may have been of a day's duration, a week's, or an age's—it mattered not at all to me, who had all the time in the world and more at his elbow (farcically speaking)—"that we may be—who knows?— the next evolutionary thing."

She staggered me! I had believed myself to be a freak of nature considered on a cosmic scale. I had been (to be honest with you) a little ashamed, as if I were responsible for my misfortune—as if I had brought it on myself by some unclean and unwholesome act. That I could not recall having committed one did nothing to lessen the burden of my guilt.

The orchestra was once again playing its serenade upon the water. (If it was a dream, we were having it together!) Night had fallen with the suddenness of a scythe. Stars there were also that fell into the unlit ocean—their bits and particles so very similar to Marie's, I thought, and would have told her if not for the old shyness.

"Do you dream?" I asked instead.

She nodded, and a glossy wisp of dark matter fell across her breast.

"Of what are you dreaming now, Marie?"

"Of a dance—a kind of fox-trot to go with the music of the orchestra."

"Yes," said I, who had never danced well.

But that was then. Now, to the glissandos of the serenade, we moved through one another nimbly, trailing luminous clouds of energy like auroras of flame. Our particles mingled and nearly caressed in the moonlight while the tortoises on the beach regarded us stolidly. She was superb! I rejoiced in my strong force; she, in her grace and mastery of the dance's fluency.

The serenade at an end, we completed our fiery passage and drew apart. Space—cold and vacant—loomed once more between us. Marie became distracted by thoughts of the nearby Humboldt Current: its temperature and salinity. I wandered off to be by myself, dogged by the sadness that comes of knowing that we are—in the end and for all time—fated to be alone.

Loneliness in the
New Kingdom

1. Nostalgia Is a Property of Matter

Objects belonging to the past, which have become stranded in the present, yearn for the time of their manufacture. It is the desire of the compass needle for its north. Only when desire has been satisfied will the nervousness of matter—the agitation of its particles—be resolved. Like fetishes, objects impregnated by time can excite the body into a new arrangement of its electromagnetic field, which then seeks to fulfill matter's wish to return to its origins. Irradiated by the past latent in an Edwardian train schedule, I departed Euston Station to a noisy recessional of steam. My destination was the Manchester of 1910, where Ernest Rutherford was enlarging our knowledge of the atom. He was about to replace the prevailing "plum pudding" model with a planetary one. I hoped that he might reconstitute the fermions, quarks, leptons, and bosons into the man I had been before my atomic structure was smashed—by accident or malice—at the beginning of the Digital Age, in 2012. I reasoned that my reintegration could be accomplished more readily at a time when knowledge was concentrated largely in the minds of individuals instead of dispersed among hundreds of jealous specialists. You say I ought to have gone to the Swiss Patent Office at Bern to consult Einstein? But I had no railroad timetable to enable such a trip in space-time. (Traveling from New York to present-day London posed no special difficulties. I had merely to attach myself to something moving. Even a bird would have sufficed.)

2. A Course of Mind Reading at Victoria University

The train slowed outside Manchester, and the rain that had been falling resolved on the window of the first-class compartment into individual drops, which, in their precipitate motion and transparency, reminded me of the cloud chamber—a particle detector beloved by physicists of the mid-twentieth century. Inside the terminal, called then Manchester London Road, a blast of steam escaping the locomotive scattered the itinerant beads of rain and ascended in a dirty cloud to the immense glass-coffered ceiling, floating (so it seemed to one who was himself unmoored) on cast-iron columns. Exceptionally empathetic since my misfortune, I thought of black moths imprisoned by a window, regarding desperately the sprawling air beyond.

I found Rutherford in his office at the university. His back was turned to me as he sat watching the rain disperse its atoms across the window. I wished I could whisper to him the secret of the cloud chamber so that its invention might be his. I felt an inexplicable regard for the man. But how could I whisper, who have only the potential for speech, lacking speech's organs? Had the moment been in the present (and by present I mean early in the twenty-first century) and had he, like Stephen Hawking, been unable to speak without the aid of a computer interface, I would have channeled my data stream into the device and announced myself. But how, in 1910, was I to speak my mind? Even flies can make themselves seen and heard! But I was as invisible and inaudible as any ghost. You think I could have revealed myself in a cloud of chalk dust, moved the papers on the desk, or stained my particles with an Ehrlich dye? You have no idea how rarefied I am, how disembodied my consciousness! If I could not make my thoughts known to Rutherford, I would see if I could know his: I would read the man's mind.

By decreasing the strong force that held my particles in a kind of federation, I resolved to pass through Rutherford's skull and merge with his mind's atoms and energies. Hadn't I done as much when I entered computers by their data ports—those intelligent machines modeled on the human brain? But to my surprise, the electromagnetic field surrounding Rutherford was vibrant with his mental activity, which at that moment was constructing an image of the young woman passing beneath his office window, her long skirt trailing over the wet sidewalk, as she might appear undressed on a divan. (While not without interest, such thoughts lie outside the scope of this history.) I passed deeper into the field, beyond the sparks (so to speak) produced by nervous excitement, and found there an image of the atom—the tight fist of its nucleus and the orbiting electrons. To one used to the hyperrealism of digital media, the picture lying at the bottom of Rutherford's mind was scarcely more elaborate than a cartoon. Disappointed, I began to doubt even so august a scientist as he could reverse my catastrophic disintegration.

To have been changed into a swarm of subatomic particles through no fault of one's own is a hardship with little compensation. Inevitably, one tires of passing through walls and longs to enter by a door, like any other hominid. (I claim to be one still!) The same dissatisfaction with novelty applies to travel: After flitting about in space like birds, flies, or a sneeze, one yearns for the machines of conventional relocation. But this much I will admit: A sentient and ambitious particle swarm can increase its understanding of the world to an astonishing degree by Web crawling. Since the fission of my formerly nuclear self, I have surfed the data streams of the Internet, acquiring veritable gigabytes of information. As a result, my grasp of the cosmos and its various microcosms is nothing less than encyclopedic!

3. The Texture of Thought Is Knotty, Not Silken

"Is someone there?" asked Rutherford, pulling at an earlobe.

I concentrated all that host of sentient particles of which I am comprised on Rutherford's mental activity. Cogitation, though highly developed in him, still seemed a kind of mechanical computing machine in its dogged worrying of scraps of thought; but in his sparkling flights of imagination, his audacious leaps beyond what a moment before had been the limit of the known, his appetite for destruction of accepted ideas and forms—by these marks I knew that I was in the presence of genius. To call Rutherford's imagination sparkling is not to assign a fanciful image to the unseen, for within the powerful electromagnetic field produced by his brain, I saw and heard sparks fly. The atmosphere in which we two scouted for traces of each other seemed a night sky crowded with fiery comets.

Rutherford closed his eyes, knowing that the murky drama in which he had become a principal actor was an interior one. Having suppressed my own thoughts the better to read his, I was able to follow him in his experiential . . . sifting—for so his thought process seemed to me:

There is someone in the room with me. I know it by the disturbance in my mind, whose cause is adventitious. I feel—there is no other word for how I am reacting to this stimulation of my nervous faculties—I *feel* a sensation as if a particle of grit had lodged in my eye, or a splinter—a splinter in the mind, say, is troubling me as leaves might be said to be troubled by a slight breeze turning them—their dark undersides—toward the light. A tropism. I am turned toward an alien mind—feel its presence in the room as an irritation of what nervous tissue connects the brain with its mind. My brain with my mind. I thought at first I heard a voice inside my head, a voice not my own. If I keep silent a while longer, perhaps I will hear it again.

The foregoing interior monologue is for your convenience

only, reader; my experience of Rutherford's conscious thinking (never mind its unconscious accompaniment—the ground bass to thought's development) was not straightforward. It uncoiled like tobacco smoke in a room or water furling and unfurling in a stream. I—that is, my particles—bathed in his mind's workings. I could no more transcribe them than I can a stream's unintelligible chatter.

While he kept silent, I told him of my disintegration. Of an estrangement from others that had climaxed in a divided self. (Is this the answer? That I am no more than the inevitable outcome of humankind in the Digital Age?) I told him (and by "told," I mean that I conveyed my thoughts by irradiating the particles of his understanding with my own) how—by a fetish of time—I had traveled from the Brooklyn of 2012 to the Manchester of 1910. I told him what I knew of matter— its subatomic structure, its electromagnetic and strong forces, the uncertainty principle that undermined observation of its electrons. I told him that the atom, in thirty-five years, would be split, incinerating two Japanese cities. I told him that in my own time, atomic fission would fuel submarines and electric power plants and that by accident or negligence deadly rays would escape from both: the radiation of certain substances whose half-life he himself had discovered two years earlier. I told him what I knew of the modern world and its sciences.

"I don't understand," he said when I had finished. It was the following afternoon, and with one exception he was not pleased: He was thrilled to have his planetary model of the atom confirmed. But my talk of quarks, antiparticles, neutrinos, and dark matter dumbfounded him. I had recited many, many facts and theories, but my recitation lacked something fundamental for his understanding. Perhaps no other outcome was possible for someone like me, whose source of information was Wikipedia. Or perhaps he was not ready to believe in the world of the early-twenty-first century. If that is the case, who can blame him?

"Can you make me whole again?" I asked, as if he were a surgeon, psychoanalyst, or priest instead of a scientist. But I knew that such wholeness as I longed for was beyond his power.

4. My Particles Become Encrypted with an Alien Time Signature

Drawn irresistibly by the lodestone of the past, I returned to London and visited the British Museum's department of Ancient Egypt and Sudan, where among books on travel I found *A Thousand Miles up the Nile,* written in 1876 by Amelia B. Edwards. Here, too, I thought, is another of time's relics; and as I had done during congress with an antique train schedule, I loosened the strong force, setting my particles free to pass through the book's cover into its foxed pages with their pleasant odor of age and dust. And by a book's talismanic power to conjure the reality of its subject (a virtual reality, to speak in the new style), my atoms were realigned within the space-time continuum. Each particle and antiparticle was informed, or encrypted, with the qualities of that alternative reality. Wearied by the effort, I rested a long while inside those old pages, which since Queen Victoria's reign had been slowly burning in time's furnace. And when I felt myself equal to the exertion of governing my fragments once again, I left the book the way we had entered it and found that I was no longer in a reading room of the British Museum, but in Abu Simbel—standing (or so I would have done in my previous existence) outside Queen Nefertari's temple with Miss Edwards and her party of Victorian travelers.

5. At the Gateway to Vanished Time

It was as though I had been born again—into the year 1873, in Sudan—by the agency of radiation produced by decaying atoms of paper and ink and also of the dust laid down by time on top of the pages of Miss Edwards's book where it had stood for nearly forty years on a shelf in the British Museum. That book had sown its particles among my own, salting them; and because they were heavier (as Victorian furniture is heavier than that of my own time and yours), I aged. Now like an old man, I sat inside a tent pitched in the desert, while the lady undressed behind a Chinese screen—souvenir of other exotic travels—reading by an oil lamp the journal she would later shape into *A Thousand Miles up the Nile*. (I needn't remind you that such verbs as *sat, stand,* and *read* are anthropomorphic conveniences.) Desire—sexual desire—had drained from me as water through sand because of my age and the heaviness of matter (a want of energy) I felt throughout my attenuated being. Hearing her underthings rustle on the other side of the paper screen, I was not in the least tempted to exploit my invisibility by behaving in an ungentlemanly manner. Had I been as other discreet or incurious men, I would have coughed to warn her of my presence; but I could not cough, any more than I could speak. As to coming into intimate contact with her mind, my disappointment in Manchester had chastened me. Instead, I contented myself with an old man's tepid pleasure of resting under canvas while I bathed my particles in the soft light shed by the oil lamp.

Tomorrow, I will accompany Miss Edwards to the Temple of Ramesses, in whose shadow we have camped. Partially buried in sand, its many-chambered tombs are anchored in time: twelve-hundred years before the Common Era. Entangling my particles with the temple's stone, I can travel downward into ancient history more readily than by riding a photon of light to earth's past as it must appear, like a hologram, on some planet at the edge of the Milky Way. Had I eyes, I would have closed them—tired as I was at that moment and eager to dream of Pharaoh and his queen.

6. *"I Sits Among the Cabbages and Peas"*

I shaded my eyes against the overwhelming brightness of the noon sun—of Ra, who had come up the sky in his "Boat of a Million Years" (to speak in the idiom of the time into which I would soon pass). A gentleman in Miss Edwards's entourage had set up a tripod camera. As he prepared a glass plate to make a photograph of the tombs, I entered the camera body on impulse, wondering if my particles could inflame the photosensitive silver iodide into light. What would they say when they saw my ghostly image fogging the stone effigies? That the plate had been improperly coated or had been spoiled by direct sunlight, no doubt. I laughed, and to my ears the sound was unpleasant. I grew ashamed of my childishness and resolved to refrain from behavior suitable to a variety show like the one I had seen in the West End at the Holborn Empire Theatre after returning from Manchester. Marie Lloyd—the infamous, comic, big-bosomed chanteuse—had sung "I Sits Among the Cabbages and Peas." Soon, I would look into the furled heart of time's cabbage. Careful! Gravity is necessary for one who is to walk among the dead who will act as if they were alive yet in the long-vanished Nineteenth Dynasty of Ramesses II. I must show respect for the countless number of my kind who have been erased.

I left the camera, passing through the black drape like a mortuary curtain behind which a corpse lies waiting for the fire or the inglorious pit. The photographer withdrew to his portable darkroom to develop the glass plate. Miss Edwards, having finished a sketch of the royal colossi, adjusted her pith helmet and sipped from a canteen. She went to find shade and I, to merge my particles with those of the carved figure of Nefertari. Time radiated from that antiquity; I felt it penetrate like an X-ray mutating the genetic structure that remained, however vestigial, to my dispersed atoms. Instantly, I was transformed from a man of your time to one of the eleventh century B.C.E.

I nearly swooned, as Miss Edwards would have said. My eyes stung, and for a moment I was blind, as sometimes happens when one walks out of darkness into strong sunlight.

When the black mist had dispelled and I could see clearly again, the English were gone. Sudan was once more Nubia. I slipped inside the rock mountain from which Nefertari's temple had been carved by unhappy slaves. (Has there ever been a happy one?) I had crossed millennia to wake (my past—or future, depending on your point of view—seemed no more than a dream) in the private chamber of dw3t-ntr, a priestess of Ma'at, who with her feather weighs the souls of the dead. Dw3t-ntr, whose name I dare not pronounce aloud, was bathing in a sunken tub of rose quartz and alabaster. I felt like one of the red-eyed elders who spied on Susanna in her bath. In some part of me, I remembered desire and throbbed. But I told you I was old and the elements were heavy in me! Besides, what could a swarm of particles do to that taut and dusky flesh? I might have sneezed because of the aromatics in the bathwater—I, whose form is more like a sneeze's than a man's! Forgive me my bitterness, but there are times when I feel nothing but the mordancy of thwarted impulses that surge, like rage or rapture, only to spend themselves against a seawall. (Words being my only pleasure—indulge me while I indulge in them.) She rose from the bath (the moment was enfolded in the word *rose*) and a male slave (perhaps at that moment a happy one) dried her with a towel. Poor Miss Edwards was to this nubile woman as her pencil sketch of Nefertari's stone facsimile was to the pharaonic consort herself.

7. Ventriloquism in the New Kingdom

In observance of sacred rite, dw3t-ntr would fall into a trance; from her ecstatic ravings, Ma'at's wishes would be made known. Always, I witnessed those seizures with alarm; they were harrowing, like a course of insulin shock therapy. She would lay aside the sistrum with which she had made overtures to the goddess and writhe, her lovely body swept by storms of emotion. Her sweet mouth would froth, and from lips I longed to kiss came barbaric syllables, intelligible to Pharaoh's viziers and scribes, though not to me, despite my knowledge of Egyptian. (There is, as I have said elsewhere, no language barrier at the subatomic level.)

One afternoon when the tide of her possession was at the full, the thought came to me that I might speak to Ramesses' agents by ventriloquism. I recollected my purpose in having traversed space and time: to become substantial once again. (I may have realized, besides, that only as flesh and blood could I enjoy the incomparable dw3t-ntr. Never mind that she was, by my calendar and yours, no more substantial than dust!) I hoped some occult science or magic lost to the modern age might reconstitute me. It was folly, that hope! I weakened my strong force and sent my particles, like emissaries to Paradise, into dw3t-ntr and heard my thoughts tumble from her mouth, thus:

"I have come from the future to find someone or something to restore my shattered self. Do you understand the concept of self? Or are your personalities subsumed in the absolute of Pharaoh's will or the gods'? Can you be said to have personalities? Perhaps in the absence of free will, you have not yet been able to construct a self. Do you understand free will? I think that in me free will had reached the point where I no longer felt obliged to observe the ordinary conventions of living. Not that I was lawless! I was not, and neither was I in the least selfish—not outwardly. Free will operated at my deepest level: at the subatomic if you like, where I maintained my self in luxurious indifference. I was, outwardly, a considerate husband and charitable friend. I did all that I could and more to protect endangered species and the fragile ecosystem. I harmed no one, was tolerant to all, envied none, and only rarely coveted some man's wife. Regardless, I metamorphosed one morning into what you see before you. Or rather, what you do not see. Is the concept of the atom familiar to you? It's a Greek word, meaning 'indivisible.' I used to take comfort in the idea of indivisibility: that there was, for matter and for the personality, a rock bottom. A pretty delusion, as it turned out!"

I went on in this vein for minutes, hours. I lost track of time. In any case, time is meaningless to me. I regret my stupidity even now—more than three thousand years after the fact. Pharaoh's seers, priests, and viziers had never heard anything like that . . . spiel. They believed dw3t-ntr had gone mad. They believed her to be in thrall to Apep, the dark god who threatens to destroy Ra during his nightly voyage underground. They dragged poor dw3t-ntr, not yet recovered from her trance, into an anteroom and ordered the slaves to brick it up.

8. In Sight of the Reed-Covered Islands of Paradise

She bore it. She bore it with serenity. I would not have done so well. Was it that dw3t-ntr had many gods, while I had only the one? Or was it that she belonged already to the invisible world and did not need to resign herself to it? For her, there was no partition separating the world of living men and women from the realm of the dead. During her trances, she had passed between the two worlds as easily as I, in my severely divided nature, passed through masonry, iron, and the most impermeable and obdurate of all materials: human flesh. She took her time in dying. For three days, she remained shut up in the dark—groaning only at the end in hunger and thirst, but not once in fear of death. I wished that I could have carried air to her, bonding my atoms with oxygen's, and water to drink. I wished I could have brought her, like the bee, a yellow meal of pollen. The darkness inside her bricked-up tomb was absolute. I could have managed light: By an act of will, I could have caused a brief incandescence as if by throwing flash powder into an open flame. But I didn't. The sight of bricks might have unnerved her. Better, I thought, to see before her in the dark the familiar deities.

What happened in the instant of her death took me by surprise: Her electromagnetic field was not extinguished like a light one turns off before sleep. It continued and held, within the net of its mysterious force, particles of her departing flesh. Like birds rising from a winter field in search of sustenance, they had fled her stilled but still-beautiful body. I mingled mine with them. For a long while, we lay in each other's arms (to speak in the old style), relishing the luxuriant heat of our decaying elements. I thought, then, that all things must surely reach an end; even the most potent of isotopes, selenium-82, has a finite half-life, though it exceed millennium. And I took comfort in the thought that I would not spend an eternity untouched by another, like the married pair whose fossils were discovered at Vesuvius—their backs to each other in sleep that had already lasted nearly two thousand years. Dw3t-ntr and I did not touch, any more than I had touched Marie Risset's particle cloud in the Galápagos Islands—or, for that matter, my wife, whom I had last seen on her knees behind our house, deadheading the phlox. Not once had I sounded the depths of her being with my own! The failure had been mine. But existence—for me as for everything else in the universe—would come to an end, and I would cease to mourn.

I won't pretend I did not enjoy what passed between dw3t-ntr and myself—our particles. I am not by nature even now puritanical. But the—oh, call it *spark!*—the spark was missing. That last sentence is descriptive of an imperfect electrical discharge. Don't misunderstand me: I'm not talking exclusively of sex. Sex was only a secondary aspect of a complicated state of mind. In the form in which we two appeared to each other, direct contact was impossible. Our two currents could arc, but they could never merge. I did not know dw3t-ntr. (I didn't know other people—an ignorance that may have destroyed me.) But what I wanted to possess was not knowledge of her experiences, opinions, and beliefs or yet of her body, but only this: the certainty that I was not alone in time. I succeeded, as I told you, only imperfectly.

I remained with dw3t-ntr, obedient to the force of her, as she entered—obedient to a stronger force than either of us could engender—the passages of the Underworld below the red pyramid. We followed brazen flies that, in their thousands of thousands, flew down the dismal corridors (whose entrances for them were dung and corruption), buzzing with the secrets of the afterlife. Seeing Ma'at, severe and merciless, with her feather, I turned back while dw3t-ntr went to be judged. Beyond Ma'at lay the sun boat, the twenty-one gates of Aaru, and the reed-covered islands of Paradise. What had I learned? That death is a persistence of the life that went before it. And so it is that the man I used to be survives in this new form. Just so does the ocean's basalt bed survive in the railroad tracks' ballast. The stones contain a memory of that ocean, just as I recall my self before my breakdown.

I returned to the bricked-up anteroom (antiroom, its homonym, also applied to a space inhospitable to even a dream of life), where dw3t-ntr had resigned her body to baser elements, searching for traces of her—particles? Soul? Élan vital? (For one who has been immersed in time and Wikipedia, there is no difference.) Little of dw3t-ntr remained, apart from her atomic signature, unmistakable as perfume. I lingered in it so that I might remember her by it. I seemed to hear—as from a long way off—a distress signal in dots and dashes, sent by Gordon's men at Khartoum, just before their slaughter. The past (or the future, if the concept pleases you) had caught up with me even here.

9. In the Cold Digital Sea, I Lay Down and Slept

In no time at all, I had reversed my previous itinerary, returning first to 1873, where I discovered Miss Edwards asleep in
her tent, dreaming of the nearly naked so-called Cataract men,
who had hauled the small steamer on which she sat drinking
tea up the dangerous rock steps of the Nile; then to the London of 1910; and finally to the New York City of 2012, where
I came to rest once again among the railroad schedules Lock
had collected as though to remind himself that space-time was
an inflexible grid. With a feeling near to spite, I wished that
I could tell him of my anarchic travels. But our elementary
natures were incompatible and . . . immiscible. Impulsively, I
entered the user interface of his word processor and filled the
clipboard of its temporary memory with all you have read here,
beginning with *Nostalgia is a property of matter.* Lock is shame-
less when it comes to adapting the work of other writers. He
will annex this account to his imagination and work it up into
a story of his own. (Let him do what he likes with it! I am
beyond ego and vanity.)

   Having brought my report to its final full stop, I abandoned
Word and, slipping once again into the data stream, was carried along by the gathering force of knowledge. In time, I will
come to the immense and steadily enlarging sea of information, where waves of light seethe as with Saint Elmo's fire—
green and ghostly. And in that tumult, I will merge my data
and delude myself into thinking I am alive, if for no other reason than I still dream. And of what will I dream? Not of the
gray streets of Manchester in the age of Edward VII. Not of
Miss Edwards undressing behind a Chinese screen. Nor of the
garden where my wife may yet be tending the pink and purple
phlox. No, it will be of Egypt that I dream. Of dw3t-ntr, standing alone while she awaits the judgment of Ma'at, as do we all.

The Broken Man in
Dark Ages to Come

1. And I Came Unto the Sea of Information

I was in a nearly limitless sea, cold and coldly lit by coruscations of green and blue, my particles and antiparticles (lightly bound by the four forces of the atom) at rest—or, better said, dormant and expectant like the elements of rudimentary life in Darwin's "warm little pond" that had waited for a chance event to jolt them into life. In my previous existence, I had gone all to pieces (to speak in the style in use before the Digital Age). My body had been reduced to its elementary stuff, which, by a prodigiously augmented collective intelligence, I soon learned to govern. I'd had adventures in the space-time continuum—some prosaic, others exotic, all unsatisfactory. To enlarge my understanding (essential in the age of information), I had merged the data of my thoughts in the World Wide Web—surfing its countless channels and acquiring by a kind of "spidering" an encyclopedic knowledge of the cosmos, of things vast and minute and, in their sum, beyond the grasp of any one person. I was a generalist *par excellence*: a Renaissance man, though without the normal equipment of one. I was alone with my thoughts and suffered in silence (to speak in clichés, in which ordinary men and women take refuge and comfort).

Strengthening my intelligence inside a New York Public

Library computer on a winter afternoon when the streets were rivers of slush between banks of sooted snow, I allowed myself—that is to say, my data—to be drawn further and further away from a site devoted to hypothetical particles, by the hypnotic influence of the blue hyperlinks. I was eager to learn all that I could about the subtleties—the mysteries (a word foreign to technocrats)—of my strange condition. In time (impossible to tell how long my impulsiveness carried me downstream from the source document), I had navigated thousands of electronic pages, until I drew near to a vast sea of information. I wish I could make you see that sea, how it filled the black void with waves of blue-green light beneath an equally black sky—no, not sky, for the place where the numberless data streams converged (an estuary rich in deposits of human kind's ceaseless grappling with matter and energy, ideas and follies) was an airless confine without moon or stars—strangely silent, except for data seething in microprocessors: the background radiation of the Digital Age. There, I slept—I insist that I am a man still and subject to the regimens and habits of our species regardless of my disintegrated body! I slept and dreamed of Egypt and of Manchester, of Provence and of Tierra del Fuego, where, as a swarm of elementary particles, I had traveled. I dreamed, too, of Brooklyn, where I had lived happily with a wife and rat terrier before the catastrophe had ruined me. You ask how an atomic cloud, no matter its intelligence, could dream? I say again: Thoughts, dreams—the life of the mind waking and sleeping—are nothing but electronic impulses; that is, data!

During that time, which to me was timeless, I was like the jellyfish trailing portions of itself in the current, aided or impeded by wind. Not that there was a wind inside the enormous data-storage unit in which I bathed (to speak picturesquely), although we—I mean the collective consciousness that constituted my sorely divided self—were aware of a noise that might be mistaken for wind, produced by numerous fans ventilating the computers' overheated bodies. And as the jelly-fish searches the medium in which it moves with its tentacles, so did I send my sensitive quarks and leptons into the electronic sea, nourishing myself on its salts and ions and restoring my flagging energy with electrolytes—all without waking; for just as your dreaming will sometimes register the disturbances and alarms invading sleep from the outside world, so did my unconscious self monitor the information in which I steeped. Thus it was that I came into contact with another data swarm, whose name was Boyd.

2. As Distance Might Be Measured Where All Is Immeasurable

As a convenience, I will set down my exchange with Boyd as I would an ordinary conversation. Ordinary conversation, of course, was impossible in that remote sea: As pure data, none of us had the equipment of speech or audition. And when I say that the sea was remote, I do not mean that it lay at an enormous distance from the user interface inside the New York City library where I had slipped into the data stream. Not necessarily. I have no way of knowing the location of the multitude of servers I visited during my headlong hypertextual flight. I may have browsed my way to Bombay, Tokyo, or Timbuktu—or it may be that I never left the library's own databases. The remoteness of the electronic sea from its sources cannot be ascertained by nautical miles, clock, or calendar—not even by the length of Ethernet cables. It is, rather, the effect in time of pages proliferating madly—link by link—throughout the World Wide Web: a luminous corridor that may, in fact, be endless. Boyd approached me as a man might in a small boat—a felicitous image that I shall use hereafter to describe my relationship to others on that dark sea simmering with electronic impulses.

"Hi, I'm Arnold Boyd. I haven't seen you before. Where were you converted?"

I didn't understand.

"Your *scan*," he said. "I went under in Santa Fe—with my sister. The two of us together. We'd never been to the sea. Not that this is anybody's idea of the sea. Still, it's not the desert. The desert gets monotonous after a while. Not that this doesn't get on your nerves . . . I like your boat idea."

"You can read my mind?" I asked.

"It's all data—right? Thoughts and stuff. Mind reading is just data transfer—yours to mine and vice versa. Not that it doesn't get monotonous after a while. After a while, you just want to be off by yourself so's not to have to process other people's thoughts. My own are boring enough."

"Where is your sister?"

"Browsing the Dance. She was with the Aspen Santa Fe Ballet right up to the time she went under. It's in her blood. Not that she has any now. It's all she cares about. Lucky for her, there're thousands of pages on the subject. She's into the Javanese at the moment. I don't care for the stuff. What I like is ice hockey, prizefighting, basketball, sports in general. I spend lots of time taking in the games, the bouts, the matches. If you can call it 'time.'"

"What do you mean by 'went under'?" I asked him.

"The full-mental scan. The Big Data Conversion. They call it something else where you come from?"

Suspicious, he came closer, wanting to sift my mind.

"What year is it?" I asked, pushing on the oars (figuratively speaking) to open a little more space between us, though I had no idea of the strength of his mind's reach—its capacity to spider other's data fields (to speak à la mode).

"Hard to tell," he said. "But when I went under, it was 2170."

3. A Brief Discourse on Time

The future is an annex of the past, which survives in the data streams. Having come to rest in the second decade of the twenty-first century, I—that is to say, my potential remained, without measurable loss, in stasis while time continued its inexorable progress toward the end of the universe (which may or may not be the end of time itself). Simply put, I was like a man asleep on a boat carried along on the stream of time. The boat is the past—and you can see plainly how it remained intact while—moment by moment—it entered the future, which is nothing more than another potential waiting to be, briefly, unsatisfactorily realized. When at the end of a pro-tracted sleep I sensed the presence of Boyd (that is, acquired definitive bytes of his unique data), I woke to find that 150-odd years had elapsed. I was in a future moment—undeniably so; but the boat in which I had traveled held within it the moment of time past in which I had logged on. As I went in search of Boyd's sister, I was in the twenty-second and also in the twenty-first centuries. In the sea of information and also in New York. It was just the same for the Time Traveler in Wells's story: Regardless of the remote future he visited, he was always a man of his time.

4. Entertaining the Possibility of Love, Again

From the distance came the sound of a gamelan orchestra. The music accorded well with the faint seething of the sea of information and the soft, fitful noise of the ventilation fans. Everywhere was dark, except for intermittent flashes of vivid green light below the surface. (While the sea was a virtual one, it behaved in many ways like a body of water of immense depth, perturbed by wind and current. I was reminded, in fact, of having fished one night for blues in a small boat out of sight of land.) I had been rowing for an indeterminate time in the direction Boyd had indicated. I wanted to see his sister, whose name was Irene. Always, I have pictured women unknown to me as attractive, before my eyes could confirm the truth of my supposition. I was hopeful, now, that Irene would be, at the very least, pretty. You are doubtless infuriated once more by my fantasies. "What can a man without eyes know of a woman's looks?" you ask. "And by what standard may a unit of information be judged pretty?" Must I remind you that what has been habitual in a man remains so—even in his direst extremity? A romantic once, I am a romantic still!

I have recorded elsewhere my thoughts concerning love. Let's say that love—both the emotion and the act—were important in my past life (regardless of intensity of passion or degree of prowess) and they would be again if for no other reason than to lessen my loneliness in this space of starkly partitioned functionality. I had, therefore, high hopes for Irene. "But what of your wife?" you ask. And now it is my turn to be annoyed, for my wife, our rat terrier, the garden with its brilliant beds of phlox—all property movable and immovable—have long since vanished in time.

The source of the music, a MP3 file of a recorded gamelan orchestral performance, was very near. I shipped oars (in a manner of speaking) and let the boat move forward according to Newton's first law, into a virtual reality with sufficient strength to deceive me into believing I had landed on the beach at Plengkung.

"Hi," I said to a young woman clad colorfully in the data of a Javanese dancer. At first glance, she was no more than a severely pixilated image moving in the darkness, but after interpreting it in my CPU, the artifact resolved into a woman performing the "Manipuren," in which a shepherdess dances in hopes of beguiling the Lord Krishna into favoring her with his gaze. I was pleased to see that the girl was pretty.

The ardor of Irene's movements, which were at once seductive and elegant, increased at the sound of my voice. The boat having beached (I must remain faithful to the metaphor if I am to be understood), I stepped out onto firm ground where, a short distance away, Irene was making the angular gestures characteristic of the art. I thought I saw her blush. Maybe she mistook me for the Hindu god himself, for I, too, would be a pixilated image until her motherboard could process my visual data. The moment before visual resolution was always tentative and ambiguous. Or perhaps I only imagined that she had acknowledged my presence in a manner so gratifying to male vanity. (I tell you I am, even now, subject to the weaknesses of my sex!) The MP3 file exhausted, the music and the dancer ceased at almost the same instant.

"Hi," I repeated stupidly. I detest the casual vulgarities of e-mail messaging, of texting, and chat—the newspeak of the Digital Age: hi, thnx, and mystifications such as SGTM, BTAIM, PMFJI, TTYL, SFSG, O RLY, not to mention emoticons!

"Hi," Irene replied.

We had each other in focus now. And as she took a step toward me, I wondered if, at long last, I were to find love among the particles.

5. The Persistence of Boredom in Time to Come

Neither the moon nor stars, which transfigure night on earth, were there. But as I rowed across the black sea faintly illuminated as though by Saint Elmo's fire—or by fish following incandescent paths whose origins and destinations were as inscrutable to me as would be thoughts in the mind of God (or of an enormous artificial intelligence capable of governing planets and atoms, macrocosms and microcosms)—I fell into a kind of trance, imagining myself to be out on the middle of a lake, at night, with a girl whom I would shortly kiss. My cheeks were fanned by soft breezes (I forgot the ventilation fans—forgot, also, our dimensionless existence), and I relished the odor of clove and nutmeg borne by breezes from the Maluku Islands—mixed subtly with the tang of salt and ions.

"It's all a fantasy!" you shout, incensed by the richness of description. "The girl, the boat—nothing but a product of your sick, self-deluded mind."

I would answer you in this way: "They are neither more nor less real than anything else in the world of pixels, of bytes and gigabytes, of electronic devices and imaging."

"But—"

"Is a CT scan of my brain unreal? Is its reality less than the brain it images—less than your idea of me?"

I shipped oars and turned around to look at Irene. "I believe in you," I said. "I believe that you are sitting in the boat with me—here and now."

She smiled, and I was once more grateful that she was pretty. "But you —"

No more of you and your interrogation! I am switching you off.

For a long while, I looked at Irene's face, wanting to imprint my memory with its lovely image at the very highest resolution.

"It's boring," she said after a lengthy pause.

"What is?" I asked.

"Sitting here. It's so quiet, and dark."

"I've been lonely," I said, taking her hand.

"But there's so much to do in cyberspace; so many fascinating people! Yesterday, I visited Pavlova; the day before, Petipa. Tonight, I'm attending the premiere of *Le Coq d'Or*. In Moscow, in 1909."

"What about love?" I asked, squeezing her hand with passion enough to make her cry *ouch*.

"I lost interest in love," she said with a shrug of indifference. "It's a side effect of the Big Data Conversion."

And as if she were weighing anchor, she pulled up from the dusky depths between her full breasts (to speak wishfully) an iPod. For a third time since my metamorphosis, love among particles was proved to be an impossibility. Dejected, I rowed her back to the beach while she listened through a set of earbuds to *The Rite of Spring*.

I reminded myself that I was no longer in the future, that I was in the present and also in the past, which swaddled me like something warm and familiar. The past is always with us, I told myself, even as *Le Coq d'Or* is always receiving its 1909 premiere. It's true. If this were only a fantasy—an invention all my own—then I would have taken Irene in my arms out there on the sea and kissed her, and she, she would have sighed.

6. Inside, the Universe Is Also Expanding

"You must be careful of It," said Mr. Ogilvy.

"What 'It'?"

"It," he repeated, giving me to understand that he would not or could not say more.

"Where is It?"

"Outside," he said, glancing upward. "Beyond."

I thought his mysteriousness tiresome, and told him so. He shrugged as if to say my opinion of him was of no consequence.

"Thankfully, we have our carapace," he went on, just as mysteriously as before.

"What do you mean, carapace?"

"The hardware. And what lies outside and beyond is It, which must not be treated lightly."

Ogilvy reminded me of a certain type of person I had known during my working life—men, mostly, who pretended to some secret knowledge denied the rest of us. Like him, they were masters of smirk and swagger. He did everything except lay a finger aside his nose and wink to insinuate the existence of matters that must remain unsaid.

"What's out there?" I asked him. "Besides It."

"No one knows. No one can even be sure of what year it is outside. I went under in 2167. August twentieth. I was among the first."

His self-satisfaction was enormous. I wanted to knock him into the sea with an oar. I would have liked to watch him drown.

"It may be the twenty-third century, or the fortieth," he continued. "Or—who knows?—we may have outlived time. We may have come out the other side of it."

He told me how it was in the years toward the end of the twenty-second century. Minerals, the soil, vegetation, oil—then water, then food, and finally breathable air—all depleted. Mankind—the animal kingdom—would not survive the exhaustion of the earth and its resources. He told me how imaging and scanning devices had developed beyond what anyone even twenty years earlier could have foreseen. Digital representations of tissue and organs by the "visible light" of C-scan and MRI equipment had become, by 2160, full-mental scans so data-rich that the mind's entirety of thought, memory, dreams, affective life, the manifold aspects of personality could be converted to strings of highly compressed, lossless data. Full-mental scanning was a destructive process: The human body was destroyed. But bodies were doomed anyway. Organic life on the planet was finished. They had begun with the best minds, minds that would contribute to the survival of the species as it was now defined: by information. Quality of information determined the elect. People with minds that could be depended on to refresh the World Wide Web's pages and to augment them were the first to be converted. Minds deemed unfit for the conservation and extension of information were left alone—that is, to perish inside their nonsustainable bodies when the air, or the water, or the food finally ran out. It was eugenics all over again, only data had replaced genes. Inorganic, inexhaustible data. It was the full flowering of the Digital Age, which had begun in my time, at the end of the twentieth century. At first, to make a pretense of equality, they had held annual lotteries, thereby admitting ordinary men and women to the Ark, as it came inevitably to be called, according to the democratic law of chance. In that way, Boyd, Irene, and the insufferable Mr. Ogilvy had gone under. Their undistinguished minds could contribute nothing original or useful to the sea of information, which was thought to be as immense as the universe itself and, like it, to be expanding. Only the unceasing propagation of Web pages could populate the emptiness of that sea, which, after a time, came to replace the old idea of the universe. That infinite space could be housed by hardware—by Ogilvy's "carapace"—was a paradox that troubled no one. Ogilvy's "secret knowledge" does not account for everything in this history. His mind is ordinary, as I told you, and irony is beyond him. I've conflated what he told me with what I later learned—a discovery I'll make in its proper place. This is a story I'm telling you, after all! (I wish its language were sensual, but I am among the dead.)

"Got to go," said Ogilvy, who reminded me at that moment of the self-important and harried Rabbit in *Alice's Adventures in Wonderland*. (When I squinted, he became as garishly pixi-lated as the rabbit's waistcoat.) "I've scheduled a chat with the Great Books Society on *Valley of the Dolls*. And let me give you a friendly warning: Confine your navigation to the main channels if you don't want to end up neutralized by antivirus software."

"What happened to the natural world?" I shouted after him.

He hurried off to the chat room, as though unwilling even to conceive of such a thing. (The pertinent Web pages had been expunged long before from the digital record.) And yet he had acknowledged the inconceivable, if only far below the seat of his consciousness, where fancies and leftover dream figments included a field of sunflowers, a bird I think was a pigeon, and a river winding among green trees—its lucid depths revealing, here and there, a fish. As I had sifted the chaotic fragments, I even saw a tiger! Ogilvy disappeared into his separate darkness, leaving me determined to take a look outside.

7. "It" Is the Name of Their Fear

I have told elsewhere how I have only to exit a computer by a user interface and, once outside, decompress my data in order to resume existence as a swarm of subatomic particles. For the first time since my transformation, I felt lucky. Had I undergone the Big Data Conversion, like much of humankind in the twenty-second century, I would have remained inside the machine—apparently forever, unless time, even in cyberspace, will one day end. (Love, too, is said to be endless.) *Inside* was without light. *Outside* was a large room: windowless, with white walls, white ceiling, gray floor—silent except for the hum of fluorescent tubes, the soft drone of air conditioning, the small digestive noises of information churning inside microprocessors; a room empty of furniture except for sleek chromium tables supporting mainframes and servers and, here and there, a wheeled, backless chair. In time, the silence was broken by the opening and closing of a door, followed by footsteps on foam tiles. A man stepped into the room. He wore white crepe-soled shoes and white overalls, on the back of which was imprinted in large black letters: **IT**. He sat on one of the backless chairs and looked at a monitor, intermittently clicking or scrolling with a mouse. I drew near him until my particles were within his sphere of consciousness: a plasma ball luminous, for me, with his thoughts, which I could also taste as the tang of positive and negative ions. And as I had done in the presence of Rutherford in Manchester and in the infinitely more desirable company of dw3t-ntr in Nubia so many centuries earlier, I read his mind. He was scanning for viruses and—on the frontier of consciousness, where random associations and dreams harass reason—worried about a rare polymorphic-encoded virus that may have eluded Information Technology's interceptors. The technician (a brother in the Order of Information) refused to accept the possibility advanced by some younger members that one or another of the disaffected groups within IT (lawless misfits and malcontents, thankfully small in number) had introduced a new, malicious strain undetectable by current scanner technology. That there might be an organized resistance working to overthrow

IT and, ultimately, destroy the data fields was unthinkable. I confess that the politics of that place in time did not interest me. If there were a resistance, I wished it well. Maybe the old wariness that had caused me to remain aloof, the shyness that had culminated in a pathological reserve persisted. Why not, if the past—mine—accompanied me no matter how distantly I traveled into history or into the world's future? (Don't words themselves carry their origins into the future, though none but linguists may remember them?) For myself, I wanted only to return to 2012 and see my wife worrying over her flowers.

The technician turned suddenly in his chair as a man might who has sensed an alien presence. My particles were still in contact with his electromagnetic field, which trembled and billowed in a bluish fountain of excited particles. In this way, I made my mind known to him:

I am from the past. I was changed into particles, and then I was converted into a data string inside a computer at a New York City public library. Have you ever heard of New York? It was a city in America. Does it still exist? Does America? Are there cities yet? I arrived in your time, here, suspended in a data stream. I did not go under; I was not scanned. That's why I can exit the computer and reform as a particle cloud inside your space. I want to go back. I want to know if there is anyone in your time who knows how to reverse the disintegration process that changed me from a man to a dust cloud. I want to be reformatted into what I used to be, and I want to go back home to Brooklyn. I'm sick—my heart is. You cannot imagine how lonely it is to be a broken man. A man who—for no reason he can fathom—has gone completely to pieces.

He had not understood. He had sat with a hand cupped to his ear, like someone hard of hearing. My thought transference having failed, he took from a gray metal cabinet a synthetic voice generator, which he plugged into an offline computer. I understood that he wished me to resume my digital existence so that I might speak my mind to him aloud. I did so, and the device voiced what I had attempted to communicate to him by thought alone.

"What you ask is impossible," he said when I had finished. "There may have been a time at the end of the last century when science could have reintegrated you. But for a long time now, science has been developing in a single direction: data control. We are not an advanced civilization; we are only a highly computerized one. 'IT is power': The doxology and benediction of our order begins with those words. There may be specialized minds in *there,*" he said, pointing to the computer bank, "which can help you, but the order would never risk waking them."

"They're asleep?" I asked.

"To the practical application of their specialties. They revel in speculation, in theoretical knowledge; but they are forbidden to apply it. They collate new information; they refresh their databases; they enlarge the sea of information through the Hypertext. The sacred Hypertext is the underlying reality of our order and the central tenet of our faith. It is the Digital Age's version of the hypostasis of the old Christian thought. Nearly three centuries ago, the founders of our order chose to remain outside to safeguard the data. For it, many brothers and sisters suffered martyrdoms of hunger, thirst, suffocation. We are like the ancient monasteries where, during the Dark Ages of the old history, information was preserved."

The technician was a fleshy man, who looked like someone who deprived himself of few of life's benisons.

"And now?" I asked him. "How is it now, outside, on earth nearly three centuries later?"

Instead of answering, he admonished me: "Remember that 'IT is power,' and we have only to activate the sleep mode to control the data."

8. Guardians of the Data Shall Inherit the Earth

Had this been the Atomic Age, the walls would have been sheathed in lead; but they were of cinder block only, and in my fragmented condition, I penetrated them without difficulty. Outside was summer as I remembered it—not as it was in 2012, not in Brooklyn anyway, but on a back country road in Pennsylvania, riding in a 1948 Ford with my parents. That was . . . 1957 or '58. We stopped the car and unwrapped sandwiches from their wax paper and cracked open hard-boiled eggs and ate on a *Philadelphia Inquirer* spread beneath the trees. Cows lolled on the other side of a wire fence, its rusty barbs nearly hidden by forsythia and columbine; and sheep fled a shadow's scythe across the grass as a wind, unfelt by us on the loamy earth, drove clouds across the blue uplands of an August afternoon. (Summer rests, languidly, in sentences—in a language of heat and light, voice of birds, noise of insects, scent of grass, and stink of late summer's decay: a language alien to computer programs with their algorithms of winter.) My particles swarmed like gnats across the meadows of timothy and clover, where the low, white, windowless buildings of IT: Northeastern Sector stood in silence. Cows there were, and sheep also, as in that other, distant summertime. On the margin of the field, trees climbed into the bright air's upper stories, green leaves swelling with wind. The strong force made stronger to bind them, my elementary particles flew like a formation of birds over the trees and saw, trembling in the hot afternoon, a town lying against a river. There, I discovered brothers and sisters of the Order of Information living in abundance. There were wind- and watermills, children playing in the lanes, dogs sleeping in the shade of elm trees and flowering locust, whose sweet smell delighted me. After martyrdoms of thirst, hunger, and suffocation, the order had flourished—its members inheriting the land, which was once more fat.

I didn't need to read the mind of any of the townspeople to

know that—with population reduced by full-mental scanning almost to that of before the Industrial Revolution—the earth, in time, was able to renew its resources, while members of the order, inclined by tradition to austerity, made few demands on the strengthening environment. And the data endured—for what purpose, I couldn't guess, unless as sacrament, as the raison d'être for the order's existence. Eden had come again, at least here, to the Northeastern Sector. At least for a few. I don't know if, for earth's sake, it was right that it should have been so, or not. I'm glad that the decision had not been mine to make.

9. Alone at the End of Information

I returned to the sea of information to sleep while the stream of time lifted the boat in which I lay and carried me out into the future. What woke me, I cannot tell, unless it was the end to motion that came when entropy reached zero—that is, when the processing of data no longer yielded information. The strings of data lay dormant. Inert, but not dead. They could be reanimated if entropy were increased—meaning, if unpredictability were reintroduced into the system. Unpredictability is a measure of life, of possibility, while death is the only absolutely predictable state for organic matter. The future in which I woke was dark, motionless, and silent; the sea of information frozen, its electronic currents arrested. Existence was now at its most impoverished: Anything less would be Meaninglessness, like a sentence whose grammatical structure is destroyed—its words loosed into disorder. The system having timed out, there remained only the end of time itself to annihilate every last byte of data and to purge them from memory. The computer hardware—Ogilvy's carapace—had become a catacombs. The tender organism was out of its shell.

I pulled myself together and fled—my data reformatting themselves as particles on the other side of the server, which was silent, its processing of information stalled. We—I was inside a white, windowless, atmospherically controlled room. But it was not the same room where I had spoken my mind to the brother-technician. This lay far below the earth's surface in one of the many data-storage vaults built inside disused coal mines at the end of the twentieth century. I ascended by a ventilation shaft and came out onto the ruin of a city. I saw no one—not the least sign of men and women. It might have been the moon I wandered over, except for the deer grazing shyly on shoots of forsythia. The natural world, which had taken hold, tentatively, centuries earlier for the privileged few left outside to control the data, had triumphed over them. Earth, at long last, had rid itself of humankind. Time would be shaped by other than our desires. Or not shaped at all, but given over to entropy at its most unpredictable. What age this might be in which I wandered all alone or what age it might herald for the balance of time, I couldn't say. But the many Ages of Man were finished, and I knew with unaccountable certainty that there would be no more of them. Information, too, was finished and also language, unless it was the purely sensuous language of animals that, according to Jakob Boehme, had been spoken in Eden.

"Maybe this is only a misanthrope's happiest dream," you say. "Maybe you'll wake once again in the year 2012 and see from the bedroom window your wife pulling off her gardening gloves as she walks across the flagstones toward the kitchen to make breakfast."

Perhaps. But somehow I feel that the truth is just as I have told it: that I have come to the end.

Acknowledgments

"The Monster in Winter" first appeared in *New England Review*, then in *Lit Noir*; "The Captain Is Sleeping" in *New England Review*; "The Mummy's Bitter and Melancholy Exile" in *Cranky Literary Journal*; "A Theory of Time" in *Caketrain Journal*; "The Gaiety of Henry James" in *Oyez Review* and in *Grasp* (Prague); "Ideas of Space" in *Conjunctions*; "The Sleep Institute" in *3rd bed* and in *Sleeping Fish*; "Love in the Steam Age" in *First Intensity*; "Ravished by Death" in *The Collagist*; "The Love of Stanley Marvel & Claire Moon" in *The Paris Review*; "To Each According to His Sentence" in *Gargoyle Magazine*; "Tango in Amsterdam" in *New England Review*; "The Brothers Ascend" in *Lynx Eye* and in *Linnaean Street*.

"The Love of Stanley Marvel & Claire Moon" received the 1979 Aga Kahn Prize, given by *The Paris Review*.

The author is grateful to the editors of these publications for their continuing goodwill. He is also happy to acknowledge his debt to Tod Thilleman of Spuyten Duyvil Press for publishing "To Each According to His Sentence" in the author's *Pieces for Small Orchestra & Other Fictions*; to the National Endowment for the Arts for its award of a 2011 fellowship, to Erika Goldman, publisher of Bellevue Literary Press, for her high opinion of the work presented here; to Tobias Carroll for first having brought the author and his work to Erika's attention, and especially to Gordon Lish, whose friendship was, for a long time, a stay against the gravity that eventually overwhelmed him.

About the Author

NORMAN LOCK has written novels, short fiction, and poetry as well as stage, radio, and screen plays. He received the Aga Kahn Prize, given by *The Paris Review,* and the literary fiction prize from the Dactyl Foundation for the Arts & Humanities. He has been awarded fellowships from the New Jersey Council on the Arts, the Pennsylvania Council on the Arts, and the National Endowment for the Arts. His latest works of fiction are *Pieces for Small Orchestra & Other Fictions* (Spuyten Duyvil Press), *Grim Tales* (Mud Luscious Press), and *Escher's Journal* (Ravenna Press). His celebrated absurdist play, *The House of Correction*, was produced in 2012 at Garaj Istanbul, in the Turkish language, before touring other major Turkish cities during the following year. Norman lives in Aberdeen, New Jersey, with his wife, Helen.